THE WORD IS DEATH

Mary Clayton

First published in 1997 by
HEADLINE BOOK PUBLISHING

10 9 8 7 6 5 4 3 2 1

All characters in this publication are fictitious and any resemblance to real persons, living or dead, is purely coincidental.

British Library Cataloguing in Publication Data

Clayton, Mary, 1932–
The word is death. – (A Cornish whodunnit)
1. Reynolds, John (Fictitious character) – Fiction
2. Detective and mystery stories
I. Title
823.9'14[F]

ISBN 0 7472 1965 6

Typeset by Avon Dataset Ltd, Bidford-on-Avon, Warks

Printed and bound in Great Britain by
Mackays of Chatham PLC, Chatham, Kent

HEADLINE BOOK PUBLISHING
A division of Hodder Headline PLC
338 Euston Road
London NW1 3BH

For my children and grandchildren – With love

May they live and thrive

ACKNOWLEDGEMENTS

My sincere thanks to my editor, Andi Blackwell, for all her suggestions and help, and to my agent, Arnold Goodman, always a great advisor and friend.

My thanks too, to Nellie and Deborah for all their suggestions. And as always, my gratitude to Ron for his loving support and encouragement.

Chapter 1

When the crown used for the coronation of St Breddaford's Mayday 'Queen' disappeared, everyone blamed Mrs Varcoe, a notorious scatterbrain. Although she swore she'd stowed the missing item safely in the church hall cupboard after the last rehearsal, no one believed her. Not when her niece, a pouty girl of eleven, had expected to be selected Queen herself and was wildly jealous of her younger successful rival! And not when the only clue was a scrap of paper with what was called a 'smiley face' drawn upon it.

The inordinate glee of the Varcoes that the crowning could not take place as planned and the anger of the Alsops that their little June's chances had been thwarted, created factions in the village out of all proportion to the crime, until the vicar mildly pointed out that the crown was actually more valuable than it seemed. Explaining that the cardboard gilded circle (bedecked every year with fresh garlands and ribbons) was actually an early Victorian replica of a much older model, he also was the first to suggest, somewhat tactlessly, that it should have been put in a museum years ago, as a symbol of pagan and Christian ritual, an idea which pleased nobody.

St Breddaford's festivities might pale in comparison with the more famous Hobby Horse of the nearby port at Padstow, but the villagers were proud of their traditions. The first day in May, rain or shine, children assembled at daybreak to pick sprays of may blossom (in recent years substituted by bluebells and primroses, easier to reach and less thorny)! After which, accompanied by the local brass band, they danced to a distinctive tune through the streets, finishing up with a traditional feast of jam buns and cream. Finally, the crowning of the Queen took place outside the church beside the sixth-century Celtic cross, amid much oohing and ahhing from admiring relatives and the clicking of many cameras.

Faced with the historical or rather antiquarian value of what they'd thought a gilt cutout, the rivals' claims and counter-claims of defamation of character and sabotage subsided. Renewed attempts were made to find the missing article; a tearful Mrs Varcoe offered to let her house be searched (an offer refused because, as someone put it, 'no telling what else the old biddy's shoved out of the way and forgotten – including her former husband!'); finally the local police were summoned. But for all his patient probing Sergeant Derrymore could make no headway, and was still puzzling over the case when the second incident occurred – to eclipse the first completely and set new rumours buzzing.

Chapter 2

'I hear the verger discovered it when he unlocked the door first thing this morning. Nearly fainted, poor soul. And they say the vicar was so angry he tore up the only clue, a poster above the altar of another smiley face.'

Mazie Derrymore was speaking. She was the sergeant's mam, a dumpling of a woman, with rosy cheeks and the dark hair and eyes of the typical Cornish. She was sitting at the dining-room table while her visitor sat opposite, in the place of honour.

Mazie was still wearing her best dress, her work-roughened hands clasped around her teacup. Although the day had been warm this last Saturday in May, firelight flickered on the whitewashed walls of her little cottage near the centre of the village, and the oak furniture gleamed with polish as if in contrast with the scene she had been describing.

Mazie was a methodist of long standing, but as a village elder had been asked to help in the emergency and had already spent most of the morning scouring the church clean. She had also stripped her garden of flowers to redecorate it and although invited (belatedly) to the reception afterwards in token of appreciation, had done as she had always intended, merely attended the ceremony to watch.

'The whole community had done their utmost to make the church beautiful for Matty's wedding day,' she went on. 'Even the bell ringers practised every evening last week. To my mind it's an insult to the village as well as Vicar Tamblin and his family.'

Before her visitor could reply, Mazie couldn't resist continuing. 'The main aisle swimming in it,' she said. 'Buckets of it, splattered about in fury. Walls, ceilings, floors. Even the matting on the altar steps was sodden, they'll never get out the stains. And guess where they found the buckets? Hidden behind a gravestone. Blasphemy, I call it. No wonder the vicar was angry. The verger thought there'd been a murder but they say it's animal blood.'

When she explained that Matty was the vicar's daughter, her visitor, a young woman herself, made sympathetic noises and closed her eyes, as if the vision of a bride in white greeted by a scarlet flood was somehow more than disgusting; it was weird, disturbing.

The visitor was Sally Heyward. She and Mazie had met during the course of a previous police investigation when a firm if unlikely friendship had sprung up between them. Since then Sally often came to see Mazie, and stayed to chat. If these visits gave her the chance to see Mazie's son as well, Mazie never mentioned openly that this was her intention. Although if not exactly desperate to drive her giant fledgling from the nest, she was for ever nudging him towards flight and as far as she was concerned Sally Heyward presented the best prospect so far.

'We'll have to wait until Derry comes home with the details,' Mazie said when Sally made a move to leave. 'It's been hard on him, so many questions, the one real clue destroyed, and everyone frantic to clean up before the guests arrived. Thank goodness the verger is an old worry-wart, I say. Suppose he'd waited until the last moment to open the door, just as the groom's family arrived! They're said to be something "Big in the City," whatever that means.'

She took another sip of tea. 'Of course Derry's known the vicar's family for ages,' she went on. 'The sons and him were good friends. And here's Derry now,' she added as a door banged. She gave a pleased smile. 'I knew it was worth your waiting,' she said.

She bustled off; her voice could be heard down the narrow hall, scolding and cajoling at the same time. After a while Sergeant Derrymore came into the room. He was a very large young man, a former Cornish wrestler, considered handsome with dark hair and eyes, like his mother. But the most attractive thing about him had always been his good humour – not much in evidence this evening.

His broad, usually cheerful face, a larger version of his mam's, wore a worried look and his shoulders sagged. Although he made an effort to be pleasant, and greeted Sally as an old acquaintance, it was clear from the way he sighed as he sank into a chair that the last thing he wanted was to be bothered to play host to anyone.

His mother bustled in with the pasty she'd been keeping warm in the oven. 'Eat that up,' she said. 'And then tell me, how did my flowers look? I was that pleased in a way to be asked to provide them; those church people are so proud of their own gardens they think we villagers grow nothing but potatoes and onions.'

Derrymore sighed again, but under his mam's spate of questions gave way, although if prodded, he probably would have said he was old-fashioned enough to hide such horrors from womenfolk. And after he had reassured Mazie that her flowers had saved the day it seemed natural to go on to discuss the events that had shocked the whole village.

Derrymore didn't dwell on the condition of the church. But he did say that the saddest part for him was the way the vicar's wife broke down. 'Never seen her like it,' he explained. 'Suddenly, when we were trying to make sense of what had happened, she burst out that it was a retribution. It was her fault, and her husband's; God was punishing them for having let Matty run wild.'

He stared at the fire, and shook his head slowly. 'I mean, Mrs Tamblin's always seemed so calm, it was awful to see her berating herself, like, like . . .' He thought for a moment, came up with, 'Like some old churchman scourging himself at confession. Even the vicar looked taken aback, as if he hadn't enough on his hands without his wife ranting on at him. Fortunately Matty was still in tears in another room, so I don't think she heard, and after a while Mrs T. settled down, but still, it makes you think.'

Seeing his listeners' expressions, he said briskly, 'Well, it's over with now. The marriage took place in the end, and the couple are off on their honeymoon, none the worse. And all the more credit to the village for rallying round.'

'That's a truth.' His mam stood up, shaking out the folds of her skirt and picking up her hat from the dresser. 'Never thought I'd see some of those fine ladies on their knees scrubbing out the porch,' she added, with a smile of satisfaction, quickly repressed. 'And now I'm off to bed. Keep the fire up, Derry, and mind you drive Miss Heyward home. It's no night to be taking a bus. And if you ask me, which you haven't, I'd say this is certainly a case for ex-Inspector Reynolds. No call,' she said firmly as she went stiffly up the stairs, 'to have anyone outside the village involved.'

After she had gone Derrymore still did not relax, despite loosening a tunic button, and although Sally now sat by herself on the sofa he did not join her. He did cut several large chunks of cake (which she refused) and opened a tin of beer, after which he sat for a while, gazing into the fire.

'You poor thing,' Sally said, with a look that suggested she knew what a hard day he'd had and appreciated his need for quiet. 'I expect you're fed up with the whole thing and want to forget it.'

She was about to add, 'Don't worry about me, I'll see myself out,' when Derrymore interrupted.

'Oh, it's not just that,' he said bluntly. 'There's,' he hesitated, then came out with, 'a lot on my mind what with this today and then the ruined May Queen procession. As if someone has it in for the village and is out to make trouble.'

He lapsed into silence, still gazing into the fire, rousing himself to say at last, 'It preys on you, you know.'

Sally had never seen him so depressed before, and his mood puzzled her. He seemed to be saying that as well as the incident in the church he had something else on his mind, something unspecified that he didn't want to talk about. Her intuition was justified when instead of lapsing once more into silence Derrymore began to go over the events of the day again, as if indeed they did prey on him.

But after he'd finished explaining how he'd ascertained where the break-in point was (through a door with a weak hinge, damaged months ago); when he'd admitted that his search for fingerprints had been unsuccessful because doors and even buckets had been wiped clean; when he'd complained, with some justification, that the vicar's hasty action had lost the one real clue and that although he had located a possible source of the blood at the local slaughterhouse (their unhelpful comment had been that they had so much blood a few gallons here or there wouldn't be missed) she had the impression he was trying to convince himself that he had followed all leads and had done a thorough job, an impression heightened by his reaction when she commented that surely the drawings must link the two events and mean the criminal must be local.

'Why do you think that?' he flared. Then, calming down, 'Anyone could have heard of the first drawing and reproduced it. And could have got through that door. All it needed was a shove, although I know the vicar insists that it was locked when he and the verger made the rounds together last night. Everything was in order then, he said. He even admitted picking up a fallen rose petal, the floor was so shiny he couldn't help noticing. Presumably later that night, or more likely early this morning because the blood was still wet, someone broke in.'

Resisting the urge to say that only a local person could have explored ways into the church before the actual break-in itself, or know the exact details of the wedding, Sally asked instead why anyone would hold a grudge against the Tamblins. Or why her mother had called poor Matty wild.

Derrymore shot her another sharp look as if he thought her question had a secondary purpose. After all Sally's former lover was no secret, but they had never yet discussed him so neither knew the other's thoughts. But she suspected that it made a difference to Derrymore, he was so straight-laced sometimes it made her want to smile – except it was also why she liked him – and if truth be told, why sometimes she hoped that he liked her.

At last, as if making up his mind that Sally wasn't being devious, Derrymore rallied enough to say, 'Matty was always a bit weird. Even as child she shocked the village with her tomboy ways. Then she became devoted to good causes, off at protest rallies and such. And the boyfriends she brought home!' He whistled. 'Probably her family's glad she eventually chose someone respectable. Better than one I met, some scruffy fellow who played a guitar in the main street.'

'Sounds reasonable,' Sally agreed. 'I presume she didn't leave a local suitor dying of a broken heart. And even if she had a succession of boyfriends, that's normal enough these days.'

She looked hard at Derrymore until he in turn looked up so their gaze met. If she had thrown down a challenge, Derrymore didn't pick it up. However the turn taken by their conversation seemed to have shaken his composure. Again he turned to stare in the fire until Sally, with the common sense that was typical of her, brought them back to neutral ground and possible suspects for the crime.

'What about the groom?' she asked. 'Could he have jilted some girl and her family be out for revenge?'

Derrymore made a face. 'I'd say he's as harmless as a piece of wet lettuce. However, I suspect one of the real reasons for Mrs Tamblin's hysterics was having to explain to him and his sophisticated London relatives why her husband's church looked like a medieval shambles.'

'So if the criminal isn't an ex-suitor with a grudge,' Sally said, 'for the sake of argument, could he be a business acquaintance of the groom's father wanting vengeance for some shady deal?'

She achieved her purpose. Derrymore laughed. When he did his face lit up and showed what he really was like. It was something worth looking for – if any girl these days had the time and patience to look for it. It encouraged Sally to ask, 'Any other clues? I mean, other than the torn up drawing?'

Derrymore ran his fingers round his collar as if it had suddenly become too tight. 'I'm checking on them.' His answer was abrupt, as if again convincing himself. 'Mind you, the whole world was in and out of the church all day Friday, which doesn't help. It may explain, though, how the criminal was able to bring the buckets up without rousing suspicion.'

'But are there really no hints who he might have been?' Sally persisted. 'No suggestions what sort of man?'

At that, Derrymore suddenly stiffened. 'All these questions,' he said, half angrily, 'you ought to be the police sergeant, not me.'

Sally's laugh was uncertain. 'And now, I suppose like ex-Inspector Reynolds, you're going to ask why I'm so sure it's a man?' she started to say. Then, as Derrymore turned away without answering, she cocked her head somewhat like a cheeky robin, before adding, 'And why aren't you going to consult him? He's helped you out a score of times.'

She shook her finger at him playfully, although there was no playfulness in her voice when she went on, 'Don't tell me you believe the rumours about him? Because if you do, shame on you!'

Chapter 3

The remark wasn't exactly tactful, and Sally was known for her tact. But then she worked these days as Reynolds' part-time secretary (the main reason for her frequent trips to St Breddaford) and could be excused for being prejudiced in his favour. And she was right about several things, namely that Derrymore had more on his mind than the actual crimes. As for the rumours about Reynolds, they were so irrational and vague at this point he should have known better than to listen to them.

She had the sense not to continue the argument that evening – which ended as such evenings full of misunderstandings always do; in growing silence, punctuated by stilted conversation and a sense of relief when the time came to part. Nor was their relationship close enough yet for her to probe for answers. Mazie had no such inhibitions. When, a day or so later, a third event rocked the village, Derrymore's mam had no hesitation at all in telling him what she thought of him, and taking the law into her own hands.

This third event was mild in comparison with the second, but did underline the gossip now beginning to surround the ex-inspector. On the Monday evening, sometime after midnight, the fire brigade were summoned. A fire had been started in the yard behind the local bookshop, fed by packing cases and cardboard boxes. To add to the conflagration, the shop window had also been smashed and a special display of books taken from it and flung on the pyre. And of the books burned, every single one had been written by Reynolds!

'No reason to behave like a bear with a sore head.' Next morning, buttoning her raincoat on, Mazie glared at her son. 'It's absurd to say this burning proves his books are encouraging all these horrors. We ought to be proud of having him in the village, not trying to drive him out, like that old cat, Mrs Basset, was saying in the greengrocer's.

' "You look here," says I, and I banged my bag down good and proper. "You haven't opened a book since you left school. So don't go making judgements about things you know nothing about. If some criminal person thinks he can hide behind Mr Reynolds' writings and blame them for corrupting him, he needs his head examined." '

Out of breath, she sat down again, for she seldom quarrelled with her son, and when she did, was never happy until she had made things right. But Derrymore looked sulky. When he did answer, he sounded even more agitated than she was.

'Of course I don't believe the inspector is personally behind the mischief,' he snapped. 'And I don't say I don't enjoy his books, always have. I only repeat if people are claiming that since he came into the village and began writing there's been nothing but trouble, at least I should take notice. That's why I'm a village policeman; I listen to people.'

And as his mam continued to glare at him, 'And it explains why I don't think he should be professionally involved,' he added lamely. 'It might cause trouble.'

'It already has.' Her rejoinder was as sharp. 'And you've never been afraid of trouble before. If you ask my opinion, like Sally, I think you're hiding something.'

At mention of Sally's name, Derrymore stiffened. 'Don't drag her into it,' he shouted. 'She's nothing to do with it.' A most unloverlike observation, which didn't endear him to his mother and strengthened her resolution. But he didn't deny her last accusation, as she was to remember when she confronted Reynolds himself on his doorstep, a round figure reminiscent of a homely Buddha, glaring at him through the rain that had finally quenched the fire and sent a smell of wet soot through the village.

John Reynolds was the village celebrity, a well-known police inspector who had retired to St Breddaford to write the detective books that had won him as much, if not more, fame then his previous profession. In the subsequent years he and Derrymore had become firm friends and at Derrymore's specific request he had frequently helped the village policeman solve difficult cases, the pair of them working so well together they often reached solutions in spite of opposition from headquarters.

At the moment Reynolds was so preoccupied it had never occurred to him his books were being blamed as the underlying cause of violence in the village; in fact it is doubtful if he had even heard of the violence, or would have remembered if he had. What kept him engrossed these days was writing a new book, an occupation he usually enjoyed; not so this time.

Ever since he had begun his second career, to his great astonishment the actual work of creation had come easily, as easily as solving crimes when he'd been a police inspector. He had actually engaged Sally Heyward to help him with the new manuscript, arranging to give her a certain number of pages every other day or so, for her to retype in final form – a more satisfactory arrangement for him than wrestling with a word processor. But the earlier halcyon moments of authorship had vanished. For the first time he knew what it was to sit at his desk for hours without putting pen to paper, or to wake at nights with a scene just slipping from his dreaming grasp. Whatever he tried, the plot wouldn't gel and the characters remained wooden – and the deadline was approaching fast. No wonder when Mazie knocked at the door of Old

Forge Cottage, he answered it with unshaven chin and crumpled clothes as if he had slept in them (although instead of being offended, Mazie's motherly instincts were so roused she almost offered to cook him breakfast and wait on him while he ate it).

She refused to come inside but stood on the step to tell him bluntly that things in St Breddaford were going from bad to worse and if his books weren't to blame, he himself certainly would be, if he didn't pull himself together and give her Derry a hand.

'And if they say your writing detective stories encourages people in crime,' she concluded bluntly, 'and what's more writing them is wrong, and if they've got to burn them to prove their point, my answer is that I believe in freedom of speech. And that goes for writing as well as talking. Although at the moment I'd willingly gag some old gossips in the village, like they used to in olden days, and enjoy it.'

And ignoring her own lack of logic she proceeded to tell the ex-inspector exactly what had happened since the ill-fated May Day, a torrent which left Reynolds totally confused. The only thing she omitted was Derrymore's own opinion, but she did add that he 'was in some state', an expression she used to describe someone out of sorts with himself and the world in general.

When she had finished, Reynolds said at last, running his hand through his thick, cropped hair so that it looked more than ever like a brush, 'You mean people are saying that writing, and presumably reading, my books is encouraging crime? That's ridiculous. Surely the object is to show crime doesn't pay. And why on earth would I encourage someone to burn my own books?'

He stared back at her. 'But if someone's gone to all that trouble,' he said slowly, 'there must be some reason. And when you think of it,' a sign that his detective instincts had begun to function, 'apart from the drawings, there're similarities between sloshing blood about and starting fires – both actions are meant to shock – and to call attention to the perpetrators. But I can't interfere unless Derrymore asks me; it wouldn't be correct. Besides, I've a manuscript to finish . . .'

'Correct.' She repeated the word scornfully. She stood her ground, her umbrella resolutely planted, and glared up from her dumpy height to his tall one. 'That's something else Derry was blathering about. Well, I'm his mam and my guess is that he's as unhappy as you are.'

When Reynolds looked suitably startled she shook her umbrella open. 'If Derry won't, or can't, ask you, I will. We need you, Mr Reynolds, sir, no matter what people say. And since it was your books that got burned, I'd go and talk to that bookshop keeper straight off before I'd bother about any new one. If writing it keeps you that busy and makes you that miserable, it can't be doing you much good.'

And off she marched, leaving Reynolds in his doorway without a word in his defence, and his own self-absorption (which, in the normal way of things, he would have been the first to laugh at) dangling in tatters.

Her comments about Derrymore surprised him. He'd never heard her criticise her son before and would have said that one of the best things about him was his dependability. Then, too, Mazie's last words rankled. They almost made him angry. He came behind her to close the gate and leaned on it to watch her trot down the lane, her head high under the umbrella. Long after she had gone he stood there, his shirt soaked but the air so mild he scarcely noticed.

To have this fierce little lady suggest that he ought to put his manuscript aside and occupy himself with something really important until he got over his writer's block, startled him. The idea that it was necessary at all was disagreeable, to put it mildly, and a blow to his self-esteem. Nor had he ever thought before about the possible consequences of writing detective stories, although he knew his editors were always careful to ensure that his fictional criminals were suitably punished. In fact, if one thought about it seriously, the idea could have horrible implications – if someone for example decided to imitate an actual crime. There were certainly worse crimes than burning books or stealing children's head-dresses and he certainly had written about them . . . but presumably village gossip hadn't yet latched on to them and he hoped they never would.

By now the rain was easing off into a drizzle and behind the old high wall his garden, smelling of rich earth and growing plants, was clamouring for attention. Down the lane he could hear the little brook that gave St Breddaford its name gushing in a late May flood, and the sound of the bell ringers practising came in gusts, blown from the church on the soft western wind. Damn, he thought, damn, and damn again.

Making up his mind, he strode back to the house more energetically than he had in weeks. Resisting the temptation to make a detour to the sitting room, where a stack of crumpled paper waited in mute accusation, he shaved, changed, and was out of the front door before he could change his mind again – and with a feeling that could only be likened to liberation.

He knew where the bookshop was, the only one in St Breddaford. Sandwiched somewhat incongruously between the pub and a row of small cottages, on the opposite side of the green from the church, it was well positioned to attract the type of tourist he himself felt the village could do without. He had only been in the shop once, when it first opened, but had been waited on by a young girl assistant so had never met the owner. He had no idea that its bow window had been given over to a display of his books, and if he had known, might not have been pleased. It smacked of the sort of blatant publicity he most disliked.

When he reached the green, the smell of damp soot was even more pronounced but fortunately the rain had driven off the crowd which had surrounded the shop earlier to comment and commiserate. Now only one man was left, presumably the proprietor, for he was standing on a ladder, struggling to nail a plank of wood across the shattered windowpanes. Shards of glass still lay scattered underneath.

Hearing Reynolds' step, he looked round. Bespectacled, with a scanty thatch of long black hair, his tall thin body, engulfed in a flapping raincoat, gave him the appearance of a distracted heron, precariously perched on a ladder. But his 'Good morning' was cheerful. Reynolds felt a twinge of empathy.

'Here, let's give you a hand,' he said. Resisting the impulse to take over the hammering, for it was obvious that the fellow had no experience at home repairs, he steadied the ladder, and after watching one or two ineffectual tries, eventually completed the job himself. After which, it seemed natural that he should be invited inside and offered coffee from a little machine installed at the back.

Divested of the raincoat the shop owner – 'Sinclair's the name, Robert. Doctor, literature not medicine' – looked more like the professor he had been. Explaining he had given up a teaching career for a quiet Cornish life, he went on to add that he was merely 'following your example, Inspector', his surprisingly brilliant eyes beneath the glasses sparkling with fun.

'Oh, I recognise you,' he went on, his eyes still sparkling. 'I mean from the photograph on the back cover of your latest book. We don't see you much in person.'

If there was a reproof it was soon forgotten in the bustle with the coffee which he dispensed with the typical fussy air of a confirmed bachelor. When Reynolds, angling for a chance to examine the yard, said he was sorry to hear about the fire, to his chagrin Dr Sinclair didn't take the hint.

'Not much damage done,' he said, shrugging, as if shaking the whole incident off. 'Although one doesn't expect arsonists in a village like this.'

He took off his glasses and began to polish them. 'Of course the loss of the books is serious, but I can order up another batch and hope insurance will cover the expense. What I mind is the book-burning itself. It smacks of censorship, to say nothing of spite.'

He didn't volunteer that the burnt books were all ones written by Reynolds, perhaps he was too polite, and if he knew that Reynolds' work was being attacked by people in the village, he didn't mention it. His intention to reorder the books suggested he hadn't heard.

Putting down his coffee cup, Reynolds wondered if he should enlighten him. There was a sort of other-worldliness about Sinclair that he found sympathetic and wanted to protect. Instead, he asked if there were any clues who the culprit was, to be answered by a vigorous shake of the head that sent the tatters of hair flying.

'And you didn't hear any noise?'

'Oh no,' Sinclair's hair wisps flew again. 'Nor would anyone else. The pub was long closed, and my neighbour on the other side is an old dear who's deaf. But perhaps you think I live here myself.'

His eyes sparkled a third time. 'The upstairs of the shop is a loft, only suitable for storage,' he explained. 'I can't afford a period house in the village. Not on my pension. The shop took all my capital so I make do with a small place on the outskirts. It's one of those new monstrosities you village people hate, but it does have all the mod cons and is within walking distance. I don't drive much.'

A long-winded explanation. But again, if there was a reproof, a sort of bitterness in the phrases 'can't afford', and 'you village people hate', it was mild and quickly hidden by a smile that lit up his thin face and made it attractive.

'So I didn't know anything until the police rang. And by then the damage had been done. Speaking of the police, here he is in person. Good morning, sergeant, you're in time to join us. I was just answering Mr Reynolds' questions about the incident.'

And he bustled off to make more coffee, leaving Reynolds and Derrymore facing each other in what was distinctly an embarrassing situation.

Not wanting Derrymore to think he was interfering, and yet at the same time realizing that was precisely what he was doing, wanting to tell the sergeant about his mam's visit, and yet not happy at revealing all she'd said, Reynolds muttered something about just passing and stopping to help.

'So kind,' Dr Sinclair said from the background, and then, as he rejoined them, 'I'm hopeless with my hands.'

He put the coffee down and held them out, long-fingered, thin-wristed, the backs surprisingly covered with fine black hair; the sort of hands, Reynolds thought, that go with academicians and so-called 'artistic' folk.

'And I hate heights, even a ladder's too high for me,' Sinclair was adding, with a smile. 'Inspector Reynolds really saved the day. Or should I say ex-Inspector? Although you are on the warpath, aren't you?'

As the brilliant blue eyes sparkled with mischief, the professorial idea of a joke, Reynolds groaned to himself. That sort of remark wasn't likely to placate Derrymore, if, as his mam claimed, he was 'in some state'.

Derrymore began to ask the same questions that Reynolds had previously, and received the same vague answers, with the added information that Sinclair himself knew of no reason why he should have been selected for trouble. By village standards he was still thought of as a stranger, a 'newcomer', but as a so-called 'newcomer' he had no enemies here as far as he knew. 'Unless newcomers by definition are disliked,' he added. 'On the other hand, the child whose crown was stolen is local. And so is the vicar's family.'

Looking worried, he turned from Derrymore to Reynolds, as if for confirmation. 'Seriously, Inspector, do you think the events are linked? I wouldn't want to become part of some village vendetta. And you do know there was another drawing, a sort of smiling face, scratched in the dirt in the yard, but the firemen trampled over it so it got erased.'

Reynolds saw Derrymore's gaze also swivel towards him. He guessed this piece of evidence was important. For a moment again he hesitated, wondering if he should comment, then thinking he might as well be hung for a sheep as a lamb, said, 'My advice, for what it's worth, is that you hold back on reordering, or even stocking, my books for the present. I rather suspect in this case they're the real target.'

And as Sinclair's expression clouded, 'If it helps, and you would like, that is, when this blows over perhaps we could arrange a book-signing.'

Sinclair brightened. 'I won't deny that you're a real inducement,' he said. 'The number of strangers who come in and ask where you live and so on, they all want your books. But if you suggest it, I'll wait.'

'Right.' Reynolds steeled himself to the prospect of a book-signing in the future, the least he could do, he thought. He moved towards the door, said, 'I must be on my way. A word, if I may, Sergeant, when you're through here. I'll wait outside.'

And with that time-honoured phrase he got himself out and across the green, before Dr Sinclair could do more damage. After a short while he was joined by a grim-looking Derrymore, not inclined to idle chit-chat. Abandoning his original idea of explaining in detail why he was there, instead Reynolds turned to neutral ground, asking if Derrymore had looked at the remains of the fire, was it really arson?

'That's what the fire chief says,' Derrymore was brusque. 'Besides, those books didn't walk into the yard by themselves.'

'Apart from these drawings, any connections with previous events?'

He hoped Derrymore might comment but the sergeant merely shook his head. 'Can't see one,' he admitted, almost reluctantly. 'That's what's really puzzling.'

As if he felt obliged to fill in the details of the earlier incidents, he began to stride back and forth along the banks of the swollen stream, elaborating as he went. And as so often in the past, Reynolds strode beside him, listening carefully.

Side by side, certain similarities between the two men became apparent. Both had dark hair, in one greying at the sides; both were tall, although Derrymore was broader, while in both, their upright carriage and military walk marked them out as former soldiers whose previous army experience had stood them in good stead, Reynolds in the Middle East, Derrymore in Northern Ireland. Finally, both were dependable; the sort of men to stand at one's back in a tight place, the sort whose friendship is worth keeping. And since each knew his own worth, Reynolds hoped eventually Derrymore would remember it, and confide in him.

But after the sergeant had rehashed all three events and Reynolds asked again if there really were no other leads, for the first time Derrymore hesitated. 'Not exactly,' he said, but his voice lacked conviction. 'Sinclair has no enemies, as he pointed out. And of course newcomers to the village aren't disliked but they are, well, different, aren't they? I mean, it takes time to get used to them.'

That's an understatement if ever I heard one, Reynolds

thought. It takes years for a newcomer to become part of village life; sometimes they are never accepted at all.

'The only thing he's complained of before,' Derrymore was continuing, 'is about kids wandering in the shop, browsing they call it, but he's sure they swipe stuff when his back is turned, small things like pens and cards. I'll follow that up; someone might hold a grudge.'

He didn't sound impressed by his own arguments. He's clutching at straws, Reynolds thought. Setting fire to shops and selecting which books to burn sounds a tad sophisticated for mere schoolboys, shoplifters or not. And even if they did set the fire, I still can't believe kids got into the church. Although they might steal the crown for a lark.

Seeing a chance here to bring Derrymore round to the discussion of the point so vital to himself, he added, with a half smile, 'If boys are involved, surely you'll accept that their motive was probably macho one-up manship, the egging of each other on that the young engage in these days? Likely to have more influence on them than, say, reading detective stories?'

He smiled to take away the sting but the sting unfortunately was there. And Derrymore reacted to it with more antagonism than Reynolds had anticipated. He stopped in his tracks and turned on Reynolds with a look that alarmed the older man. But all he said was, 'Is that what my mam says?'

Cursing himself for being stupid, Reynolds considered his reply carefully. He certainly didn't want to cause bad feeling between mother and son: neither did he want to hide behind Mazie. But even if she hadn't told him that Derrymore was out of sorts he would have guessed it by the younger man's behaviour. And by the look of strain he'd never seen before.

'Mazie mainly said I'd better watch my back,' he replied at last, 'or words to that effect. Said strange things have been happening in the village that as a villager now myself I ought to know about.'

It was a fair answer. Derrymore, always the soul of fairness, accepted it. 'Look,' he began less stiffly, 'I haven't come to you myself like, for several reasons.' He hesitated, as if about to reveal them or at least list them in some sort of order, then thought better of it. 'I don't know if you're aware,' he finally came out with in such a way as to suggest that he was trying to be tactful, 'there's an undercurrent against your writings. I've never known anything like it, there's the truth, and this book-burning just about puts the finishing touch. It's all over the village now that only your books were burnt.'

Again he considered for a moment before finishing more firmly, 'I don't hold with arson, of course. And if I find who's responsible, I'll clap them in prison, see if I don't. But it does make complications about asking for your help, you can see that I'm sure.'

Something about the way Derrymore said this suddenly made Reynolds angry, as if in attacking his books the sergeant was attacking him. He'd always taken pride in keeping aloof from criticism of his work, and was somewhat surprised to find objectivity was so much more difficult now he was having trouble writing anything at all! Before he could stop himself he barked, 'Meaning that you yourself agree with my detractors. You think my books, if not burnt, should be withdrawn from circulation?'

Derrymore drew himself upright until he was standing to attention. Sweat had beaded round his hairline. But the expression in his eyes was pained rather than hostile.

'Yes, I do think so,' he said finally. He wiped his face with a large handkerchief. 'For the time being.' And as Reynolds started to protest, 'You suggested so much yourself, a few moments ago.'

This remark didn't improve Reynolds' temper. Nor did

Derrymore's next comment. The sergeant still faced Reynolds squarely, although to give him his due, he continued to look embarrassed. 'It's not even a matter of what I think,' he said. 'It's what other people say. Besides, there's been so much copy-cat crime these days, it's always on the telly, no one wants the criminal faction in the village to get the wrong ideas.'

And having got that out of his system, he finished equally stiffly, 'And I didn't like to disturb you when I heard you've been busy with your own affairs, or so Miss Heyward says.'

There was something in the way he slipped in the name that made Reynolds bite back a hot response. Sally Heyward, he thought. I didn't know he and she were on such friendly terms. But bless my soul, surely he's known all along what I hired her for – and precious little of it at the moment. I think Mazie's right, something else is biting him, and he can't bring himself to say what it is.

He resisted the impulse to argue – to say that in his opinion if anything encouraged copy-cat crime, television was more to blame then books; and if Miss Heyward had explained why he was so 'busy' surely she would have also explained with what little result. Damn it all, he thought, why should I apologise for my own problems just to make Derrymore feel better because he can't cope with his own?

By now, they had returned to their starting point. The sun was beginning to come out from under the bank of clouds, gilding the edges of the stream, and a duck or two quacked loudly under the bridge where they were playing in the current. The bell-ringing practice was apparently over and the ringers were beginning to come out from the church on the far side of the stream. As if regretting his outburst, Derrymore said as awkwardly, 'Well, this won't buy the baby a bonnet. Back to work I suppose.'

But his heart wasn't in what he was saying and his joke fell flat. He made no mention of Reynolds accompanying him as he normally would, in fact he deliberately waited as if expecting Reynolds to leave.

Reynolds felt strangely deflated, a feeling he wasn't used to. 'If you haven't any leads, except for graffiti, which seems unfortunately to get lost,' he said, keeping his voice even, 'then you'd better go hunt some up.' As if an after-thought, he added, 'Drop in sometime and let me know the outcome. Good luck.'

And although aware that sounded more like a brush-off than he intended, and yet equally aware he wasn't in a position to do the brushing-off, he hurried away in the opposite direction, anger rising at every step.

It wasn't all directed at Derrymore; poor Mazie got her share, wasting her efforts and his. And so did Dr Sinclair, at first appearing to defer to him in an ingratiating way, then not revealing anything!

Suppose it was one of his little jokes, he thought, part of his absent-minded professor routine. And suppose Derrymore let me tag along just now because refusing to do so would really be insulting. Well, if they want to play games for some reason, it's all the same to me; I've no axe to grind – and was suitably ashamed of the bitterness behind his thoughts.

It was little consolation, after a long walk along a moorland track had cooled him off, to reflect that probably there would be no further need of his services anyway. The troubles in the village must have run their course by now, and Derrymore would pull himself together to manage on his own. He could never have been more wrong.

Left on the green, Derrymore still didn't move. He was watching the bell ringers. By now they had come through the lych gate and were milling about the old cross, all except one. This was a strange figure who broke away from the others and loped off with a curious half-running trot towards the eastern end of the village. As he ran, his corduroy trousers, tied with string above his thick boots, creaked stiffly, and his heavy moleskin coat, its large pockets flapping about his knees, gave him a conspicuously old-fashioned appearance, like a nineteenth-century poacher.

Derrymore knew him well; even from a distance the misshapen head with its fringe of red hair, the full lips that smiled like a child, the blue, china-doll eyes, meant Rab Tremayne could never be mistaken for anyone else. And he knew where he was going, back to the isolated cottage on the moors where he lived, like a fox to its den, away from the village where his presence aroused curiosity and dislike.

'Didn't think he was capable of bell ringing.' 'Didn't think he could speak.' 'Didn't know he was capable of any thing, should be put into a home.'

Useless to defend him, say that he isn't stupid, only different; that in the old days he'd be thought of as an innocent. As for bell ringing, he started when a boy because his father taught him and he can learn things by rote. And no good to say, my mam and I have always been friendly with him since his father died. And in return for what he can't put into words, he's left us signs of appreciation: a fresh-laid egg, a bunch of flowers with the dew still on the petals, a bundle of firewood – strange, unique gifts from a strange, unique person.

It's all very well to say I'm a good policeman because I listen, he thought. 'Keep your ears to the ground, boy,' his predecessor had said, and he had. But these days there was too much to listen to, too many foreign sounds; it was difficult to judge what was important, what was trivial.

Sometimes, he thought despondently, I'm like an old person in a young man's body; I don't move with the times. That's what people used to like about me, stability they called it, and it made them trust me. Not any more. Village life is changing, and I'm already feeling, what's the expression, redundant, as if getting the sack sounds better with a new word.

He gave a sigh that came from his boots. If only he could get over this feeling that worse was to come, the sense of foreboding, of warning. If only he hadn't come down so heavily on Mr Reynolds as being at the root. I can only defend my position with Mr Reynolds, he thought uneasily, by saying he's able to take care of himself. He's strong enough to bear the brunt; I can't be responsible for him too. But although he spoke forcefully he wasn't really convinced. As far as he was concerned Reynolds was the lesser of two evils; he just hoped he'd made the right choice.

The running figure had disappeared by now. Derry knew he should chase after him and speak to him but already it was too late; he'd be lost among his moorland haunts, no knowing where he went. Derry sighed again. After all, it wasn't his fault, he couldn't waste precious time; he'd other things to worry about.

His personal problems seemed to heap themselves upon his broad shoulders; he'd never felt such weight – if his mam's wishes and hints and prods could be called problems and if Miss Heyward didn't add to them. He knew what his mam was after, mind you; she made no bones about it, but he himself didn't like being rushed. He was pretty sure but not yet sure enough to venture out into deeper water. Slow and steady was his game.

And then there was Sally herself. Too good for him by far he knew, he was the last man to have expected such luck. And if she was too good for him, while he dawdled and hung back someone else might be interested enough to snap her up and there would be an end to it. Except that would break his mam's heart – and probably his.

Of course his mam would say he was being a real dog-in-the-manager, and so he was. Look how he'd reacted when she'd defended Reynolds and she merely worked for him. Was that why he'd treated Reynolds the way he had, to pay him back perhaps for her show of loyalty? And yet if he was in her position and had to choose between the two of them, he knew who he'd put his money on, so much did he admire the older man.

He knew he was usually considered affable and good natured; he tried to be a friend to all. But if village affairs suddenly had become too complex to manage, so had the complexities of his own life. And if I turn out a mere turnip head, he thought despondently, a simpleton like my mam says, then I'd better give up my job as well and go live like a hermit with Rab Tremayne. And only one thing is clear in all this mess, no one can help; we've got to sort it out ourselves and do the best we can. I'm doing Mr Reynolds a favour if only he knew it; he's better off not involved.

Like the ex-inspector, he, too, could never have been more wrong.

Chapter 4

Either the long hike did Reynolds good, or perhaps it was the meal he ordered at a wayside pub, with a bottle of wine to top it off: he slept better than he had for weeks. He woke early to sun and shadow chasing over the bedroom wall, and the rustle of wind in the branches of a flowering pear tree. He lay for a moment luxuriating. Mazie was right about one thing after all, writing didn't have to be martyrdom and if necessary, deadlines could be altered. He wasn't a slave and his publishers weren't ogres! He'd phone Sally Heyward today and tell her not to come again while he took a holiday from work. In the meanwhile there was nothing to stop him doing whatever he felt like doing, even tracking down the source of the rumours about his book. And after he had shut the gossips up once and for all, he'd return to his neglected manuscript, invigorated, full of ideas.

For a moment he felt pleased at the prospect. Then common sense took over. Mainly, that it hardly seemed fair to put Sally out of work because he needed time off. To begin with she was the best secretary he'd ever had. And he had the impression, although she'd never said so, that things hadn't been easy these past months since her former job had folded and she'd had to make do with part-time work.

He suspected all this had come about mainly because of the notoriety of the case in which she really had been an unfortunate bystander. And as he had been the reason for its ending as it did, he had felt some responsibility for her welfare afterwards.

He grimaced. He hadn't thought much about all this, or even much about her personally; another example of his selfish absorption. He only knew he had come to rely on her showing up three times or so a week, often his only human contact during this period. If asked, he might have admitted looking forward to seeing her, if he hadn't been so irritated by his own unproductiveness.

He knew she was efficient and good-humoured, willing to put up with his grumpiness. Now he remembered how once, when she had ventured to suggest that the motives of his 'hero' had scarcely appeared 'heroic', he had cut her short coldly (although, on reconsideration, her criticism reflected his own dissatisfaction with the book). At the time, her smile had faded, and the brightness had gone out of her eyes. After that she had never volunteered another opinion, never commented on his progress, or lack of it. No real conversation had taken place between them – so again it was just as well that she and Derrymore apparently had found pleasure in each other's company.

He began to think about her in light of this new relationship. When they had first met he'd been impressed by her lack of conceit, rare in so attractive a girl – and by her sense of loyalty, also rare. But she was a sophisticated young woman who might think of looking higher than a village policeman when she had recovered from the trauma of her former love.

The sound of the telephone broke in on his musings. Reaching for it out of habit he barked his name, heard someone say, 'There's been an accident.'

Not another, he thought dismayed, listening to the voice fade and blur on a mobile phone as presumably a car bounced over rough terrain. It wasn't a voice he recognised although it soon identified itself; Brad Nicholls, Inspector, of the Devon and Cornwall Constabulary, and could Reynolds come along? It was the sort of thing they thought he'd be interested in and they could do with his help, did he know where the disused quarry was?

Reynolds sat bolt upright, almost rubbing his eyes. Given the number of times he'd been positively banned from official investigations; given the usual hostility of the place where he'd once worked (now dominated by an old enemy who had done his best to ruin him) this offer of friendly co-operation from headquarters took him by surprise. It was not until Brad Nicholls asked again if he knew where the quarry was that he pulled himself together to get directions.

'A mile or so from the village,' Inspector Nicholls explained, sounding agitated. 'To the left of, where's the damn place, the St Breward Road. Apparently a rock fall. I'm on my way there now.'

A pause, while the background static increased. The 'Can you join us?' was again blurted out as if the inspector expected a refusal. Only after Reynolds' assurance that he would be with him as soon as possible, did he add in a muffled voice, 'If what they say is true, we've got a damn disaster on our hands.'

Reynolds heard him take a breath as if about to elaborate. Instead, after another great burst of static, Nicholls hung up, leaving Reynolds with a strange mixture of feelings. It was nice for once to be asked to help. It was only when he turned on to the St Breward Road that he wondered where Derrymore was, and whether, ironic in the circumstances, the sergeant (who would normally be informed first about local accidents) would have consulted him at all!

Actually the quarry wasn't far from the outskirts of St Breddaford, and he'd heard it often mentioned as a rendezvous for courting couples on summer evenings. As he came up to it he thought it a gloomy sort of place, the lane leading to it surrounded by straggling brambles and gorse bushes, and pitted with stagnant puddles of ochre mud left behind by the rain. Discarded rocks lay scattered beneath the undergrowth, as if, at a given signal, the workers had downed their tools and let the stones fall at random.

At the entrance to the quarry itself, the lane widened into an open area where old machinery was slowly dissolving into rust. On the right was a parking space; on the left, a large pool, whose water was so still and dark its surface had taken on the oily sheen that denotes great depth. Behind both pool and parking area, forming a semicircle round them, the face of the quarry rose up in a jagged cliff, adding to the gloom.

So far, only two police cars had arrived, neither of them Derrymore's. They had drawn up at the edge of the open area, and a few people had gathered around them while an officer, again unknown, attempted to take evidence. Another man, out of uniform, was crouched beside a third car which was parked beneath the cliff, broadside to it, as if trying to hide itself, or make ready for a quick get-away. But it wasn't a whole car. Its newish white front stuck out from a pile of rocks as if someone had tried to drive through them, while its rear was completely buried under what was obviously a landslide.

As Reynolds slowed down, the uniformed officer came forward then, hearing his name, waved him on. Conscious of several strange glances, Reynolds drew up. As he got out, a man with a fishing rod in his hand came running up, self-importantly pointing out the obvious. 'Now then, now then,' the officer said, 'we've already had your statement.' And to Reynolds, 'Inspector Nicholls is over there, sir. A sorry business.'

Close up the cliff glinted, its layers of rocks dark grey and ominous, except where the scar of the fall had left a broad, lighter streak. As he approached, Reynolds' feet made loud crunching noises on the gravel, and the sound of the chief witness wailing about his lost morning's fishing took on operatic dimensions – the effect of an echo chamber formed by the encircling walls.

At Reynolds' approach, Brad Nicholls straightened himself up. Of medium height, with a square open face, topped by a thatch of short brown hair, he stood summing Reynolds up with knowing eyes. A typical police detective, Reynolds thought, assessing him in turn, a face so commonplace it becomes anonymous, lost in a crowd. Yet the handshake was firm and the dark brown eyes, if shrewd, had laugh wrinkles round them. So far so good.

When Inspector Nicholls spoke his Midlands accent, blurred on the phone, became more pronounced. A stranger to Cornwall then, Reynolds thought, a real unknown. That explains a lot. And helps us start on even terms.

Quick introductions over and the necessary polite formalities observed, Brad Nicholls beckoned to Reynolds to look inside the remains of the car. The rear was mangled out of recognition. Peering through the window, under the tangle of metal Reynolds could just make out the white shape of two bodies, both naked, their arms and legs entwined like tentacles. And obviously dead.

'Ye Gods,' he said, startled. 'Any idea who they are? And what in heaven's name were they doing here?'

His question was fatuous. Why else did lovers come to this deserted place, if not to make love?

'Car belongs to Frank Barker,' Nicholls said. 'Identified by the fellow who alerted us.' He gestured to the man with the fishing line. 'Says he came here to catch perch this morning, and Barker is his neighbour, down at Mill End. Says they usually play snooker together of a Tuesday evening but he didn't show last night.'

'And the woman?'

Nicholls lips worked. 'Well,' he said at last, 'we've had a second call. From someone who says she's Mrs Barker. Reporting her husband missing. And if she's his wife, then the woman in there certainly isn't!'

Reynolds gave a silent whistle. Frank Barker was the middle-aged bank manager of the local branch, a conscientious little fellow, bristling with self-importance. A stalwart on the village council, a great church-goer, he was always squeaking on about law and order. Here was scandal in the making.

After a moment or two spent in contemplating the wreck of the car – and the grief and shame its discovery would cause: two presumably upright citizens caught out in the most compromising position – he asked the leading questions: 'Any idea what caused the rock fall? Was it an accident?'

And when Nicholls didn't answer directly, more specifically, 'What makes you think it was deliberate?'

The answer was reluctant, and revealed at least in one thing headquarters hadn't changed. 'It would be just my bad luck,' Nicholls said slowly, 'to be stuck with a humdinger of a case that'll drag on for weeks. And as far as I can tell, there's not been a natural rockfall here for years.' He looked miserable at the possibility of being kept in the country, in what for him was a foreign backwater. Although if he's just joined the Devon and Cornwall Constabulary, Reynolds thought, he should have expected rural crimes.

'We may draw the obvious conclusions what the couple in the car were doing,' Nicholls went on, even more miserably, 'but if someone else was around to start the rocks rolling, he must have been up there.'

He pointed towards the cliff behind them. 'And if he did so deliberately, how the hell are we going to get up to find the proof? I'm no rock climber, and neither is anyone on my team.'

He lapsed into silence, as if the prospect of scrabbling about rock quarries was as daunting as living in a village. If what he claims is true, Reynolds thought, with sudden understanding, no wonder he's latched on to me. This is the type of work I thrive on these days, and I bet he knows it. He looked at Nicholls more carefully. He hadn't been wrong then about the shrewdness in those eyes. But where on earth was Derrymore? He ought to be here by now. This was his patch.

As if he realized he'd already revealed too much, the inspector added somewhat apologetically, 'We've sent for your local man; should have done so first off, I suppose, but as it happened the calls came through to headquarters so they picked me to come down. And when I realized it was your neck of the woods, so to speak, I couldn't resist getting in touch. The rest of the team is on their way, by the by, and we've just called out the fire engine to deal with the car. If there's proof waiting for us up there we need it, and someone should get it for us before it's lost.'

It was as good as asking Reynolds outright. Reynolds stared at the cliffs. He suspected there were easier routes to the top, from the side of the quarry, for example, but if time was important, and he accepted that it was, at least in the search for the kind of evidence Nicholls had in mind, the quickest way was to climb up. He said to Nicholls, 'If I find anything for your team to look at, I'll signal you from the top. If I get there. And I may not be able to come down the same way.'

As far as he could tell the best place to start was halfway round the pool, where a few small bushes and plants springing out of the cliff face gave some possibility of hand and foot-holds.

He turned to the others. 'Anyone ever climbed from here?' he asked. And when there was no response, 'What about the pool? Any path round it?'

The fisherman now came forward reluctantly, as if afraid of being asked to volunteer. 'Used to be when I was a lad,' he said at last. 'Some slippy, mind. Fish from the shore these days. Safer like.'

His nervous laugh was drowned in the common mutter that only a fool would try to scramble round the pool, let alone go up the cliff. Reynolds wasn't listening. Miraculously, he'd seen a line to take between the terraces of granite that looked relatively easy. He had already removed his jacket and was picking his way over the rocks, thanking his stars he had worn thick boots; they'd come in useful on the climb.

As the fisherman had said, the rocks were slippery, covered with green slime, and the sheerness of the cliff behind them was intimidating. He slowed down. If Brad Nicholls had made it clear he didn't like climbing, Reynolds didn't like water, and the possibility of falling into those murky depths was frightening, especially because he couldn't swim. Instead then of leaping confidently from rock to rock as Derrymore for example would have done, he found he was clawing his way along, scrabbling for holds, his boots soaked where they slid into the water. When he missed his footing and almost crashed head first, he clung to the point of rock that had checked his fall and cursed himself. So much for curiosity, he thought, so much for letting myself be conned. Didn't I tell myself I'd nothing to prove? It was only when he came to the actual cliffs, that he found the strength to forge ahead again, this part of the climb having no dangers for him although in fact it was probably the hardest part of all.

It took him longer than he expected to reach the top, by then out of breath and covered with scratches from the sharp edges of the rocks. Do that a couple of times a week, I'll be in shape again, he thought, as he heaved himself to his feet and peered down.

From this height the people and cars below looked like toys. Beyond the actual quarry he could see towards the moors, where the outcrops of Brown Willie and Roughtor were just emerging from mist. Westwards, a faint line between horizon and cloud suggested that on really fine days there would be glimpses of the distant sea, never far from sight in Cornwall. Behind him, as he had expected, an overgrown wilderness dipped down into a mass of gullies and steep rocky gorges which he presumed would eventually emerge into an equal maze of fields, from which somewhere there would be lanes or roads connecting to the real world. For a moment, the sound of the fisherman still protesting, the lap of water, seemed to belong to another time – until the far-off whine of a siren brought him back to the work in hand.

The top of the quarry had obviously not been disturbed in years; it was an animal haven. A couple of rabbits scuttled into hiding and there was a rank smell of fox. Here too bits of broken cables and winches littered the ground, poking out of the brambles like red skeletons. Gingerly he picked his way back to where he thought the rock slide must have started – and found it easily enough, running down from a gap in a sequence of granite posts or pillars which marked the edge of the quarry, although the wooden rails which had connected them had long rotted away.

The gap was freshly made; the raw earth where the missing post had been was the same faint ochre colour as the scar beneath. And beneath again, buried under the accumulation of rocks and stones, lay the crushed remains of the car – at first glance a natural disaster, caused perhaps by the rain, the main pillar giving way and bringing down everything else with its fall. He was about to shout these observations down to the waiting inspector when he spotted the first clue.

He almost stepped on it, a scrape on a flat rock near-by, a faint line made by the claw of some animal. But once properly identifying it as a nail mark from a boot, he soon found the boot-print itself, the outline of the toe cap with the nails, distinct in the mud.

It had been dry all last week, so the mud must have been caused by yesterday's rain. And the boot mark belonged to a countryman's good hob-nailed boot. And yes, here's another thing. His attention had been caught by something hanging in the gorse bushes that leaned over the quarry beside the gap. Bending down, he began to push his way beneath them, hoping they wouldn't give under his weight. They crackled and bent ominously, the thorns catching at face and hands, until he had crawled far enough in to identify what he'd seen – a tuft of grass with its roots still on, dangling from a branch. And stuffed underneath it, more tufts, these with fresh muddy roots, recently dug up, possibly pried out in clumps from around the pillar, and then hidden deliberately.

Reynolds crawled back from the edge. Brushing the gorse prickles out of his hair he stood up, looking around him for some sort of bar that could have been used to dig up the grass or pry out the pillar. There were many suitable pieces; it would be worth a search. He formulated his thoughts. Someone, his guess a local man, the boots were certainly meant for rough country wear, had pried a granite pillar loose by first tearing out the grass which helped hold it in place, afterwards hiding the tufts in the gorse bush. As the roots were still wet all this must have been some time yesterday, probably before dark. Afterwards, all the person had to do was wait until the car arrived and parked underneath; he had only to set the main stone pillar going and the rest of the landslip would take place as a matter of course. But had he been waiting for that particular car? Or were Mr Barker and his partner unfortunate victims of chance?

He looked around him again. 'But no matter who the victim,' he told himself, 'if the slide was set deliberately, that means murder.'

He spoke to himself, but using the word aloud made it seem probable at last.

He was suddenly silent then, thinking of the effect of that swift and deadly fall upon the car's occupants. As the first rock crashed on top of them, did they feel a moment's panic as they realised their danger? Had they had time to struggle to escape before being crushed? He hoped not, for their sakes better quickly over and done with.

After a while he roused himself to practical realities. Someone official ought to get up here quickly to examine and record the evidence. But he couldn't imagine anyone from headquarters climbing up the way he'd come – and as he had suspected, descent by the same route was impossible. Nor could he follow the lip of the quarry round, as its previous workers had done, because the way was blocked by a chasm created by an old rockfall. He would have to force a route through the dense scrub behind him. And he wasn't sure exactly where he'd hit the line of the road. He signalled down the news of his findings, and the direction he was planning to take, waited for Brad Nicholls' response and, after several consultations with maps, was rewarded with an enthusiastic waving of hands.

The fire engine could be heard more clearly now, clanging its way towards the quarry floor. Another official car had arrived, the portly gentleman getting out was the police doctor. Still no sign of Derrymore, but Reynolds couldn't wait any longer. Mud dries out fast and the day was promising to be hot. The boot print might be lost, and grass roots are hard to identify unless still fresh.

Before he set off he paused to listen. There was no other sound, no birds' calls, no rustle now of animals in the dense undergrowth in front of him. It had already occurred to him, although he'd deliberately suppressed the idea, that if someone had pushed those rocks off the cliff he had to be strong – and clever. Strength and cleverness combined always spelt trouble.

He still hesitated. The area was one of the patches of really inaccessible terrain he was always coming across in rural Cornwall, often surrounding the derelict workings of some ancient mine, all that was left of former days he supposed, when much of the countryside must have looked like this. And there was no way of knowing where the murderer was now, or if he had actually left the scene of the crime. Stay alert, he told himself.

Moving swiftly, wherever possible keeping under cover (skills he had learned from his wartime experiences) he plunged silently down into the first gully where bracken fronds which might have shielded him, had not yet uncurled. The dead stalks of last year's growth tangled in knots round his feet and pockets of moss-covered stones poked up through the heather roots, traps for the unwary. Soon he was deep in a sort of rocky cleft where long grass and brambles entwined and tore, and it was impossible to see ahead, the underbrush as dense as any jungle.

Even for him the going was hard and he began to sweat. When eventually he reached a ridge covered with low stunted trees, he was reminded of a time in his multi-faceted career when he had taken part in a tiger hunt. That the tiger was old and maimed, the cause of its becoming a man eater, hadn't dimmed the memory of the first piece of advice he'd been given: 'Step off the path and the tiger will be waiting.' Only to be topped by the second: 'Stay on the path, the tiger knows it better than you do!' The fact that there was no path, and as far as he could see no visible signs of a tiger, didn't offer much consolation – if the equivalent of a tiger was lurking somewhere. With more relief than he liked to admit he came eventually to the first hedge, hauled himself up and over, and found himself standing in a ploughed field.

Several fields on, by now muddied beyond recognition, he still was no closer to a road. As he wearily struggled through another hedge, again cursing his own officiousness – there was no reason to volunteer like this, he didn't have to be involved – he was finally rewarded with the last clue he'd been looking for. Beside an overgrown stile, a set of boot prints showed someone else had been this way recently. And as far as he could tell, the prints matched those on top of the quarry. The glint of a tarmac road on the other side of the stile was an added bonus, as welcome as the eventual hooting from an official car when, half an hour later, it caught up with him.

The car was Derrymore's. There was no time to ask Derrymore where he'd been, or explain how he himself came to be there – in Derrymore's wake followed a procession of other official cars, manned by people from headquarters, all of whom looked appalled at the prospect before them, dressed as they were in their city clothes. He caught their covert glances and almost laughed.

They also commented loudly and not unfavourably on his presence, (which, thank God, he noted they didn't challenge). In fact, before they set off towards the quarry, one said, with a wink, 'Knew you must be about once rock climbing was mentioned. The guv actually admitted himself he'd asked you to try it out first.'

Reynolds allowed himself a grin. He understood from this cryptic message, as he was meant to, that the team was being sympathetic – and as long as Derrymore didn't bring up problems, all looked set and fair.

It was therefore with some satisfaction that he gave directions, and watched the team straggle over the stile and begin the work of measuring and photographing the first prints before starting across the muddy fields, carrying their various apparatus with them.

'That should keep them busy,' he said, easing himself in the car beside Derrymore. 'While they're slashing through the undergrowth, let's track down the actual tiger.' An observation that caused Derrymore's mouth to purse, although he was perhaps too accustomed to Reynolds to ask what he meant. It was not until they had been driving a while that it occurred to Reynolds that Derrymore hadn't asked any questions about anything.

Chapter 5

Back at the quarry they found everything under firm control. The fire engine had gone. The customary blue plastic covers had been set up to facilitate the gruesome task of examining the bodies and the time of death had now been tentatively set shortly after midnight. In short the investigation was proceeding at a normal pace; only the officers sent to the quarry top had so far failed to arrive, and their comments, coming in over their mobile phone, suggested they were really struggling!

After filling in the details of his findings, and assuring Brad Nicholls that his subordinates were in no immediate danger, except from mud, Reynolds asked who the woman victim was – to be told that she had been identified as a Mrs Caddick, and both families had been informed, although Mr Caddick had failed to report that she was missing.

'Under the circumstances,' Brad Nicholls took Reynolds by the arm and led him out of earshot, 'that looks suspicious, don't you agree?'

He smiled hopefully at Reynolds, still looking for a quick solution, and although again not quite asking outright for Reynolds' services, left the way open for him to volunteer by going on to suggest he needed 'someone experienced' to 'squeeze a confession out'.

'Under the circumstances,' he repeated, a favourite expression, Reynolds was to discover, 'either of the relatives could be prime suspects. Although I put my money on Caddick.'

Although not agreeing at all with this analysis, in fact from long experience already suspicious that the solution should be so simple, and after a mental battle in which once more curiosity outweighed sense, Reynolds finally offered to go to the interview – providing someone official accompanied him to do the talking – namely Derrymore who was hovering in the background, looking distinctly harassed.

'Good man.' Nicholls' relief was obvious. 'Never was much of a hand myself with country people. And by all means take Derrymore with you; I know how well you and he co-operate.' He grasped Reynolds' arm even more confidentially, to whisper, 'By taking the original phone calls, I'm afraid we've really put his nose out of joint.'

Reynolds refrained from arguing that Derrymore wasn't petty-minded. But given the number of times he and the sergeant had been prevented from working together, Brad Nicholls' affability had a humorous side – and made the tension between him and Derrymore all the more absurd.

For there still was tension between them, and as Reynolds drove himself back to change into decent clothes, he tried to pin-point the cause. For his own part he admitted he was still irritated with the sergeant; he couldn't quite get over Derrymore's apparent willingness to go along with current gossip so far as to seem anxious to exclude Reynolds from participation in the investigations. As for Derrymore's own position, in normal circumstances he would have been as amused as Reynolds at the change in headquarters' attitude. But presumably if his disapproval of Reynolds' books hadn't altered, then the behaviour of Brad Nicholls, and of headquarters in general, must be especially galling, no doubt accentuating his stated reluctance to work with the ex-inspector.

Joining the sergeant in the official car, he resolved to downplay his own feelings, and try to get to the root of

Derrymore's troubles. Although Derrymore could be stubborn, like his mam, he was honest. Whatever was wrong eventually would come out into the open, if Reynolds could restrain his own impatience.

Leaving the village they drove in silence, however, and excepting for Reynolds' involuntary gasps as they approached every corner – Derrymore's driving was notoriously erratic – any attempt to justify his presence remained unspoken. It was all very different from other occasions, when, on the way to an interview, the two men discussed the situation and decided what questions they should concentrate on – or rather Derrymore asked for advice, and Reynolds gave it. As the official representative, of course Derrymore usually did the actual questioning, but in the past he'd always relied on Reynolds' superior knowledge of tactics.

The odd thing was it wasn't exactly that Derrymore seemed resentful of being obliged to work with Reynolds. Rather, he was more preoccupied than ever with something he didn't want to talk about. Reynolds began to feel seriously worried, especially when this lack of interest showed itself during the first interview.

Their destination was Mill End, a few miles from St Breddaford, the site of the Barker residence, a modern house. Set back from the road and shielded by trees, nevertheless it looked incongruous compared with the simple stone cottages in the village.

'Supposed to be farmland.' As they got out of the police car, Derrymore revived sufficiently to pass on this information. 'Gossip has it that Barker used his influence to get the plans passed.'

Reynolds gave him a quizzical look but made no retort although it was on the tip of his tongue to ask if the gossip had the same origin as that against him. In general, village gossip never ceased to amaze him; city life had nothing to equal it unless it was in the news passed on by informers who lived by their wits. He never knew when to take gossip seriously although Derrymore seemed to, instinctively. If he's hinting that Barker dabbled in other illicit ventures besides keeping a mistress, he thought, that's a valuable lead. But he didn't ask for details, and Derrymore gave none.

Mrs Barker answered the door, a thin, narrow-faced woman in a surprising pink suit. Her cheeks were blotched with crying and her nervous hands twitched at her jacket as if it were too tight. She doesn't look criminal material, Reynolds assessed, as they followed her into her living room, but sometimes appearances can be deceptive.

The living room was also pink; he felt he were sinking into a bowl of strawberry jam as Derrymore, a solid and uncompromising blue, stationed himself in front of the patio windows, and after offering official sympathies began to question her. She herself, half-hidden beneath the sofa cushions, peered up at him, her pointed nose twitching like a frightened pink rabbit.

Usually Derrymore was a good interviewer, showing just the right touch of sympathy and knowing when to turn on the screws. Today he seemed conspicuously uninterested. His tone was leaden, allowing Mrs Barker to burst into tears at any mention of her dead husband, while the conditions of where he had been found and the cause of his death brought on hysterics. It was only when Derrymore was preparing to leave that she let her true colours show.

'And if it's murder,' she exclaimed, her lips narrowing even more thinly, 'I could have murdered him myself.' An unfortunate admission which she immediately tried to rectify, without success.

'Imagine what I put up with,' she added virtuously, as if, once embarked on confession, she might as well do it thoroughly. 'Never knew when he'd be back. Always some excuse, as if I didn't know him well enough to tell when he was lying.'

When, taking up the questioning which by now Derrymore seemed to have dropped completely, Reynolds asked tactfully what various commitments Mr Barker had, outside office hours that is.

'Monday it was bowling,' she interrupted. 'Tuesday he played snooker.' Again her lips twitched. 'Wednesdays was the philatelist club. Thursday was council meetings; Friday, a night out with the lads. All contrived to hide his goings-on with her, the bitch, and half the village knew it. They were too afraid of him, or too mean, to tell me straight out.'

'They may not have wanted to upset you.' Reynolds was still being tactful.

She snapped at him, 'They didn't mind a little titter at my expense behind my back.'

'And did you and Mr Barker ever discuss the, er, situation?'

'He wasn't likely to.' The answer was sharp. 'And why should I bring it up, just to hear him lie again? At his age too, like some silly teenager.'

Here the memory of her husband's 'goings-on' in the back seat of the family car brought on another attack of tears, at the end of which she thanked God her son was away from home, although that wouldn't spare him the humiliation of seeing her name plastered all over the papers.

Reynolds had spotted the son already in a large photograph, prominently displayed on the piano. The photograph revealed a young man, closely resembling his mother down to the pointed nose and narrow lips. He was dressed in white tie and tails and his conscious simper suggested he was enjoying the effect.

'A university dinner to celebrate his doctorate,' his mother said, noticing Reynolds' glance and pride getting the better of her. 'Of course he knows nothing about my troubles,

Inspector. I never told him, not when he was so busy with his thesis and all. He's just been made a lecturer. Imagine, and him so young.'

She went on to name the institution, in the next county, but although Reynolds was curious to know more about this younger paragon of learning, and indicated his interest to Derrymore, the sergeant ignored the hint. Instead he went off at a surprisingly abrupt tangent to question Mrs Barker about her own movements, specifically on the night of the murder.

He'd got no further than, 'And while your husband was out, what did you do?' when naturally she bristled.

'Not amuse myself with a fancy man, if that's what you mean,' she flared. 'But I didn't stay at home either. There's a lot to do even in a small village. I play Scrabble twice a week and belong to a book club. And if,' she added shrewdly, 'you're trying to find out where I was yesterday evening, talk to Elsie next door. She and I went to the pictures and didn't get back until eleven. We went in her car, he had ours.'

Again she began to sob, although the thought of that smashed car might have been the cause this time.

Reynolds changed the subject. She was village born and bred, he believed, not like her husband who came from up-country. He waited while she compiled a list of the short-comings of Yorkshire men, then asked if she knew of anyone in the village who might hold a grudge. She gave a grimace. 'A bank manager isn't popular,' she told him. 'Not these days. All those business closures, those failed mortgages. People always blame the banks, not themselves.'

She had a point. Like other places, St Breddaford had suffered in the recent recession, which still kept its grip in the west country. Reynolds made another mental note to suggest that Mr Barker's banking activities should be looked into.

'But nothing personal?'

It might have been a trick of the light: her eyes narrowed for a moment. 'How do I know?' she said with a return to her original virtuous tone. 'He didn't tell me. But,' she leaned forward, 'I can't believe there aren't people who disliked him because of what he was doing. Bringing disgrace upon the bank and council, for one thing. And on the church. And him claiming to be such a devout Christian.'

She spoke defiantly now. 'And what about the other woman's husband? If anyone had a right to kill he did.'

'She's supplied us with a nice list of motives.' When they were outside Reynolds couldn't resist summing up. 'And left us in no doubt that she was well aware of her husband's wrong-doings. Although how much she accepted them in a Christian spirit herself is less certain. She sounds pretty bitter to me.'

'But not bitter enough to go trotting through the under-brush to push a heap of stones on him and his girlfriend.' Derrymore was surprisingly sarcastic. 'If she did, she's a better cross-country expert than you are.'

'Oh, I don't say she did it herself.' Reynolds ignored the sarcasm. 'But there's nothing to stop her getting someone to do the nasty for her. A bribe perhaps. Or blackmail. I'd certainly check if she really was with Elsie, as she claims. And what about that son of hers? I'd like to know more about him. Where was he last night? If he's at the university she mentioned, he could get back here in a couple of hours.'

He mused for a moment. 'And then there's Barker. If he's been abusing his position as councillor by changing planning laws, who knows what else he might have been up to. Suppose he's been dealing out the bank's money for favours – and it's gone sour, leaving someone with a grievance.'

He was improvising now, well away into his favourite

exercise of playing with ideas, some probable, some not. Yet in the past many of his best solutions had come from this type of theorising, even of the most improbable kind.

Usually Derrymore enjoyed going along with him, keeping his feet on the ground and playing the 'straight man' to his fancies. Today Derrymore made it clear he wouldn't play at all. When Reynolds suggested, 'Supposing one of his dissatisfied clients decided to get his own back,' Derrymore broke in with, 'Just because he builds his house where he's not allowed to, doesn't mean he's been diddling the bank or its customers.'

He stared at the ground. 'Anyway, until we check it out there's no point in guessing.' An even more brusque dismissal.

'Stalemate for the moment then.' Giving up, and again ignoring Derrymore's tone, Reynolds fitted himself back into the car. 'All the same I'd like to know who Mr Barker's friends or enemies are.'

Derrymore wasn't listening. He didn't start the car, instead sat staring ahead. At last he burst out, 'I can't get it out of my mind.'

He didn't say what the 'it' was, in fact when he added after a pause, 'You see, I know that quarry. Used to play there when I was a kid,' Reynolds had the impression that he had thought this up as an excuse to hide what he really meant to say. But when Derrymore went on to explain that he had almost thought of going there himself the other night, when he was taking Miss Heyward home, except she 'wasn't keen', he did believe him. He presumed that Derrymore was hinting he'd had thoughts of a little courting session himself and had been talked out of it. And it seemed to him the name had been slipped in intentionally.

He sat back without comment. The friendship was beginning to sound more serious than he'd given credit for.

Damn, Reynolds thought. If Sally's 'not being keen' means what I think then no wonder poor Derrymore is in a state, as his mam put it. But it's not like him to discuss his love affairs, and surely he's too experienced to let personal matters cloud his professional status. He waited for Derrymore to explain further but, as if ashamed of his outburst, the sergeant said nothing more. And so once again they drove on in silence.

Their next stop was to talk with the murdered woman's husband, Dave Caddick. Again, if Mrs Barker was right, there were plenty of people in the village who could have named him and his errant wife, including Mrs Barker herself. Now that the identification was official, they had actually been given her picture, a pretty, vivacious woman in her mid-thirties. Her face, laughing at them from a photograph, was especially poignant.

Her name was Betty, and although married to a local man, might have been thought of as a 'newcomer', like Frank Barker, as she originally came from Penzance. She and her husband had lived in St Breddaford since their marriage some ten years ago. They had no children but, according to Derrymore, seemed happy together despite the fact that she was a real extrovert, while her husband was a stay-at-home, who kept to himself.

Betty worked at nights in a restaurant so her husband was used to her coming home late, and wasn't alarmed that she hadn't returned this morning, explaining that sometimes she spent the night with a friend at work.

'I don't know anything else about him.' Derrymore finally roused himself to own, his satisfaction that he knew so much just showing. 'Not surprising, as he keeps to himself. But she was always on the go, a real live wire.' Suggesting that he had liked Betty.

They found Dave Caddick at work in the local sawmill,

where trees from a nearby estate were made into fences and posts. As they approached the mill, set deep in a plantation of firs (which Reynolds always thought looked out of place in Cornwall) the smell of pine resin became overpowering, and the sound of several high-powered saws made the air throb.

The foreman, a mild-mannered man in dark blue overalls, recognised Derrymore, but, unable to make them hear over the noise, gestured towards a distant shed where the loudest sounds were coming from. There they found the new widower, a large hairy man, bare to the waist and sweating from his exertions, pulling and pushing at a huge circular saw.

It was not the ideal place to hold an interview, and, as they soon realized, not the best time. When Caddick finally became aware of them, he too made gestures, unwelcoming ones. Finally he stopped the motor and with a distinct scowl, asked what the devil they wanted.

'You've already been round to my house once,' he shouted, as if he were so used to making himself heard over noise he couldn't speak in a normal voice. 'So what's up this time? I don't know I've anything to add. And you sure as hell told me all I want to hear.'

This inauspicious beginning went from bad to worse when Derrymore began to ask where he'd been last night. 'Account for my actions, you mean,' he cried. Seemingly unaware of the sawdust that stuck to the sweat, he leaned on the half-sawn tree trunk and glowered. 'If I say I was in the Fox and Goose you'll counter it's not one of my usual haunts, and you'd be right. B-b-but then no one told you last night that your missus was no b-b-better than she should be, and that everyone in the village was t-t-talking about it.'

When he spoke the wildness of his words was enhanced by a slight stutter. His bloodshot eyes watered. He's been drinking all right, Reynolds thought, suddenly enlightened, and isn't used to it. But if he was in the Fox and Goose, easily checked, where did he go later? If the pair were killed after midnight, there was time for him to have got up to the quarry even if he walked. He tried for a glimpse of Caddick's boots, and failed.

As if aware of the effect he'd made, Caddick straightened himself up. 'And I didn't kill her,' he bellowed, the words echoing loudly through the large shed. 'Although, by God, I wish I had. If she'd come home last night there might be some sense to your questions. As 'tis, someone rang me up and told me in no uncertain terms what was going on between my wife and Barker. And then did the job for me. So you bugger off, and find that someone. That's what you're paid for.'

'Who rang you?' Derrymore asked quickly.

Caddick snarled, 'Damned if I know. Some fool woman, that's for sure. Rubbing her hands and gloating I don't doubt. So if you're going to question anyone, question the whole village while you're at it; if they knew what was going on for so long and did nothing, to my way of thinking, they're partners in crime.'

'We're here to help.' Derrymore spoke lamely, his heart not in his reply, as if, Reynolds thought, he'd gone off into some world of his own again. This gave Caddick the chance to steer the questioning away from himself into a different line.

'A likely story,' Caddick said, with a sneer. 'Speaking of which, I've a question of my own. How come he's here?'

He jerked a large thumb at Reynolds. 'I recognise him! And these days, what I hear is that everyone's talking about his books. Dirty, they calls them. Full of the sort of smut that changed my Bets into a slut for all the world to laugh at. So you clear off, mister.'

He made a threatening step in Reynolds' direction. 'I'm not having you laughing at me. Or taking down everything I say to use in some new book.'

Too late, Derrymore tried to intervene but Reynolds waved him off. 'Let him be,' he said calmly. 'Better to have it out.' He turned to Caddick. 'Who says my books are "smut", I think you called it? Have you read them yourself?'

'Not bloody likely.' Having found a vent for his anger, and possibly, Reynolds thought, his grief, Dave Caddick held on, like a dog worrying a bone. 'Too many have read 'em already, more's the pity. But I hear they were burnt in a fire, and good luck to who done it. Burn the whole bloody lot while they're at it.' And he shook his fist again in Reynolds' direction.

Seeing that his presence was inciting the man to possibly even greater violence, Reynolds decided discretion was called for. 'I'll wait outside,' he told Derrymore softly, and withdrew to the back of the shed, to hear Caddick protest, in the sort of voice that drunks use when they feel sorry for themselves, that even his own foreman had lied to him. Said he didn't know nothing, when for a fact the man's wife said she'd spotted them together, almost six months ago. 'Everyone knew, I tell you,' Dave Caddick was sobbing, 'and I'm the fool, aren't I, thinking she was working to save up for a new kitchen and pulling the wool over my eyes all the time. When I found out yesterday I . . .'

His voice died away as Reynolds came out from the shed and found himself at the foot of the first row of pine trees. With a sudden pang of memory for his own, long ago, failed marriage, mixed with distaste at the way this second interview was being handled, he began to pick a path across the thick layers of needles. What anonymous woman had chosen last night, of all nights, to ring Caddick? And why? Had she told him the truth yesterday by chance, or had she deliberately tried to incite him to anger and possible violence? If so, her reason must be especially vicious. Already the thought of Mrs Barker as a possible suspect had come into his head. And if Caddick, surely a non-reader if ever there was one, was so outspoken about Reynolds' books, could he have set fire to them? He concentrated on these questions, hoping Derrymore would pick up on them, although he doubted it. Derrymore was sufficiently under stress that if he himself were in charge he would have taken over completely.

At the same time he kept at bay his rising indignation that even here his books were under attack. His other conviction that, offered a chance of nailing a suspect quickly, Nicholls would hang on to Caddick, didn't help. Whatever harm Caddick may have done him personally, he still felt the man's mixture of anger and grief was genuine.

He'd reached the top of the ridge before he knew it and was looking over the woods towards the river which coiled and twisted towards the estuary and the open sea. Clouds were banking in the west, sign of impending rain, but at the moment the afternoon sun was still out. For some reason the rich scent of the fir needles made him think of hot blackberry jam. He cleared a place and sat down with his back to a tree, straddling the ridge so that he had the view before him on one side and the entrance to the shed on the other. Warning himself to keep his irritation in check, and to expect the worst as regards this interview (which certainly hadn't improved his position with Derrymore) he came across what he was to think of later as the first coincidence.

He was leaning against the tree wishing that Derrymore would hurry, when he realized that the trunk was hollow. Putting in his hand, he felt something long and hard, surrounded by a hairy cover. He pulled it out, by instinct careful not to handle it in any way that would smear possible fingerprints – a long piece of hessian, with a wedge inside.

The wedge was thick, made of metal, the sort used for splitting logs. But it wasn't covered with sawdust, it was covered with pale ochre mud. He sat staring at it. When he saw Derrymore emerge and look round inquiringly, he replaced it inside the hollow and hurried down through the trees.

Derrymore's manner was surprisingly relaxed as if he was feeling pleased with himself. 'Can't say I got much else out of him,' he said, 'except in my opinion he's a prime suspect. Practically admitted he'd have killed her if he'd got his hands on her. Poor blighter.'

Reynolds shook his head slowly. Derrymore might be right to take such a claim seriously, given the unexpected discovery he himself had just made. But again from long experience he'd usually found that prime suspects in murder cases weren't likely to draw attention to their murderous inclinations – although funnily enough, when Mrs Barker had almost said the same thing, he could have believed her!

He was about to tell Derrymore of his find, and ask if he'd got anywhere with details of the woman on the telephone, when Derrymore added more slowly, 'And strange too how he blamed your books.'

He turned towards Reynolds as if he had made up his mind. 'It's the same all over,' he burst out, 'I told you I've never known anything like it. Nothing but trouble and more trouble. And now this. Shouldn't wonder if Caddick's even behind the book burning, too. Well, in the circumstances I think Nicholls should know the way the wind blows. He'll understand, even if you don't, that you are too closely involved to be part of this murder investigation. And he's bound to hear all the rumours about you eventually even if we don't tell him first.'

I suppose he's offering me the chance to tell Nicholls myself, Reynolds thought. Decent of him I suppose – if I've any reason to admit responsibility! But damned if I do. And damned if I will, to let Derrymore off. If he thinks there's anything worth revealing let him do it himself. If he doesn't want me on the case for some other reason that he's still not saying, let him be a man and come out with it, instead of hiding behind some improbable excuse. And damned if I'll wait around to be given my marching orders; there's no need for me to let Derrymore have me dismissed like some underling.

By then he had worked himself up into a fine temper, the sort that later he would regret. It blurred his own sense of proportion. 'I shouldn't bother,' he snapped. 'I'd just as soon spend my time tracking down those rumours myself. As I should have done from the start, if I hadn't been side-tracked by your mam, running to ask me for help.'

Derrymore looked shocked. Serve him right, Reynolds thought. But he was too angry to be ashamed of his own meanness. 'In the meanwhile,' he said, 'you might take a look at that hollow tree up there.' He pointed towards the ridge. 'The big one on top. You can't miss it. Whether what is inside is important or not, that's for you to decide – although how anyone could be expected to come across it beats me, unless . . .'

Another thought was nagging away that he couldn't keep to himself. 'Unless it's a set-up. And another anonymous call tells you where it is!'

He started off down the yard before stopping to shout over his shoulder, 'For God's sake before you jump to conclusions, trace that phone call. And take a look at Caddick's boots. Most of all, if Caddick took the trouble to carry a thick iron wedge all the way to the quarry top and back, ask him why in hell he didn't take the trouble to clean it off!'

And with these last pieces of advice he set off again, full of self-righteous anger, leaving a confused Derrymore to climb the hill and make what he could of the find. It was not until he came to the main road that he remembered he'd come in Derrymore's car!

Chapter 6

Nothing worse than making an exit with nowhere to go, and no way to get there! Several hours later, stubborn as a mule himself and willing to walk all night rather than ask Derrymore for a lift, a weary Reynolds reached home after a complicated and lengthy journey involving bus and foot. Drenched to the skin by the rain which had started as threatened, this time his hike did not improve his temper. It did strengthen his resolve to withdraw completely from the murder case, and concentrate instead on who, and what, lay behind the smear campaign against him. It wouldn't be the first time he'd been excluded from an important investigation and yet found the solution on his own. As for Derrymore, let him go his own way and see how far he got! Or better still, let him team up with headquarters. He'd done so in the past and a fat lot of good it had done him!

Before he went to bed, he made a list of specific leads he wanted to explore and the specific people he wanted to interview, excluding Caddick from his list. Even if Caddick proved to be an arsonist he didn't seem the sort to spearhead a smear campaign; that wasn't the sort of work home-loving males usually thrive on.

His list was not long, but he knew enough about village life to accept that if gossip spread like wild fire, like fires it always had a starting place. Presuming there was some pretence of logic behind the attack, he was looking for a hard core of readers, probably females, who disliked his books, again presuming they had read them! If so, they would have had to get hold of them first. His priority therefore was to chat with Dr Sinclair, as well as sound out the local librarian. But before he did anything, he'd pay a visit to Mazie Derrymore. He owed her an apology. And if anyone understood the underground workings of the village, she did.

He was especially sensitive to the awkwardness of his talking to Mazie. Just as in the beginning he'd had scruples about coming between her and her son, now he warned himself to avoid all questions about the ongoing murder, or the new developments, although he was honest enough to admit he was intensely interested in what was happening, specifically what Derrymore had made of this last interview with Caddick.

Eventually, curiosity getting the better of him, he couldn't resist compiling a list of possible suspects in the murder, for his own benefit, including not only the obvious people like Mrs Barker and Caddick, but others, such as Mrs Barker's son and the unknown woman on the phone. He had a feeling, call it an instinct, that they might be more important than they seemed, the same instinct (again so unprofessional he was reluctant to admit it) which kept telling him that, despite all the evidence stacked against him, Caddick wasn't the murderer that Derrymore, and by now Nicholls, would probably think.

It wasn't only instinct. For what it was worth there was also logic. And behind the logic lay the main puzzle: what connection had the murder with the previous events in the village? Assuming that there was one.

In Reynolds' experience, a string of events like these didn't happen 'by accident'; there had to be some link, however obscure. And of the people he'd talked to so far the stay-at-home wood-cutter seemed the least likely to provide it, for all he'd made no secret of his dislike of Reynolds' books. On the other hand, apart from the drawings (of which only one survived) the only other link seemed to be with the church, which had been involved, at least indirectly, in the first two incidents. If Mrs Barker hated her husband as much as she indicated, she might have found pleasure in attacking any event connected even vaguely to her husband's place of worship. She was also, by her own admission, a reader and a member of a book club, and she had recognised him, he was sure of that. And was nasty enough to get up to all sorts of tricks.

But more than any of this, the way the events themselves occurred seemed ominous. Was it his imagination, or had they happened in a kind of pre-planned sequence? True, the first had taken place at a certain time determined by the date of the May Day procession, but it seemed to him that the others had followed too close behind each other for comfort. Did the despoliation of the church, the book-burning, and the murder, happen in that order by chance, or was the perpetrator becoming used to his crimes, as it were, enlarging upon them, 'warming up' to even greater ones?

It was an alarming idea, bringing back not only his sensations at the top of the quarry, but his repressed concern that if he and his books should be blamed in a general sort of way, as Caddick for example seemed to blame them, it was an easy step for some criminal to use them more specifically.

He had little hope that Nicholls, or even Derrymore, would think along these lines, but his own line of reasoning worried him. The impression he'd had today of someone clever, and dangerous, returned to haunt him. If he had the chance he'd like to check on the previous incidents, to see what light they shed, but for the moment found no way to do so without major complications. With these and other thoughts swirling in his brain, he shut his notebook firmly, and put it out of temptation.

Next morning, he waited until he was sure Derrymore

had left, before strolling round to Mazie's cottage. It was cool for almost June, the sky still overcast with intermittent rain. He noticed that Mazie's roses were already out and spared a thought for his own neglected garden.

At this time he knew she'd be busy with her baking, and sure enough a warm smell of rising bread and freshly-made fruit-cake filled her little kitchen. Whatever her son had told her, if anything, of the split between them and his churlish remarks, she made no mention of them and invited the ex-inspector in with her usual display of hospitality.

He waited patiently while she chatted on about the weather, about the coming weekend. Derrymore was working all hours, but still hoping to take Sally out some evening, now the days were drawing out. Reynolds noted Sally Heyward's name was mentioned freely, so perhaps the differences between her and Derrymore weren't too deep-rooted after all – unless Mazie had no knowledge of them – or unless she refused to take them seriously. It was only after he had drunk several cups of tea and eaten a slice of cake that he came to the purpose of his visit and although it wasn't easy to say what had to be said, he plunged in.

'I want to apologise for my outburst yesterday. I didn't mean it. In fact I've come again to you for help.'

Mazie put down her teacup with a clatter. 'You know,' she began slowly, 'Derry isn't happy about any of this. Not at all. And nor am I. But he never told me anything you'd have to say sorry for.'

She smiled at him. 'So if you feel you lost your temper I expect it was because I'm an interfering old busybody, and should know better at my age.'

It was generous, just like her. He felt humbled by her. After a while she asked him how she could help him, and when he told her about his plan of tracking down the gossip about his books, without taking any further part in the ongoing murder case, she stood up, and after peering in the oven, an old-fashioned Cornish range, rummaged in a battered tin box on the mantel-shelf.

'There,' she said, 'It came in the post several months back. I thought nothing of it, not my sort of caper, although I hear several younger women take part.'

Her voice suggested that she disapproved of these younger women, whoever they were. Reynolds unfolded the form letter she'd given him. It was typed and photocopied, a harmless open invitation to 'all those interested', to join a reading club. The aim, to discuss books as well as to meet others with similar tastes, was equally innocuous and one in normal circumstances Reynolds would have approved of, although, being by nature a non-participator, he might not have joined had he been asked.

The date for the first session was several months earlier and the meeting place near St Breddaford, at Grange Manor. 'Where the organizer, lives,' Mazie explained. 'Mrs Jenifer Murdock. A newcomer. Very smart.'

Again more by her tone of voice than anything said, Reynolds received the impression that Mazie didn't approve. 'She bought the manor several years back,' she added, 'and they say changed it for the better, but I haven't seen it so can't judge. I wouldn't have thought she went in for reading, but you can't always tell. Anyway, I didn't go that first time, but a neighbour did, and said it was all too much for her, too much chit-chat and too much drink. I'm surprised you didn't get an invite. I know they've had several guest speakers.'

'May I borrow this?' At her nod, Reynolds put the paper in his pocket. It was as good a lead as any, at least a focal point for readers to gather to discuss books – or censor them. And he remembered something Mrs Barker had said about a book club. If this was the same one, it occurred to him again that her being a member might have some significance in the murder case too. He put the thought aside hastily. Having just assured Mazie he'd no intention of meddling in the ongoing police investigations, he certainly shouldn't break his promise while still in her kitchen.

'Mrs Murdock doesn't come into the village often,' Mazie was confiding. 'So we thought it strange, her starting a club, because she's not that popular. Of course, being lonely like, she might have hoped to use it as a way to make friends. She originates from London, I believe.'

Her voice suggested that by default all Londoners were so fond of company they were never happy unless whooping it up and partying all night. 'I think I heard the vicar's wife joined,' Mazie continued. 'But she doesn't go every time. And Daisy Abbot, the butcher's niece, cleans for Mrs Murdock after the "do's" and complains about the mess. As for the books they read, I never paid much attention, but I did hear they were the sort you'd have to buy so that cut out several people right off. But there, the bookshop does well enough out of them I suppose.'

Reynolds rose to go. 'Now mind,' she told him, 'In the beginning I told Derry he was wrong to take the gossip about you so to heart, but since then so much has happened, including murder.'

She shivered. 'I'll have to let Derry know you've been calling. I don't want him to think I've been doing things behind his back. I can't always be turning against my own son, can I?'

Consorting with the enemy, you mean, Reynolds thought. He found the idea depressing, but as he opened the door, Mazie broke out, 'I wish you and Derry could make up your differences.' For the first time her voice faltered. 'Then you could come again freely, like you used to. He's missed you, you know. And so have I. But he's like his father, my Derry. As kind and gentle as a lamb, when you know how to lead him, shy and awkward about his feelings, like a schoolboy.'

She paused, then continued in a sort of rush, 'Especially around women. Like his dad. His father was so shy I had to do the proposing. But after we were married he wouldn't let me out of his sight. He once swore he'd knock a neighbour down because he saw us talking! And 'twas only over the garden wall, comparing the state of our cabbages.'

It could have been an attempt to explain her son's behaviour, or it could have been a warning. Reynolds couldn't decide which. On a sudden impulse he bent and kissed her soft cheek, more flushed than ever from her baking. 'I miss you too,' he said.

He went down the path with her farewell admonition to be careful ringing in his ears. He already had a premonition that being careful would be the least of his problems.

Reversing the order of his visits, he decided to leave the library and bookshop until later, instead drove straight to Grange Manor. It lay south of the village in one of those little valleys or combes that spin off the moor, and from the old-fashioned lettering of its name on the map he presumed it was very old, possibly a monastic manor farm founded before the Reformation.

There was nothing monastic or farm-like about it now and as he parked outside the iron gates, he saw what Mazie had meant about changing it, he'd have thought not for the better. The original old granite stones had been rendered over and faced with coloured spar chippings and the windows had been replaced by PVC models, brown, double-glazed. A conservatory had been added at one side, with a cupola that made the whole building off balance, while the front lawn had been covered with crazy paving, over which straggly plants of Mediterranean origin drooped from soggy pots.

There was a large Mercedes parked on the paving stones; presumably Mrs Murdock was at home. She answered the door so promptly Reynolds thought she must have been standing inside, and although she waited for him to introduce himself and state his business, as if he were a travelling salesman, she gave the impression, he wasn't sure how, that she actually knew who he was before he told her his name.

Again he'd planned what to say, a rather lame excuse although one she couldn't actually quibble at, but when he started to explain he was interested in the book club he'd heard she started, she invited him in, not without a little smile of satisfaction, quickly suppressed, as if she'd landed a celebrity without really trying.

Jenifer Murdock ('Call me Jen') was a brisk woman in her forties with a brightly efficient air. Big breasted and hipped, her figure was what in a previous generation would have been called well-corseted. And in some ways she seemed old fashioned; her silk dress, its tight waist and short hemline surely not modern, swished as she walked and her high-heeled shoes, from another era, pattered as she led the way into her sitting room. After making a fuss about where Reynolds should sit, she pattered off again to make coffee, giving him the chance he'd been hoping for to find out what he could from her surroundings.

These seemed normal enough, but right from the start something not quite right put his professional antenna on alert. Her taste in decoration for example left an uneasy impression, everything reeking of wealth and yet everything slightly off-kilter, from the Spanish flamenco dancer doll, a swirl of black and red lace, to the surprisingly red table lamps and curtains. There was a smell he vaguely identified as incense, and there was no sign of her literary interests, in a room completely devoid of any printed matter, not even a magazine on the marble-topped coffee table.

Like the way she walked and dressed, the silk, the high heels, the immaculately coiffured black hair, nothing matched easily with country living. Yet she knew how to make a visitor welcome, positively fawning over where to place the coffee cup and insisting on his trying her imported biscuits.

'I love books,' she began, with a simper that immediately suggested she was lying. 'When I retired and came here to live, I felt I couldn't be without them. I started the club by my little self, but of course soon found kindred spirits.'

She batted her eyelashes, so long they had to be false. 'If you would join us, we'd be so pleased,' she cooed. 'Overwhelmed in fact. But we may not be intellectual enough for you, Mr Reynolds. Or should I call you Inspector?'

The simper that accompanied this last question put him even more on guard. It certainly confirmed his impression that she had known who he was from the start. If she was now making him aware of her knowledge, was that a mistake? Or was she using it to warn him off? Whichever, it made him re-assess her. Here was a shrewd woman, who, underneath an outward silliness, knew how to use her cleverness when she wanted. But if she were flattering his intelligence, or flexing her own, at this point he couldn't be sure. And surely she was too young to talk about 'retiring'? He made a mental note to check on her former employment.

When she asked specifically how he'd learned about the club he made noncommittal mutterings, to the vague effect he'd merely heard talk in the village. When in turn he asked who else were members he heard her deploy similar vagueness. Finally, after he had asked for a copy of the current reading list, she made a great to-do of searching for, and not finding it, eventually promising to send one on without fail, 'as soon as possible'.

'We usually decide on a book each time we meet and then read and discuss it at the next session; we're very informal, Inspector,' she added, with a throaty laugh. 'You'll think us ever so inefficient but we don't follow any special trend. We don't have any special likes or dislikes, just go where sweet fancy takes us, as the poet says.'

Whatever poet that was, he thought when he regained his car. And whatever list she's supposed to send 'as soon as possible', that's whistling in the wind, for all her 'without fails' and 'promises'. And never gave a thing away, except as near as damn saying that she's not responsible for any campaign against me – although I never mentioned it. In fact, and here his temper, still smarting from yesterday, again began to rise, she's managed the whole interview surprisingly smoothly, as if I were the one being interviewed. All I'm left with is the impression of things slightly off-balance and of nothing being as it seems. And nothing to base that impression on except my own damn instincts.

And she had deliberately been vague about the other members, an important objective. Deciding speaking to Mrs Barker or the vicar's wife at this point might be construed as interference, as would finding out what Daisy Abbot thought about her employer, he put them on hold, instead returning to the village to confront Dr Sinclair.

The glass in the bow window had been replaced and a new display of books, dealing with local history, filled the gap left by the book-burning. It was almost one o'clock now and the shop was empty of customers. 'Just about to shut for lunch,' Dr Sinclair began from behind the counter where he was emptying some boxes, then glancing up, 'Oh sorry, Inspector, didn't think it would be you.'

There was something in his tone of voice that suggested not only surprise but regret, as if he would have liked to have been expecting him, and against his will Reynolds suddenly remembered Mazie's observation about Jen Murdock's possible loneliness. Perhaps all 'newcomers' to the village perforce felt lonely; after all, they must realise too how difficult it was to make headway into a tight, closed circle. He himself hadn't cared one way or the other, in fact had chosen village life originally because it offered anonymity and quiet, but as a former member of a bustling community like a university, Dr Sinclair might have reason to feel cut off and excluded.

About to say, 'It's nothing that can't wait,' on an impulse he couldn't quite justify afterwards, he said instead, 'I've not had lunch either. What about a pint at the Fox and Goose?'

He regretted the offer almost at once. A look shuttered down on Sinclair's face; Reynolds almost expected him to say something severe, like 'I don't drink', or worse, 'I can't afford pub meals'. He was mistaken. 'Let me get this stacked away,' the ex-professor said, pushing his glasses back on his nose. 'And I'll join you with pleasure.'

While he was kept busy with his unpacking, Reynolds passed the time browsing. He was surprised at the range and variety of books, unexpected for such a small village shop, almost like a well-thought-out personal library. And he was even more surprised when he saw what was in the boxes; a large number of fancy pens and pencils, note pads, key rings, pencil sharpeners, the sort of articles that would attract juvenile shoplifters. He almost mentioned it, decided not to, waited until Sinclair had locked the shop door and then led the way round to the Fox and Goose.

Although it too had gone through hard times, at one point having been closed down, nowadays the pub was always crowded during the lunch period. He and Sinclair managed to find seats in a corner where, if not secluded, they could talk without having their drinks knocked off the table or their plates shovelled into their laps.

'Not bad,' Sinclair took a great draught and looked round him as if approvingly. 'Always full, I'd say, now that the tour coaches make a point of stopping. And the food is better than you'd think. At least better than I manage for myself; I'm no cook.'

Attacking his pallid ravioli and chips with gusto, he went on, 'Of course the more customers they attract, the better I do myself. A real windfall, you could say. After they eat and drink, they just have enough time to stroll down the street to oh and ah at the stream and church. With luck, one peep in my bow-window, and they're caught.'

At last Reynolds understood. Sinclair's enthusiasm was for tourists rather than local pub-goers, the passing visitors he presumably catered for by keeping Reynolds' books. And of course that was why he had so many 'novelties' on display – they too would attract casual buyers.

Seizing the chance to bring the conversation round to his main interest, 'You've got a wonderful selection of books,' Reynolds said, and meant it. 'I doubt if even a university shop would be so well stocked.'

Sinclair took off his glasses to polish, looking pleased. 'I love books,' he said simply, making Mrs Murdock's similar remark sound all the more insincere. 'That's why I became a professor of literature, of course. But these days students are too lazy to read. They want quick digests, condensations, even, for God's sake, mass produced literary criticisms they can plagiarize for their own miserable essays. So I gave up teaching and went back to my first love.'

He sounded more amused than angry, benign almost.

'So who are the lucky ones you cater for now?' Reynolds asked with a smile. The question was not an idle one. It was only as he put it that it occurred to him, whatever the answer, he himself didn't count among the number, the more shame to him.

'You'd be surprised.' Sinclair's voice was sharp, as if he had anticipated Reynolds' question and resented being patronized. 'All sorts of people live in Cornwall nowadays, you know; they aren't all peasant farmers or out-of-work miners. And in the course of a long life, I suppose I've built up quite a following of former students.'

He added this mildly, without trace of pride. Reynolds was impressed. One of the bonuses of a teaching job would be finding out how your pupils got on in the real world outside, and keeping in touch with them. 'Mind you,' Sinclair was continuing, 'I suppose one should be grateful for small mercies. I mean just the ability to totter on, year by year. Bookselling isn't very lucrative; that's why I have to stock up on so many bits and pieces. I even put the coffee machine in because an American magazine said it attracted customers.' He gave a wry smile. 'Still, I admit I get a charge out of meeting so many people who're nice enough to say that my shop adds colour to their lives. And then, a lot of my ex-students live hereabouts. Some of them come miles just to chat again. They're very supportive. They tell me what they want in the way of reading matter, and I get it for them.'

And like any real enthusiast he was away on a flood of reminiscence, of books he'd tried to find, and failed, of rare books he'd picked up for a song at some local boot sale, of books that were his favourites so he couldn't bring himself to sell them on – they had come to the end of their meal when Reynolds finally broached the last question he'd been leading up to. 'And is it only tourists who buy my books specifically? Anyone else in the village keen on them?'

And when Sinclair, concentrating on paying his share of the bill, didn't answer, 'That village book club I've been hearing about, what sort of thing do they read?'

Sinclair put away his change, sorting it methodically into the separate sections of a small purse. 'Now then,' he said with another professorial twinkle which this time didn't hide the astuteness, 'you're asking a leading question here. Or should I say questions? To answer them in order, first, as the old saying has it, I regret the prophet is more honoured abroad than he is at home. The average St Breddafordite reads, in order of preference, the *TV Times*, the *Sporting News*, and *Country Life*. As for the second, the so-called village book club,' another sharp twinkle, 'if you're really interested you presumably know who to ask. But if you're trying to find out if they're at the bottom of some smear campaign, I doubt if they're organised enough even to consider it, let alone mount a concentrated attack. Not that I'm ungrateful for their patronage,' he went on, as they emerged into the street, 'but God knows what they do with the books they choose. I don't think half can understand them, even if they do get round to reading them.'

He stood still, a tall wispy figure with his shabby tweed jacket buttoned tight. But there was something fiercely professorial in his tone as he added, 'As for the murder in the quarry, surely you've heard the latest news? They're saying that the woman's husband has been detained for questioning. That means they've already got a major lead. And if it solves who fired my shop, I say well done to them.'

He wagged a finger in mock reproof. 'So there's no need for you to go fishing for clues, if that's what you're doing. Next time the impulse takes over, come buy one of my books instead.'

Feeling like a student who has just been reprimanded, Reynolds watched Sinclair hurry back to his shop. Blast, he thought, adding several more picturesque curses in other languages. I must be losing my grip. How did he see through me so easily? And I didn't believe Derrymore would be so hasty, although I admit things looked black for Caddick. But there're other suspects who've scarcely been 'squeezed' as Nicholls put it. And if Dave Caddick turns out to be an arsonist, I still think he's an unlikely murderer, for all his bluster. That's the beer talking rather than himself.

The thought of the missed opportunities, the missed chances he could have exploited had he stayed on the case nagged at him (although, even if he had stayed, his opinion would probably have been overridden; Inspector Nicholls had made no secret either of his intention to find a quick solution). But mostly he was angry at himself.

The two interviews he'd had this morning had not gone according to plan. He and Derrymore were still at odds, and by taking himself off the case so precipitously, without explanation, he had probably angered Nicholls into the bargain. Faced with the choice of either engineering another confrontation with Derrymore and the official team, or trying to get his views across without seeming to (impossible) instead he paid a last quick visit to the local library.

This was a hideous building, dating from the nineteen-sixties, its concrete blockwork and tinted glass fortunately tucked away in the most inaccessible part of the village, where parking was impossible and where people had to negotiate a cobbled lane full of picturesque but treacherous pitfalls.

The librarian, a small, well-mannered fellow of indeterminate years ('Newcomb, the name's Art Newcomb, and I'm glad to meet you, Mr Reynolds, an honour, if I may say so') seemed overwhelmed by Reynolds' request: that if the library had copies of his books, could a list of the borrowers who read them be provided. It was only when Reynolds suggested, without saying so outright, that this was part of an ongoing police matter, that Mr Newcomb relented enough to consider the idea.

Yes, Reynolds' books were in the library, he finally admitted, and had been very popular in the past although . . . Here he blinked his eyes, pale blue surrounded by sandy lashes, and looked at the floor as if he didn't like to admit how rapidly that popularity had declined in the past weeks. And yes, if it was a police matter (here he gave a sharp sideways glance) and if the computer was working, it wouldn't be too difficult to trace borrowers, no trouble at all. Only there was personal privacy involved.

His mouth began to twitch so badly again Reynolds felt sorry for him. 'I'll take responsibility,' he assured the librarian blandly, 'don't worry.'

A downright lie followed by a false assurance should have worried Mr Newcomb. As it should have Reynolds, who was well aware that by his request he was breaking several rules at once. So much for his personal promises to Mazie Derrymore, he should be ashamed! To his even greater shame he felt none, was in fact congratulating himself that at last he had gained an objective without too much resistance, when a voice he knew stopped him short.

'Hullo there. I've been wondering where you were.'

The speaker was Sally Heyward, a coat over her arm, smiling at him demurely as she followed him through the swinging doors. 'Christ,' he said, stopping so abruptly she bumped into him. He'd meant to ring to put her off, don't say he'd forgotten? Presumably he had. 'Christ,' he said again, 'I'm sorry.'

She laughed. 'It's all right,' she assured him. 'I've put the finished pieces through your letter-box, there're several letters that need signing, and I can pick up anything new another time.'

Reynolds was still disturbed by his forgetfulness. 'Have you been hanging about here all day?' he asked, to have her say with another smile, 'I often come into the library to wait until the bus goes. I rather like it. And you see a lot of people.'

She hesitated for a moment, biting her lip, then said in a rush, 'I don't mean to interfere, but I couldn't help overhearing what you and Newcomb were talking about. Now I don't want to add to the difficulties, and with things as they are I know there are difficulties, but I can tell you that people are still taking out your books. I saw a woman with several the other day. I don't know her name but I could describe her.'

This she proceeded to do with the graphic grasp of detail he remembered from another occasion, sketching the picture of a lady in her forties, well dressed but in a slightly old-fashioned way, tottering along the cobblestones in too high heels. Mrs Jen Murdock to the letter, Reynolds thought at once, now what the hell was she doing here?

'Thanks,' he told Sally, 'that's given me a lead. And as one good turn deserves another let me at least buy you a coffee and drive you home. Unless as you say, "it makes for more difficulties".'

She laughed again. 'I don't suppose so,' she said. 'I'd love a coffee, but there's no need to drive me. The bus comes in half an hour.'

As they went down the cobbled lane, she began to discuss the work she had returned, without, he noticed, putting any pressure on when to collect the next batch (non-existent at the moment). Unlike the woman she had described, she didn't totter, and although he supposed her clothes could be called 'modern' she looked good in them. In fact she was a remarkably pretty young woman. No wonder Derrymore is hooked, he thought, as they went into the local coffee shop and sat down.

'Today's my day for a regular feast-out,' he told her, going on to describe his lunch with Sinclair. 'But I didn't get very far with him, I'm afraid.'

'And it's all connected with your books?' she asked, biting into the sandwich he had ordered, guessing, rightly it seemed, that she might be hungry. Although why didn't she go to Mazie's? She often seemed to be there. 'Derry said you're trying to find out about the rumours against you,' she was continuing. 'Have you had any luck? And what do you think about the suspect in the murder case; they say someone's been arrested.'

Somewhat dampened by the mention of Derrymore, Reynolds' reply came slowly. 'I don't mean to cause problems either,' he said awkwardly, 'I did tell Mazie what I was doing when I went round this morning.'

'Oh,' she broke in, 'I don't know anything about that. I'm not prying. I do know how fond Mazie is of you. She's a darling. But I can't always be running to her, it's not fair on her.'

She flushed, adding quickly, 'And so is Derry, really. Fond of you, I mean. It's just these cases have been worrying him. If the murder's solved, as I suppose now it must be, he'll be so relieved we won't recognize him.'

He interpreted these remarks to mean that she hadn't spent the time with Mazie because she didn't want to impose too much on the older woman's kindness. And she was being protective towards Derrymore perhaps because she had found him, as she said, 'difficult' (although that might as well be caused by the pressure put on him by his mam as the pressure of work).

She put down her cup and smiled. He had forgotten how her smile lit up her face. 'It's been hard the past few weeks,' she stated candidly. 'You know Derry well, I suppose. Have you noticed . . .' she bit her lip, 'how defensive he is; how much he takes village problems to heart?'

Again he was surprised. Like Mazie he didn't expect her to criticize. As if she guessed what he was thinking, she added, 'Don't think I'm finding fault. It's just I'd like to help. But you can't help someone, can you, when he won't let you near enough to try.'

Despite himself he remembered Mazie's description of her son. But it wasn't his place to advise. He had no dealings with young lovers and their quarrels. Feeling more and more like some grandad, about to pat her hand and utter 'There, there', words made immortal in a hundred old-fashioned story books, he said instead, 'Derrymore is big enough to look after himself. I shouldn't worry.' Which of course was the modern equivalent.

'But I do.' She wasn't going to be put off by his platitudes. 'All this gossip business, it would drive me mad. But he takes it so seriously, worries about it, lets it gnaw at him.'

'If you lived in a village you'd have to get used to it,' he said.

'Oh, they say city life can be as cruel,' she said, with a look that suggested she spoke from experience. 'But you can be lost there somehow. You can live your individual life without everyone taking note of all you do. Don't get me wrong; I don't dislike village life.' Here she made an effort to sound more positive. 'I suppose there might be something comforting in knowing you have no secrets from anyone. It's only, you might feel you'd have to change, do you know what I mean? Alter your ways to fit in, adapt to a pattern that's not you at all.'

She leaned forward, suddenly intense. 'You shouldn't change from what you are, should you? I mean, pretend you're something different just to please.'

Her intensity surprised him. He shot her a quick glance. What most people would see was a very pretty girl brimming with vitality and enthusiasm. For the first time he glimpsed a vulnerability beneath the veneer.

'The trouble with your Derry is he has a conscience,' he said, answering her obliquely. 'And he's been too well looked-after for too long.' He gave a rueful smile. 'That's a common problem with live-at-home bachelor sons. Most of the rest of us poor sods make do with our own cooking and appreciate any attention we can glean, whatever the source. And I agree with you. One shouldn't change because one feels obliged to.'

She laughed, looked at her watch and grabbed her coat.

'Must run,' she said. 'Thanks for the coffee. And the food. I seem to have eaten most of it.'

Scattering a handful of money on the table he hurried after her. 'Look,' he said, again feeling like a schoolboy himself, 'for the moment I've given up on my new book. It wasn't going anywhere, as you must have sensed. But while I'm on holiday, as it were, there's no reason why you shouldn't have a holiday from me and my manuscript. Paid in advance.'

The smile faded. 'I can manage,' she said. 'I have other part-time jobs, you know.'

'But I'd like to retain your services for later,' he persisted. 'When I get down to serious writing I'll need you, and you won't thank me, I assure you. If I'm a bear with a sore head now, wait until I'm really in action. So if anything comes up in the meanwhile may I get in touch? I have your address and phone number.'

Her reply was lost in the run for the bus. He was left standing on the corner of the green, opposite the bookshop, feeling deflated. And conscious for the first time that if Derrymore's love affair had fallen on hard times, he himself had presumably committed a cardinal error by flaunting himself with Derrymore's girlfriend in front of everyone.

As the bus jolted round the green before taking the main road out of the village Sally forced herself not to look back. Having stuffed her coat in a luggage rack she resumed her seat and stared out of the window at the passing hedgerows, with the little fields behind them. Usually the hedges were too tall and thick to see through. It was only when you sat high up on a bus like this, that you could peer over at the hidden beauty on the other side, the special blend of green and brown of pasture and ploughed land, the clumps of trees, the little valleys, each with its own stream, that made up the Cornish countryside. Life in a village should be like that, she thought, beauty hidden until you look for it.

How could she have been so silly to suggest she didn't like village life? How could she have spoken so freely of her own feelings to an almost stranger whose kindness she had reason to know and whose professional detachment she now felt she had taken advantage of? What an idiot he'd think her, what a stupid chatter-box.

And with all her chatter why on earth hadn't she told him the rest about the woman in the library, the bit that had frightened her?

She knew why. Like other attractive women, she supposed, she couldn't help noticing the envious glances given her by those less fortunate, although she knew she herself made little of her appearance and never flaunted it. The worst were older women, whose own attractiveness, if you could call it that, was gone. But none had ever looked at her with such icy hatred as that one, what had Reynolds called her, Jen Murdock. Her thick-lined eyes had narrowed, her painted lips tightened; she might have spat venom.

And it wasn't just the look. As Sally herself had hurried from the building to avoid her, the woman had caught up with her in the lane outside, suddenly brushing past her with a vicious swing of her bag. That was how Sally had seen the books. They had spilled to the ground with the force of the blow that left her elbow numb. And when like a fool she had bent to pick them up, 'Get out of my sight, you filthy cow,' the woman had hissed, 'we know your sort. And you aren't welcome here.' It was almost, Sally thought, as if Jen Murdock knew enough about her and her former lover to condemn her on the spot, without mercy or understanding. And it was that implacable judgement which had been most frightening.

That was why she hadn't told Reynolds the whole of it, not merely because she didn't like speaking of the past, even less than she liked speaking of her looks. And that was what she had meant really by talking about change – blurted it out as if she were asking him to pay her a compliment and say she was all right as she was, something she felt Derrymore would never understand. Yet in the beginning she had been so sure of Derry; what had gone wrong that they seemed unable to talk of anything? She stared out of the windows as the bus now gained the main road and gathered speed.

Reynolds returned home to find the envelope on the hall mat, and carried it into the living room, in time to switch on the news. It was full of the murder in the quarry, the bizarre nature attracting even the main channels. At least the man's name had not yet been released and he was described as 'helping the police in their enquiries', the usual euphemism for suggesting he was a suspect without actually saying so. Dr Sinclair had been a bit premature in identifying him, although half the village must know by now.

The details of the case were rehashed. Hearing them spewed over and over by the various newscasters, even to the wretched wedge which was made much of, he felt more certain than ever they made no sense. But he had no way of rectifying the situation unless he set himself up in real opposition – a course of action he wasn't yet ready to undertake.

All this added to the impasse in which he and Derrymore now found themselves, an impasse which in fact seemed dominated one way or the other by the very gossip Sally Heyward disliked so much. He switched off the television, turned on some background music, and, pushing aside the crumpled papers on the floor, began to read through what he had previously written.

Almost from the start he spotted the main problem. Sally had been partially right, his hero hadn't acted 'like a hero' (difficult enough in fiction, impossible in real life) not because he had acted out of character, but because his character hadn't been drawn thoroughly enough to develop his motives clearly.

He sat back. So much for a diagnosis, now to prescribe a cure. As he had imagined the plot in the beginning, two men, who were eventually to become enemies, had been friends. He had never explained their original friendship satisfactorily; that was the first weakness in his hero.

'The two had only met once before but the liking was there from the beginning,' he wrote. 'It sprang from childhood memory, enhanced by their common attitude to the present situation . . .' and he was soon away on the flood of reminiscence and invention which people praised in his writing.

For the first time in months he wrote without hesitation, surprised, when he did stop, that the night had passed so quickly and he felt so refreshed without sleep. He did not bother to re-read what he had written. Experience told him it would stand. All he did remember thinking was, thank God the drought is broken. Now we'll swim with the tide. The next morning was to reveal another complication which he hadn't foreseen and which drastically changed matters again.

Chapter 7

The story of the complication, if that was the right word, again spread like fire through the village, was taken in with the milk, was delivered before the Friday morning papers. 'In the quarry,' ran the shocked whispers. 'Drowned in the pool.'

'Usually takes three days to surface, a body,' Mr Abbot, the butcher, became an instant authority. 'Stands to reason must have gone with the cliff slide. So what was he doing there?'

The same question had already occurred to the authorities. Suddenly the case against Dave Caddick began to weaken, and weakened still further when the body was identified. But its discovery wasn't simple, as Reynolds soon discovered.

Once more Reynolds was summoned abruptly by Nicholls. Putting his own inquiries on hold, with a certain feeling of relief, if the truth be told, he came promptly to find the quarry site cordoned off while for a second time the authorities went about their gruesome business.

The body had been spotted entangled in the reeds at the far side of the pool. As far as could be ascertained from the abrasions on it, and from the fact that it had been at least a couple of days in the water, Mr Abbot's diagnosis was possibly correct – it seemed likely that the victim had fallen in about the same time as the landslip which crushed Mr Barker's car.

He now lay on his back on the bank, clothed except for his

feet which were bare. The general impression was that whether alive or dead when he hit the water, the weight of his old-fashioned coat would have pulled him under. Reynolds bent to look at the face. Against the pallor of the skin the misshapen head looked more grotesque than ever, and something about the roundness of the staring blue eyes suggested surprise – and terror.

'Recognize him, do you?' Nicholls was frowning, tension wrinkling his forehead so the impression of what he might look like as an old man fleetingly emerged. 'They say he's a real weirdo, by name Rab Tremayne. Any thoughts about him?'

About to say, 'Ask Sergeant Derrymore,' Reynolds had the good sense to keep quiet. He had spotted Derrymore in the background and it was clear from the sergeant's behaviour he wasn't about to offer any information.

'Pity about the bare feet.' Nicholls was still frowning. 'Boots must be at the bottom of the pool, and God knows how deep it is. Probably impractical to send down divers. We've checked Caddick's boots, by the way, and although the size is right we found nothing that matches the prints you found. That's neither here nor there, of course; he could have thrown those specific boots away. But I'd like to look at this poor blighter's footwear – if he had another pair, that is.'

He added in a rueful aside, 'About Caddick. Under the circumstances I'm afraid we've acted prematurely. The evidence against him seemed cut and dried at first, too good to be true. The usual. We'll have to rethink our position. Any ideas on that?'

It was a second appeal for help. Yet, without waiting for an answer, Nicholls began to spell out the possibilities now that Rab Tremayne was the murderer instead of Caddick. He made a good case not only for the murder but for linking all the incidents together. For example, Tremayne was certainly odd; moreover he was strong, used to manual labour; shifting rocks – or carrying buckets – would be easy work for him. It may have been his bad luck to have overbalanced as he loosened the stones, thus falling into the pool and drowning. As for the earlier crimes, if he was a bell ringer he would know his way around the church and church hall; he might have been tempted by the crown's glitter. Finally, Nicholls had often found Tremayne's type fascinated by fires. And weren't there drawings left behind? Wouldn't that sort of crude clue also fit?

Reynolds was surprised by Nicholls' assumptions. He was certainly jumping to conclusions without any proof, probably in his anxiety to get the murder solved quickly. About to point this out, and to stop Nicholls' growing enthusiasm, he was saved by Nicholls eventually attracting Derrymore's attention.

Derrymore drew closer, circling them. Finally, as if exasperated with the inspector's arguments, he broke in with, 'But there's still a case against Caddick, and we shouldn't forget it.'

'Meaning?' Nicholls was surprised. He looked at Derrymore coldly, obviously not used to being contradicted by a local bobby. 'You'd better have a good story ready, my lad,' his look said.

At that, the sergeant launched into a long tirade, its main gist that if Caddick hadn't used and hidden the wedge, who had? Mid argument Nicholls turned aside to answer some more pressing question leaving Reynolds to deal with his erstwhile partner.

'You're beginning to sound like headquarters at its worst,' Reynolds interrupted, with a smile. 'Next you'll be believing their favourite maxim, anything for a fast answer.'

Caught short mid-sentence, Derrymore came to a stop. You haven't even looked at the body, Reynolds thought, wasn't Tremayne an old friend? I seem to remember your talking about him once. Why won't you go near him?

An idea struck him, an unpleasant idea. Are you clinging to Caddick as a suspect because you can't accept Rab Tremayne instead? Or do you have other reasons? Reasons you've been hiding?

He looked at Derrymore more closely. The sergeant's face had lost its usual ruddy colour and there were dark shadows under his eyes. Before Derrymore could say any more to incriminate himself, he took him by the elbow and led him quickly out of earshot. 'Now then,' he said, 'come clean.'

For a moment he was afraid Derrymore would square up to him, tell him to mind his own business and clear off. Instead, Derrymore's shoulders visibly drooped. 'It's the phone call,' he admitted. 'We've got it recorded on Caddick's answering machine. I recognise the speaker. Not by name or anything, but by voice. I've had similar anonymous calls before, from the same person.'

About to ask, 'What calls?' Reynolds again kept quiet while Derrymore went on in the same disconcerting way. 'A woman. Warning about Tremayne.'

Opening his mouth to query if Derrymore had done anything about the calls, once more Reynolds stopped himself from speaking. 'She kept insisting Tremayne was dangerous,' Derrymore was continuing. 'But the first incidents couldn't have had anything to do with him so I just ignored her. When the murder occurred I was that upset – but then Caddick turned up and I thought the heat was off. I needed him as a suspect, don't you see.'

Reynolds did 'see', and it too wasn't pleasant. Not if it meant the sergeant had been trying to suppress evidence to avoid incriminating his friend. And if any of what he was admitting was true, then it was certainly right to stop him blurting out further indiscretions in front of everyone.

'You'd better explain all this later,' he said more calmly than he felt, 'First, let's find out what we can about Tremayne.'

The same thought had fortunately occurred to Nicholls. 'I'd like you to go up to where he lived,' he told Reynolds. 'They say he had a place somewhere on the moors.' He turned to Derrymore. 'And here's the very man to show us round his hovel.'

The joke wasn't in good taste, considering Derrymore's state of mind, and the suggestion that the two men work together, although natural, was badly timed. Derrymore's face flushed. He seemed about to refuse, but Reynolds intervened. 'It'd be helpful to have you there,' Reynolds told him, in a low tone, 'and you ought to come.'

He meant 'ought to' in the sense that Rab Tremayne was one of Derrymore's own villagers, one of the people he felt so protective of. When he was alive you defended him, he wanted to say. And if what you've been telling me is only half correct, he may need help more than ever now he's dead. Fortunately this time Derrymore understood.

As calmly as before, Reynolds turned back to Nicholls to discuss the situation. He didn't reveal what Derrymore had told him. But his heart was pounding as it always did when an investigation was about to make a great leap forward. And only when they were in the car driving towards the moors did he allow Derrymore to continue his story.

'About those anonymous calls,' he prompted.

The sergeant said, 'The first was back at Easter.'

He jammed on the brakes and as the car shuddered to a halt, stared out of the window. 'At the time I thought the woman was just making mischief. He does, did, look strange until you got used to him. And you heard how Nicholls talked about him. As if he was a freak.'

'Was the woman local?'

'I never could tell from her accent and her voice was always muffled. Deliberately disguised, I think.'

'What actually did she say?'

'The first calls were vague,' Derrymore explained. 'Claiming Rab was a menace to the village, that sort of thing. Then last Saturday, the day of the wedding fiasco, she was more precise, said he should never have been allowed to go anywhere near the church, that he was responsible for the blood-throwing, and the disappearance of the crown.'

That's pretty specific, Reynolds thought. 'And?' he prompted.

Derrymore continued, 'The day after the book-burning, the very morning we met, in fact, she rang again. Saying he was a Peeping Tom, and worse. Said she'd been walking her dog and spotted him lurking. In the quarry.'

Ye gods, Reynolds thought. No wonder you were unnerved by the murder. As for my finding the boot prints – 'Countrymen's boots,' says I, as if making a real discovery – bet you recognised them straight off! But hearsay evidence and anonymous accusation aren't proof, and moreover can't be used in evidence. And why, if you didn't take gossip literally in his case, did you in mine?

He didn't mention this, merely asked if the caller could have been Betty Caddick. She would have had good reason for being scared if she thought she and her lover were being spied upon. Derrymore shook his head. 'She had a bubbly sort of voice,' he said, 'I'm sure I would have recognized it. And why would she ring her own husband to broadcast her affair? That's the last thing she'd do.'

'It's too late to track the calls to you.' Reynolds' voice was severe. 'What about Caddick's?'

'We've already traced it to a public telephone, somewhere on the main road into Lostwithiel,' Derrymore said, 'so it could have come from anyone. It's a terrible recording, mind you,' he added. 'Caddick kept talking over it. Claimed the answering machine was his wife's and he didn't know how to work it: didn't even know it was on. But I'm sure it was the same person who spoke to me.'

About to mention the possibility of the woman being his own favourite, Mrs Barker, Reynolds decided to put this line of questioning on hold. The more he probed the worse things looked. Exasperated, he glanced at his friend. No wonder you've been worried sick, he thought. Before he could stop himself, he barked, 'And you did nothing about those calls? You never tried to trace them, especially after the last incidents? You never thought they were important enough to interview Tremayne? Or detain him?'

Again Derrymore shook his head. 'No, I didn't. I told you, I thought the woman was one of those busybodies who didn't like his looks. As for him, the last time I saw him was on the green after the bell-ringing practice. But I didn't go after him even then.'

He added more rationally, 'I tell you, I used to know him well. As far as I can judge, he was incapable of planning even simple things, let alone planning crimes and carrying them out. Cause and effect meant nothing to him. And there's another thing. If I'd tried to question him, he wouldn't have understood. He'd have run off in a panic.'

More like his normal self, he went on to explain how he and his mam had befriended Rab. He trusted them. Derrymore hadn't the heart to frighten him.

There was another long pause before he added heavily, 'I know it looks bad. I know I should at least have talked to him but what with one thing and another, I just never found the time.'

All the things that Reynolds could have said seemed to hang in the air, before he continued almost defiantly, 'I know that's no excuse. I accept it's my fault. If I had acted on the information I'd been given, these deaths might not have happened!'

You're damn right about that, Reynolds thought. If Tremayne's proved guilty you'll have a lot to answer for. Although there may be mitigating circumstances, I suppose. Poor Rab, guilty or not, he obviously needed all the support he could get. But, as Sally Heyward pointed out, for a man who feels such unusual responsibility for the people in his village, you've really acted like a fool.

Again the idea jumped into his head – and if you felt you had to protect your friend, Rab, with all that evidence against him, how was it that you were willing to throw me to the wolves, without any evidence at all? I thought I was a friend, too.

All these topics were too deep for discussion at this point. Once more the two men reverted to silence – and drove on.

Tremayne's small-holding consisted of a patch of semi-cultivated land, fast reverting to scrub and heath. It was a lonely place at best, in mid-winter would have been desolate, but now with spring, even the greyness of the day was tinged with the white and pink of hawthorn bushes and the cottage itself was so hidden under a flowering cherry tree that the cracked windows and the worm-eaten door were scarcely noticeable.

A rough track led to the cottage, through a pasture where a couple of sheep looked up from their grazing. A wicker gate opened to a courtyard, surrounded on three sides by ramshackle sheds. All was surprisingly neat; someone had made an attempt to plant wall-flowers beside a large granite trough that stood by the half-open door, and the room beyond, although in semi-darkness, had been brushed clean of mud.

When their eyes became used to the lack of light, Reynolds noted how kindling had been placed ready on the hearth.

The few dishes were carefully arranged on a shelf and the wooden table was decorated with a jam jar of grass and flowers, still fresh. He felt an intruder, invading a special privacy.

'That's Rab's touch,' Derrymore said, finding his voice at last. 'But not much place to hide anything, not even a spare pair of boots.' He looked around the room before dragging aside a threadbare curtain. Behind it, a large wooden bed had been carefully made up with a blue cotton spread and white pillows. 'His father's,' he explained, 'left just as when he died. Rab sleeps, slept, in the loft upstairs.'

He closed the curtain carefully. After which, they separated, Derrymore to search the outbuildings, without success, Reynolds to climb into the loft, where his shout brought the sergeant up the ladder in a great clatter.

The loft was as sparsely furnished; the few clothes hung from hooks driven into the wooden rafters. There was a smell, not unpleasant, of old hay, and the trestle bed, where the ex-inspector was sitting, rustled, as if the mattress was made of straw.

It was what was beside the bed that had attracted Reynolds: a bookcase, made from a packing crate, with a row of books carefully arranged inside – Reynolds' books. Above the crate, taped to the whitewashed wall, was a page torn from one of them, with a section circled in red ink. Derrymore bent to read it out.

' "The container tipped with a sudden creaking sound as if a wind had rushed from one end of the ship to the other. In slow motion, the ropes holding the great steel box broke. It fell like a gigantic wave against the harbour wall, crushing the figure beneath it.'" Only an 's' had been added to the word 'figure' and the words 'in a car' inserted.

'My God.' Derrymore stared at Reynolds, then back at the wall. 'I recognise it. It's from one of your early works.'

And when Reynolds didn't respond, 'I never saw that bookcase before. It must be new. So are the books. But that passage – surely it's proof that Rab Tremayne started the rock slide deliberately after . . .' He stopped himself from saying, 'after reading one of your books.'

'Could be.' Reynolds voice was noncommittal, although his own excitement was rising – for other reasons. In fact he was almost relieved at what he'd found. Under the circumstances, as Nicholls would say, it could have been much worse. He got up from the bed, automatically straightening the rough blanket covering. 'Equally could be someone pointing out the exaggeration of my prose style. I must learn to tone it down.'

His tone was dry, ironic. For a moment, Derrymore glanced at him in his old way, looking like his mother. 'But those books,' he insisted. 'If, for example, Rab did set the fire, he could have kept some back. And I've been thinking. That trough outside, it's full of water now but it's the sort country people once used for blood-letting, when they killed a pig, for example. It would hold a lot of blood. Perhaps there's a butcher knife somewhere.'

It was as if, having admitted his own part in condoning Rab's possible guilt, now, conversely, he was out-doing Nicholls, determined to find proof of it on all sides. He came to a stop, forcing Reynolds, in a queer reversal of roles, to take up Rab's cause himself.

'Perhaps.' The way Reynolds drawled out the word showed how dubious he was. 'If he butchered an animal, where's the carcass? Don't tell me any country fellow would slaughter something and let it go to waste. And it would have had to be a damn great ox to fill a trough that size.'

He couldn't keep the excitement from his voice. As Derrymore stared at him as if he'd gone mad, 'Think man,' he shouted. 'How well could Tremayne read?'

Before Derrymore could finish explaining that he had to learn everything by heart, 'There you are, then,' Reynolds broke in triumphantly. 'Apart from the purple prose, that passage isn't easy. And I bet he couldn't write. So who got the books for him, and made the notations on the cut-out page?'

He waited. 'You mean,' Derrymore began hesitatingly, 'someone else did.'

Reynolds burst out irritatedly, 'Of course someone else did. It's so obvious, it sticks out like a sore thumb.'

He bent to examine the page pinned to the wall. 'How long has that been there?' he wondered. 'No, don't touch it. Forensic might be able to tell us. When were you last up here?'

He listened while Derrymore explained again how his visits had petered off as he realized Tremayne was coping better than he'd thought. 'He was always hard to find,' he explained apologetically. 'He had his routines, you know, his rounds as it were, that didn't deviate but were geared to his own idea of time. I couldn't spend all my off-hours hoping he'd show up: there were other things I had on hand.'

Biting down the comment that presumably Miss Heyward was one of these 'other things', and that it was unfortunate to say the least that Derrymore had left Tremayne to his own devices just when he might have most needed help, Reynolds concentrated on the torn-out passage.

'Could Tremayne learn this by heart?' he asked. When Derrymore shook his head doubtfully, 'Could he have been persuaded to act it out, for example loosen the granite pillar at the quarry in a kind of game?'

'I don't know.' Derrymore was looking more puzzled by the moment. 'He was playful but never violent. He . . .'

'Then in my opinion,' Reynolds said, making for the ladder, 'Rab Tremayne isn't our murderer either. Even if his boots are found and match the prints, or traces of blood remain in that trough (which I doubt) I think he's been used by someone else. And when you consider those phone calls to you, the first might have been vague but the later ones were not only specific, the last actually foreshadowed the place and gave a reason for the crime. Again that suggests something prearranged, part of a set-up.'

He added, 'And I don't say this because I feel sorry for Rab. Or don't want to admit he's used my writings as a model. But because everything, those books included, suggest he was a prime candidate to be a victim.'

Having reached the ground floor he turned to stare back at the sergeant. 'My hunch is that somehow he was lured to the quarry, by persuasion or fear, was again persuaded, or forced somehow, to start the slide during the course of which he fell over. He may have fallen by accident, or he may have been pushed. But since he was by then expendable, my guess is it was deliberately contrived, to make him look like the murderer himself.'

Derrymore, who had followed him, braced himself against the wall, his face darkening at the idea of someone manipulating his poor dead friend. But he kept his concentration.

'Isn't it equally possible Rab was an innocent onlooker?' he countered. 'Who came into the quarry later and then simply overbalanced?'

'It's a possibility,' Reynolds conceded, 'and of course pathology will be able to tell us more about the exact time and manner of his death. But at the moment his death at the same time as the others in the car is the only thing that makes sense of the phone calls to you, and the evidence we've just found. Both are intended to point suspicion at him.'

They had come by now into the courtyard, and again Reynolds stopped, staring at Derrymore, not really seeing him, looking through him into space. Derrymore's questions brought him back. 'What about the other things the woman accused him of?' he asked anxiously. 'Could he be set up for them?'

Reynolds considered. 'It's possible,' he said. 'If, as you say, the woman was the same as the one who rang Caddick.'

Remembering his impression at the quarry top, he added, even more soberly, 'And consider this. If true, we're looking for someone who plans well in advance, who uses other people to kill, and who takes advantage of them and preys on them. Which means we're dealing with a monster. A real man-eater. A mastermind.'

This grim possibility, as yet only a possibility without proof, united the two men in a way perhaps no ordinary crime would have done. It made them even more protective of their home village. And made St Breddaford, like some veritable Indian hamlet, appear even more helplessly exposed to the equivalent of a tiger's attack.

Only one other problem still had not been mentioned, and that was personal. As they went back towards the car Reynolds steeled himself for the explanation he hoped would clear the way between him and the sergeant, incidentally allowing them both to remain on a case which was beginning to frighten as well as intrigue.

He knew his own pride was at stake, but so was Derrymore's. Neither would want to trade on their former friendship; each, in his individual way, was too honest to deny that the friendship had been strained. He found he was eyeing Derrymore, much as Derrymore was eyeing him, reading each other's minds.

'It seems a pity,' he began, more hesitatingly than was usual, 'that we can't reconcile our differences, and continue to cooperate.' He took a breath. 'In my opinion already this case is in danger of becoming what's expected of it. For example, Nicholls would like a quick solution so anything quick appeals. And take the victims in the car, they've been branded as illicit lovers, complete with Peeping Toms and angry spouses.'

Before Derrymore could answer he went on, 'As for my books, those who criticise them will say that proof of their effect on violence has been found in Rab Tremayne's cottage. I know the evidence can't be hidden,' he went on. 'Heaven forbid. But surely the time has come to look at it, and everything else connected with the case, from a new perspective.'

After a moment he added, 'And just because you failed to follow up a lead when it was given you, Rab Tremayne can't be declared guilty or innocent. We have to go by the evidence. And that seems to point to his innocence, no matter what you did.'

Derrymore was listening intently. He reddened. 'Listen sir,' he began, 'I admit so far everything on my side has been a cock-up. I've done you wrong, and there's a fact. But I was so determined that poor Rab shouldn't be blamed, so sure he couldn't be at fault, I almost welcomed anything else that took the blame instead. And to tell the truth, I really did think that your books were causing trouble.'

He swallowed. 'Well, I see what you mean about rethinking. Although I suppose in a way proof of your writings being at the bottom of things has been found, there's a good possibility they too were a set-up. So I see no call to dwell on them, nor make more of them than is necessary. And I'd be grateful if you'd let me tell headquarters about the other phone calls, in my own way and time.'

That was fair enough. 'And I'll come clean myself,' Reynolds couldn't help admitting. 'As your mam will tell you, I've been getting help from her. And I persuaded Newcomb at the library to give me information by pretending I was on official duty. And,' he gave a grin, 'I've been wining if not dining your bird at the local caff and chatting her up. So if you're trying to get me to cook the evidence, or are cooking it for me,' here his eyes began to twinkle, 'let's call it quits while the going's good. I won't say a word about the previous phone calls you received, that's up to you. And you press the evidence about my books merely to ensure we track down who could have used them. I'll back off from looking for the source of the rumours against me; in return, you keep me out of temptation by letting me stay on the case.'

Derrymore nodded. If he minded Reynolds' joke about Sally Heyward, or even knew that they had met, he didn't show it. His question, 'So where do we go from here?' although simple, was a peace offering.

'Let me drive,' Reynolds' reply was as simple. And as he saw with relief, in more ways than one, how Derrymore willingly relinquished the steering wheel, 'Get on the blower to Nicholls. Tell him what we've found, but hold back on our theories for the moment. Headquarters never likes theories; it can only deal with facts. I don't suppose Nicholls is very different.'

As they drove along he slipped easily into his usual role, giving orders and suggestions. 'Set the team looking for clues their end. Specifically, find out exactly how and when Tremayne died and when that stuff was planted in his room. Reconsider who else had reason to kill the lovers or benefit from their deaths, namely look at Caddick's and the Barkers' backgrounds. (Another thing to exonerate Tremayne. If he did kill, what was his motive?) Stress the need to track down the anonymous phone calls. See if anyone remembers who used the call box that night; question people in the neighbourhood. And incidentally, don't let Caddick go. If they need an excuse, remind them that even if he denies hiding the wedge, he's admitted it is his.'

He added with a grin, 'And while you're at it, suggest that you and I start questioning people involved in the earlier incidents. Apart from the phone calls and, I believe, some drawings, there may be other threads that have been missed.'

He grinned again. 'For what it's worth I have another hunch that there may be motives that haven't even been explored yet. And,' sobering at the thought, 'it could be, instead of being a red herring, as it were, my books are essential to the whole situation. But I don't believe for a moment that they have anything to do with inciting crime. After all, I've dealt with criminals half my working life and never yet found one whose crimes were motivated by something they read.'

As the car bounced its way back to the main road he wished he hadn't made this last comment. His explanation, or rather defence, seemed to be challenging fate, given his secret concerns about the way his books might have been used, or might be used in the future. In any case it revealed more of his true feelings than he wanted. It was indicative of Derrymore's change of heart that he didn't comment. What he did ask was relevant, although in a roundabout way.

'It's been puzzling me,' he said, as he put the phone down. 'Why was it presumed I wouldn't act on the information the woman gave? After all, I might have had Rab arrested for his part in the earlier incidents. Exit the scapegoat before the major crime's committed.'

It was a good question. Reynolds concentrated on the ruts before answering. 'I really can't tell you,' he said. 'But let's theorize. One: Possibly the first calls were to sound you out, as it were. When you didn't do anything then they could feel pretty secure you wouldn't later. Two: They stepped up the campaign, so that even if you'd arrested Tremayne on that Tuesday morning, the date of the last call to you, and I think you said the last time you saw him, you still wouldn't have suspected a murder was planned to take place in the quarry that night. More to the point, even if you did link Rab to the other incidents, they were the worst you could have accused him of at that moment. It's most unlikely you would have climbed the cliff at the quarry or searched his house. Although if you had, given the state of the evidence on the quarry top, I guess you would have found all the "arrangement" for setting the stones moving already in place early the same morning, when the ground was still wet.

'Finally, three: Even if Rab were in custody, I suspect the murder might still have taken place. And there was always the evidence in his cottage to link him to the crime.'

He added equally thoughtfully, 'Of course along those lines, there's always another explanation. The real murderer may have known you better than you know yourself. He may have banked on your protectiveness not to do anything at all.'

It too was a sobering idea, bringing with it a host of other unpleasant ones, all involving the sort of intimate knowledge and local detail that make up what people call gossip. As Sally had pointed out, it had two sides, good and bad. But for it to be used wholly for the bad was rare – and hitherto Derrymore had prided himself on knowing how to handle it.

Chapter 8

The details of their findings roused great excitement. Reynolds was especially gratified to learn that his recommendations would be followed; here was real co-operation at last. The manner of Tremayne's death, other than by drowning, was given priority and the abrasions on the body (already mentioned) were to be examined for evidence of foul play. The hunt for his boots was reconsidered, if the depth of the pool and its underwater condition permitted, and the land behind the quarry was to be searched for new clues (even over the static they heard the groans that greeted this proposal!).

As Reynolds had suggested, Caddick would be held 'for further questioning', still without his name actually being mentioned, and Nicholls undertook to 'squeeze' him about possible implication in the earlier incidents. A massive hunt was launched to trace the anonymous phone calls, including the earlier ones to Derrymore (who had logged them even if he hadn't acted on them, an inconsistency that would presumably lead to further questions from his superiors at some later date. For the moment, 'under the circumstances', as Nicholls said, they let the matter rest). The reason for this last investigation, however, was down-played, so that the woman wouldn't be scared off from making other calls (although the likelihood of her using the same phone box again was remote).

Meanwhile, the evidence found in poor Rab Tremayne's bedroom was also given priority and, at Reynolds' suggestion,

Dr Sinclair was asked to list which specific books were supposedly burnt in the fire, Reynolds' impression that they were all copies of the same new work being thus confirmed, whereas the bookcase contained a number of different books, some out of print. Finally, a piece of good news, for once. The team had heard through the village grapevine that Mrs Barker's son had returned. Would Derrymore and Reynolds care to interview him? Once more Nicholls' obvious reluctance to tackle local people played into their hands.

They jumped at the chance. And after asking for, and receiving, Nicholls' blessing to interview other people involved in earlier incidents, they drew up at the Barkers' house, this time with their battle plan prepared.

A sports car was parked in the driveway – not a likely replacement for the Barker family car. They eyed it curiously. 'Must be the son's,' Derrymore decided, adding, 'How does he run that on a university's salary? I gather Sinclair makes no secret how hard up he is.'

When Mrs Barker again opened the door herself this time they were prepared for her vexed look as they asked to speak with her and her son.

'How do you know he's here?' Her reply was snappish. 'Barely time to take off his coat and you're hounding him.'

'Who is it, mother?' The son's voice was high-pitched, what Derrymore called 'affected', and as he came out of the sitting room, a dapper camel-hair coat draped over his shoulders, Reynolds could feel Derrymore's Cornish hackles rise.

The man ignored Reynolds and concentrated on Derrymore, lifting his eyebrows at the stripes as if to say, 'Surely I rate higher than a mere sergeant.'

'Thought we'd seen the last of you,' he said haughtily. 'I don't want you here harassing my mother.'

'We certainly understand, sir.' Derrymore could be unctuous when it suited. 'But we're investigating a murder, and you wouldn't want your father's death to go unsolved.'

'He's not my father, thank the Lord.' The man positively stiffened. 'And although I had to put up with him as a step-father, my name's not Barker, again thanks to the Powers that Be. But I suppose if we can help, you'd better come in, although what help we can be at this stage God alone knows.'

And with these three appeals to the Almighty he stood aside and allowed them to precede him into the strawberry-coloured living room, where, when his mother was once more arranged in the depths of the sofa, he stood with legs apart in front of the fireless grate.

Facing them, with the afternoon sun full on his face, the resemblance to his mother was pronounced, the same thin lips and habitual disapproving frown. Even the thinning hair was the same colour. He'll keep his students nicely in their place, Reynolds thought. And that's a useful piece of information he's given us. I'd say there was no love lost between him and his step-father.

Meanwhile, Derrymore, having suitably begged pardon, was ascertaining that the son's name was Charles Eden, his mother's surname by a previous marriage. In the same unobtrusive way he went on to suggest that Dr Eden was very kind to spare them a moment, such a busy man, did he have far to come? Charles Eden, relaxing in this flattering atmosphere, began a rambling explanation of his onerous university duties which he'd had to abandon to get here (incidentally confirming that he lived scarcely an hour's drive away).

'Are you aware, sir, of any complications in your father's, excuse me, your step-father's, business affairs that might have bearing on the case?' Derrymore broke in casually, in effect bringing the questioning round to the line he and Reynolds had already decided upon.

Cut short mid-flow, Eden's frown returned. 'I've told you

he was nothing to me,' he snapped, just as his mother might have done, causing Derrymore to ask in the same bland fashion exactly how long his step-father and mother had been married. 'It must be several years ago.' Derrymore pretended to flick through his notes.

Eden lapsed into sulky silence while Mrs Barker piped up helpfully, 'He was only a child at the time.'

'Quite.' Derrymore's tone was dry. 'So perhaps there were occasions when your step-father's influence, shall we say, was more important to you than you like to admit now. When you were a youngster, for example. Or when you began life on your own as a student. I mean most of us come to rely on our family to see us through when we start off, don't we. And money always helps.'

'Well, I won't deny my husband was good to Charles when he began college,' again Mrs Barker piped up while, with an even more ferocious frown, Charles himself snarled, 'I don't know what you are driving at.'

'Nothing in particular, sir.' Derrymore was reassuring. 'But we are looking for links between your step-father and possible adversaries in the business world. It would assist us if we had assurances that his affairs were in order. Of course we can examine the bank records, but it's the sort of investigation which takes time. And can be very intrusive.'

He slid the barb in gently before turning to Mrs Barker. 'I know I asked the same question previously,' he went on. Reynolds had never seen him so skilful. 'And I think you replied you knew of no one with a grievance. But Mr Barker was obviously a wealthy man.' He let his gaze stray round the room.

Eden rounded on his mother. 'Don't tell me the fool was embezzling bank money as well,' he cried. 'For God's sake, is there no end to it? Think of my career. You can't expect me to bail you out again.'

'Again?' Derrymore pounced. 'What do you mean by that exactly, sir?'

A second time cut off short, Eden looked stupid. 'Only a *façon de parler*,' he began with a return to his earlier superior manner, while at the same time his mother said, 'He only meant he gave me good advice.'

'I don't know about any "*façoning de parler*".' Derrymore was stern. 'But what advice would that be?'

Mother and son exchanged glances. 'When he started on his capers,' the son said at last, 'well, let's be honest about that at least, mother; there's been more than one, I told her she should stop pretending. No more covering for him, I said. And I told him the same thing.'

So much for Mrs Barker's former testimony that she'd confided in no one!

'And how did he take that?' Derrymore asked.

'How would you expect? Said he couldn't give his woman up, she meant the world to him, rubbish of that sort. Lavishing gifts on her as if he owned a gold mine.'

As if suddenly aware of what he was saying, he added in his mother's censoring way, 'Selfishness, that's what I called it, and told him so. Not caring a scrap for the rest of us, determined to have his own way. As for money matters, he's always felt he could buy his way out of difficulties. So I said, let's get rid of him.' Seeing their expressions, he added quickly, 'Divorce him, I mean.'

It was a damaging statement. Derrymore let it ride, changed the subject to ask abruptly, 'What were you doing on the night of his death, if you don't mind my asking?' Before Eden could bluster he added, 'Routine, you understand, just for the record.'

'I was at a meeting of the English department.' Grudgingly Eden went on to explain that the session had lasted for hours, Derrymore could check with the office if he wanted to.

'Oh, I don't think that will be necessary. At this stage.' Derrymore slid this second barb in as gracefully. 'But I have one other question. Did either of you know Rab Tremayne?'

The son looked puzzled but Mrs Barker preened. 'That hideous little man,' she said, 'the one they've just found drowned.'

She turned to her son, her ready tears threatening. 'I always said he was a disgrace to the village. Like his father. The old man was always drunk on the village green. To think that now they're hinting the son might have been in the quarry at the same time as . . .'

She began to sniffle while her son, stooping to pat her shoulder, said with surprising solicitude, 'There, there,' before rounding on Derrymore. 'I told you so,' he shouted. 'You're upsetting her again.'

'Just one last question, then we'll take our leave.' At Reynolds' nod Derrymore paused while Reynolds spoke for the first time. 'Mrs Barker, you mentioned a book club – are you a member of Jen Murdock's group?'

It was Mrs Barker's turn to look puzzled. Her tears dried by magic; she stared at him. 'Yes I am,' she said uncertainly, 'but I don't see it matters. I don't . . .'

Her voice trailed off as they headed for the door, although they heard it raised again when they were outside, to the effect that she didn't trust either of them and hadn't Charles recognized the quiet one, that ex-inspector Reynolds fellow, the writer of the detective books that had been burned? Why was he here? Everyone said his books should be banned.

'*Et tu Brute*,' Reynolds said ruefully. And when they were again in the car and were heading for their next stop, the vicarage, 'What do you make of them?

'Can't tell about Mrs Barker,' Derrymore said. 'I listened carefully but couldn't recognize anything about her voice. As for the son, a slimy piece of work. And he's right, I will check up on that meeting to find out how late it went on. But,' he added ruefully, 'I admit I didn't know he was a step-son. Or that he hated his step-father. Never any hint of family trouble there before. That's all news to me.'

He sounded despondent, for the second time admitting that his knowledge of his own village wasn't as sound as he'd believed. Reynolds felt sorry for him; it must be another blow to his confidence.

Reverting to safer topics, 'Mrs B said her husband had been good to Charles when he was younger,' he pointed out. 'Perhaps it was only when Barker's womanizing got out of hand that Eden turned against him. She must have told him, of course, although she said she didn't. And I wonder who the other women were. As for the "advice" that Eden gave his step-father, my impression is that Frank Barker preferred to dish out advice himself rather than be on the receiving end. And,' he added thoughtfully, 'that Audi must have cost a fortune.'

He didn't comment on Mrs Barker's reaction to his questions. Nor elaborate on the significance of her reply when asked if she knew Rab Tremayne. But he did focus on the son. In his opinion Dr Eden was what he called a smart ass, who thought he could out-wit everyone. How did Derrymore react to the idea of his masterminding a complicated murder scam?

Derrymore expressed his opinion even more forcefully. Professor Charles Eden was a conceited fop who couldn't wipe his own bum without expecting the world to stop and marvel – a vulgarism quite unlike him, showing the depth of his feelings. But, putting his own prejudice aside, he agreed it was possible, just possible, that the combination of personality and opportunity existed for the son to manipulate a murder, using his mother to make the anonymous phone calls and Ray Tremayne to do the killing. And apart from getting revenge on his step-father, Eden had another possible motive: his concern for his mother – 'If his concern is genuine.'

Derrymore's observation was shrewd. 'Like everything else about him,' he pointed out, 'it could have been put on for effect. And to tell the truth, I don't see him scrabbling about in the quarry. Or dabbling his hands in blood. Not in those fancy clothes. Or, for that matter, dealing with Rab Tremayne. Rab could scent a phony a mile off.'

Deciding unanimously to 'keep an eye on the Barkers', meaning their background would be investigated thoroughly, he and Reynolds drove off, reminding each other that even if Derrymore hadn't recognized Mrs Barker's voice they could as a last resort have her speak through a muffling device to recreate the conditions on the answering machine's recording. At the same time, Derrymore reverted back to Tremayne's own background, again inadvertently revealing his true concern for the family.

'OldTremayne wasn't a real drunkard,' he insisted. 'Something made him take to drink. I think I mentioned before he was very religious, well, my mam believes that when his wife died in childbirth, leaving him with a deformed child, he felt God must be punishing him. So he deliberately ran away from his former home, hid himself as far away as possible to conceal the consequences, and drank to forget. Of course, she's only guessing,' he added. 'But he was fond of his son. In his own way he lavished time and attention on him, trying to train him into, what do they call it, functioning on his own. And no matter how they lived, originally they came from a good background. I happen to know there was a source of income. Not much, but when the old man died it went to his son. So Rab didn't just live on welfare as some people think.'

The same idea now struck him and Reynolds – how was the money administered? When Derrymore answered his own question, saying he presumed through the local bank, 'Would Mr Barker, as manager, have known about the arrangement?' Reynolds asked in turn. 'And if Barker knew, would his wife and step-son?'

'I suppose so.' Derrymore ground the gears to emphasize the point. 'But if you're suggesting they might have used money to manipulate Rab, threatening to withhold it, for example, I'm not sure that would have worked. Rab didn't really know the value of the money he got. If you asked him to choose, he'd take a twopenny bit over a pound every day because it's a larger coin. He only knew certain coins bought certain things, and he'd learned what to buy each week and where to go for it. In fact when I think of him and his father, I'm reminded of badgers. The same sort of routines, the same neatness, the same dogged determination.'

As an epitaph it was a good one.

Reynolds was glad to see Derrymore so animated. For the moment his professional worries were in abeyance, and after the talk he'd had with Reynolds the air had cleared. If Derrymore still had personal 'difficulties', as Sally had termed them, he never mentioned them, or his actual relationship with her. But whether he thought about them, or whether he'd really paid attention to Reynolds' joke about 'his bird', again he never said.

Chapter 9

Chapter 9

They had debated where to go next and had selected the vicarage because up to now, Reynolds had only had second-hand information about the earlier events and the vicar was involved in at least two. And as Derrymore pointed out, he'd interviewed everyone so many times already about the missing crown, it would save them having to speak with Mrs Varcoe – 'she'd talk the hind leg off a donkey if you let her.' Meanwhile, he added, although Reynolds had decided to put his own investigations on hold, he might as well take the chance to ask Mrs Tamblin about Mrs Murdock and the so-called book club, thus, as he expressed it, 'killing two birds with one stone.' In fact the killing of even one was dubious: Mrs Tamblin was out and the vicar was trapped in his study by the dreaded Mrs Varcoe.

'Come in, come in,' he cried as if he were glad to see them, as well he might, for an elderly lady, arms akimbo, was lecturing him severely about 'letting things slide'.

Recognizing Derrymore, she began to protest even more vehemently that it wasn't fair and they, some unstated 'they', knew it.

'Been at me non-stop they have, and here we're already into June.' Her faded blue eyes shone at the indignity. 'As if it's still my fault that the crown's lost.'

'Mrs Varcoe's in trouble with the May Day Committee.' The vicar's stage-whisper suggested he was in trouble too and saw his visitors as welcome reinforcements. 'They're insisting she pay for a replacement but that's out of the question. Perhaps you could persuade her, sergeant, that there's nothing to be done at the moment; she'll just have to be patient until I talk with them.'

Leaving her to repeat her grievance to Derrymore, he beckoned to Reynolds to follow him into the adjacent sitting room, a pleasant, faded place where books and papers lay in untidy heaps and two golden retrievers sunned themselves by the open windows.

'I'm afraid she's got it into her head poor Tremayne's to blame for the disappearance,' the vicar continued in the same stage-whisper. 'And now she's heard Rab's dead, she wants to get her hands on some money she claims was his.'

He wiped a handkerchief across his flushed face, a bluff, hearty sort of fellow, more like a farmer than a clergyman.

'Does she now?' Reynolds looked back through the door of the study, assessing Mrs Varcoe more carefully. She was stocky, grey-haired, her own voice also lowered as she poured her troubles into Derrymore's sympathetic ears. She might be forgetful about most things but apparently remembered enough to hang on to the rumour of Rab Tremayne's little inheritance. And how many other people knew about it too, he wondered? If they did, it lessened the case against Mrs Barker and her son.

'I hope you're not here about anything serious?' Vicar Tamblin was joking but there was a worried look in his eye that didn't go away even when Reynolds assured him there was no problem. Only, like Mrs Varcoe, they were interested in the missing crown. Did the vicar have any new suggestions who might have broken into the church hall?

The vicar shook his head wearily. 'The hall was never secure either,' he confessed. 'Another thing the committee are blaming Mrs Varcoe for, although that's certainly not her fault. We never have funds enough to go round as it is, and security was always low on our list of essentials. Alas, about to be changed.'

'What about Rab Tremayne?' Reynolds cut the vicar off gently, brought him back to the line of questioning. 'Could he have been tempted?'

'I'd have said so straight out if I'd thought it.' Vicar Tamblin was emphatic. 'In fact, my opinion is that Mrs Varcoe's mislaid the damn thing, pardon my French, and it will turn up eventually. Of course I'm not denying Tremayne might have taken it if he'd seen it lying about, but again, I didn't see him as a jackdaw. They're fascinated by glitter, you know, will steal anything bright that catches their eye.'

'I gather one of the church doors was easily broken open too,' Reynolds persisted. 'As a bell ringer, would Rab know that?'

The vicar replied even more forcefully, 'I don't think Rab ever was in the actual church itself. He came and went through the belfry, you see, sidling in like some animal, one moment there, the next gone. But he was strong, you know, could ring for hours. And he learnt the peals by heart. He'll be missed.'

He added sorrowfully, 'His father came sometimes, but never brought Rab to a service although I used to try and persuade him. An interesting man, old Tremayne,' he went on, as if glad to slide away from an unpleasant subject. 'He was quite a scholar. In fact . . .'

'What about the church incident? Could Rab Tremayne have been responsible?'

'No.' Again the vicar was blunt. 'Not that he couldn't have done it physically, but the idea would be too complicated for him. In my opinion,' he went on, looking more worried again, but speaking forcefully, 'he was a gentle fellow but incapable of thinking ahead or reasoning like we do. The concept that if he did such and such in the past, such and such would happen in the future was beyond him. He just lived in the present.' His voice suggested that in this at least Rab Tremayne had been fortunate.

'Could he have been persuaded by someone else, was he easily led?'

The vicar looked horrified. 'You mean someone would use him to commit these atrocities?' he exclaimed, much as Derrymore had done. 'I suppose he was vulnerable to evil; he was trusting enough. Thought everyone was his friend. Bad luck for him.'

His voice showed a hint of bitterness which increased when he pointed out that, in case Reynolds didn't remember, it was suggested that the church had been deliberately desecrated because it was his daughter's wedding day, so much for Christian fellowship and trust.

'I know, frightful.' Reynolds was genuinely sympathetic. 'And what about your wife, she must have been upset?'

'You can say that again.' Vicar Tamblin suddenly smiled. 'Her only ewe lamb about to be sacrificed. Not that we don't like Matty's husband and his family,' he added, too quickly, 'but when you think of all my wife had to put up with last Saturday, the extraordinary demands upon her time and patience, as well as the human relationships involved – it was nothing short of miraculous she pulled herself together. And she'd never have got into such a state if it hadn't been for that damnable phone call.'

'Phone call?' Despite himself, Reynolds couldn't help pouncing. 'Who made it? What did it say?'

The vicar looked uncomfortable. 'Dear me,' he said, 'I promised not to speak of it. And I didn't on the day. Mainly because it was hard to do so in a detached way. I mean it was so deliberately vicious it made one want to . . . well, you can understand my feelings as a husband and father, and they weren't exactly priest-like.'

He shook his head at the memory. 'I really have no idea who made the call,' he went on, 'and my wife didn't either. But you can imagine the scene: the verger gone mad, shouting about murder; the wedding guests about to descend; the house in an uproar, and then some busybody of a woman chooses that very moment to ring my wife and tell her it's her fault.'

The same who chose an equally inopportune time to ring Dave Caddick. And Derrymore. For a moment Reynolds almost thought he'd said the words aloud.

'And you didn't try to trace the call?'

'My dear fellow.' Vicar Tamblin sounded exasperated. 'I can see you're a bachelor. You've no idea what a wedding is like.'

A fair observation. 'I heard,' Reynolds picked his words with care, 'that there was talk that the attack on the church was justified, that Miss Tamblin, I'm sorry I don't know her married name, was supposed to have brought it on herself.'

'Wretched rumours.' Thoroughly angry now the vicar glared at Reynolds. 'And so unfair,' he exploded, 'not just on Matty, on my poor wife too. That's another thing I meant about Christian fellowship. More like biting the hand that fed you, I'd say. I told my wife,' he added, calming down, 'that the call was the work of fanatics; there're a lot about these days. Even in St Breddaford we're not immune. Born Again Christians, or Holy Rollers, or Moonies, they're all the same. Newcomers to our church, they try to take over, upset the old folk and tip things off balance.'

'Newcomers?' Reynolds probed gently. 'What do you make of them as parishioners? Not that you see much of me!'

'Oh, we plan to catch you one of these days.' The vicar had cooled enough to be capable of a joke. 'But some of the others . . .' He made an expressive face.

'I believe one of the victims, Mr Barker, was a long-time

church warden.' Reynolds' tone expressed sympathy. 'And I've recently run into another newcomer, at least, I suppose she's still considered that, Mrs Murdock, from Grange Manor.'

'Barker was all right if you could stand his hectoring,' Tamblin said bluntly, forgetting the need for discretion. 'As for that woman, I could wring her neck. She's the one behind the present quarrel with Mrs Varcoe, demanding her pennyworth of flesh right enough, although she's rich as Hades and could buy the Varcoes out ten times over. Talk about telling people what to do and how to run the parish, you'd think she was in line to be next bishop. Mind you,' he added in the more forgiving tone that was equally part of his nature and was probably what made him so popular with his congregation, 'I suppose Murdock means well. She certainly organizes her own little committees and clubs and keeps them up to scratch.'

'Ah yes.' Reynolds looked meek. But, remembering Derrymore's suggestion, he couldn't resist the opportunity. 'She runs a book club I believe,' he asked.

The vicar grunted, 'Gossip club more like. My wife went a couple of times, mainly to be supportive, but bowed out quickly. A very decisive woman, Jen Murdock. To tell the truth I don't know what to make of her.'

Again a fair assessment.

'And what sort of books do they read? Did your wife ever mention that mine had been picked out for censorship?'

He felt awkward asking this last question, especially as the vicar, sounding apologetic, broke out with, 'Goodness me, I didn't mean for a moment to suggest . . . But no, as far as I know they never mentioned you. In fact my wife thinks the whole venture's a waste of time. She'd tell you so herself. Of course, it takes all sorts to make a world, and if it keeps Murdock off my back . . .' His voice trailed off, suggesting he'd rather anything than have her around.

'Just one last question.' Reynolds was almost done. 'I believe there was a drawing in the church. A smiling face, like the one left in place of the missing crown . . .'

'And I tore it up.' The vicar was contrite. 'But if you had seen it, grinning from the altar, you'd have torn it up, too. Horrible. Vile.'

'Did it resemble the previous drawing?'

'I suppose so. I didn't stop to think. It was certainly bigger.' He closed his eyes. 'I only saw the first one briefly but I'd have said they were the same. It was the thought behind them, don't you see, the malicious intent.'

It was as far as Renolds could go on this line. By now Derrymore had succeeded in escaping from Mrs Varcoe's clutches, promising her the case would be reopened, and they'd hope to have good news for her soon. 'For I never could forgive myself if that crown's lost for ever,' she continued to wail as the vicar showed her to the door. 'And I can't afford a new one for all they say I should.'

'Dear me,' said the vicar again once she was gone. 'It's all very sad. We've never had any trouble like this in the village before.'

He looked at Reynolds, then, as if afraid he would commit another indiscretion, coughed loudly and begged them to stay to tea as his wife wouldn't be long, she was only down at the church overseeing the flower arrangements.

Refusing his kind offer they left, to exchange notes once they got back to the car, Reynolds telling Derrymore what the vicar had said about Rab Tremayne and Mrs Murdock – and more importantly, the phone call to his wife. 'We must ask her if she remembers anything special about the voice,' he reminded Derrymore. 'As for Rab Tremayne, all personal, I know, but the vicar confirms your opinion. And incidentally, my own.'

'Mrs Varcoe still insists she put the crown away safely,' Derrymore added in turn. 'And said almost the same thing as the vicar about the state of the hall. One new thing she did let drop which she didn't tell me before, was that some of the local lads used to climb in to smoke. Said she hadn't mentioned it earlier because everyone would have been even more angry with her. They're all afraid their own children will be blamed.'

'So we could add illegal smoking in the church hall to possible shop-lifting, when we pay our visit to the school,' Reynolds suggested. 'Otherwise no real leads? I asked about the drawings but didn't get anywhere with that, sad to relate.'

'Only Mrs Murdock and the phone calls,' Derrymore began, then stopped and repeated what he'd said. 'Putting the two together makes you think,' he said excitedly, in quite his old way. 'Might she have made them, sir?'

Reynolds considered. 'I still put my money on Mrs Barker,' he said finally. 'For one thing what's Jen Murdock's motive? Besides, she doesn't seem the sort of lady to be conned into becoming an accomplice. True, she's apparently involved with church affairs as well as her book club, but your mam suggested that's because she's lonely. And the more we hear about her the more I gather she's not liked. She gives me the impression of a real outsider who desperately wants to become part of the community but doesn't know where to start. And I can't see her tottering up to the quarry, can you?'

He added comfortingly, 'We'll question her, of course. In fact she may have a lot to answer for, even if it's only driving the vicar wild.'

They had come back towards the village now, and it seemed better at this point to separate, Derrymore to catch the boys at school before they left for the afternoon; Reynolds to make a detour to the church to find Mrs Tamblin. It was only as the sergeant was squeezing his bulk back into his car that Reynolds remembered that again he was without his own – he'd left it at the quarry. With some trepidation, for he didn't want to impose on Derrymore, and more to the point, didn't trust Derrymore's driving, he asked the sergeant if he could turn over the official car to someone there and bring his back instead. Derrymore enthusiastically agreed; there'd be no problem, he assured Reynolds, who had already given him the keys when, with a return to his former stiffness, Derrymore asked in turn if he might make a detour of his own, to 'pick up a friend – Miss Heyward, actually'.

He volunteered this information aggressively, jutting his chin forward. 'Of course,' Reynolds tried to sound disinterested, not certain what line he should take. But it made an interesting codicil to his earlier observation that Derrymore was not as unaware of the young lady as he gave the impression.

As he'd told himself before, the love lives of the young were exhausting, and really none of his concern. It made him feel old, the more so, when on thinking things over, he realized his main concern at the moment was for something dearer to his own heart – the survival of his car! A quick run from the quarry back to Old Forge Cottage was nothing, but a round trip to Truro . . . he'd never have handed over the keys if he'd guessed, but, once he'd done so, it was impossible to get them back, without giving offence, or suggesting to Derrymore that the refusal was based on Miss Heyward being a passenger. Bracing himself for a burnt-out clutch at least, he went into the church.

Inside, the quiet was only disturbed by the faint rustling of the flower arrangers close to the altar and in the background the sounds of the organist practising. It put his own preoccupations into perspective, and made him feel how small they were. It also made him aware that this was neither time nor place to pursue a murder investigation, and he was about to beat a retreat when Mrs Tamblin spotted him and came over to ask if he needed help.

The vicar's wife was a cheerful woman, like her husband seemingly more used to horses and dogs for she was wearing riding boots and an old hacking jacket. As Derrymore had pointed out originally, it wasn't easy to think of her becoming hysterical. Using the privacy of a pew to put his questions, Reynolds heard her confirm her husband's version of events and reinforce his views on Mrs Murdock. Like her husband, Mrs Tamblin called a spade a spade, but lacked his more forgiving nature.

'She's a dreadful woman,' she said, her brown eyes flashing. 'And don't tell my husband this; the group she's gathered isn't at all what it pretends.'

Asked who else were members she replied she had only gone a couple of times in the beginning, and her information came from others who, like her, had dropped out. But she knew that the librarian, for example, was a regular, well, you'd think he would be if it were a genuine reading club, and she'd certainly met Mrs Barker there. Although to tell the truth she didn't know why she came, she seemed so out of place. 'But from what I hear,' she added, 'the men and women, yes, there are several male "clubies", as they call themselves, aren't interested in books at all. I won't say what I think they are interested in, certainly not in the church, but I will say some of them ought to know better and should be ashamed.'

And with this ambiguous remark (which suggested something worse than gossip mongering) she went back to her flowers, not before promising however that 'when the time was more suitable' she'd consider helping identify the anonymous phone caller, who, she finally admitted, had 'devastated her'.

When she had gone, taking the other ladies with her, Reynolds sat on for a while, trying to put his new thoughts in order and make sense of them. Gradually the light dimmed from the stained window and the sound of the organ ceased. It was hard to accept that, less than a week ago, this lovely building had been defiled, although on the surface now there were no obvious traces left.

All in all it had been a trying day. The discovery of the body, the evidence in Rab's cottage, the new leads, all seemed to bring further complications rather than offer solutions for what they already had. And still at the back of his mind, despite his emphatic denial, was his concern about the way his books could be used. The passage they had found today might have been altered to fit the actual crime, but it was rather clumsily done, far-fetched. An accident on a container ship had little in common with an accident in a quarry. But there were other passages, whole cases in fact, that could be made to suit, that, heaven forbid, were twisted and evil enough to be adapted to anywhere, if someone took the trouble to – what was Derrymore's original expression – 'copy cat' the crime. And if, as he was beginning to suspect, there was someone very clever behind all these events, someone, who for lack of anything better, he was beginning to call a mastermind, wouldn't it occur to him eventually to do just that?

He was so deep in thought he scarcely noticed the skinny figure which crept into the pew behind him; what he was to think of later as the second coincidence. He almost jumped when he heard the voice, thin, toneless, ghost-like, with the steel-like ripple underneath of what used to be called 'class'. He caught a glimpse of the woman, thin, upright, severe.

'Aren't you the famous detective?' she asked. Then before he could answer, 'I saw you the other day with Sergeant Derrymore by the stream, so presume you are taking part in the investigations. Well, the devastation of the church was bad enough, but I believe God takes care of His own. It's the fire I'm speaking of. I don't know why the sergeant didn't ask me about the fire. I suppose because I'm old and can't hear very well, he thought there was no use.'

Reynolds' attempts to interrupt were ignored as she went on in the same deliberate way, 'Because I can't hear doesn't mean I can't see.' Then he remembered Dr Sinclair's observation about his deaf neighbour. Lord, he thought, this is a problem I haven't met before!

She went on talking, a stream of words, typical he knew of those who live alone and, for whatever reason, are trapped in a private world from which there is no escape, any attempt to stem the flow making it clear that, if nothing else, she was certainly stone deaf.

'Hang on a moment,' he said at last, holding up his hand. Moving quickly into the pew beside her he fished pen and paper from his pocket. Printing the letters out large he asked the first question, 'Your name please.'

'How clever,' she said approvingly. 'I thought you looked intelligent. And I like the "please". Men today are often so impolite. Not like the ones from my own time. I'm Miss Penwithen. Originally of Penwithen Hall. I live next to the bookshop.'

Close to, she looked even more like a relic from the past, tall, her dress of some black material that rustled and her hair tied into a grey bun over each ear. He almost imagined she would be wearing mittens. The scent of lavender brought back memories from his own childhood, when all spinster ladies rustled scented skirts. And the name Penwithen Hall too rang a bell; he'd been right about the aristocratic touch.

'It wasn't always a commercial establishment,' she was saying of the bookshop. 'When I came here first there was a family in it. When it changed hands, and became a confectioner's, I remember a young girl who worked there. She . . .'

'Have you information about the fire?' he wrote, cutting her off short.

'Yes, I have.' Her reply was suitably terse to match his question. 'Two things. First, the back bedroom window in my house overlooks the yard behind the shop. The yard juts out level with my garden and in the past was always an eyesore. But Dr Sinclair was most particular, kept it so clean I'd no fault to find. Then on Monday evening before the fire, he filled it full of cardboard packing cases.'

'Brought in especially?' Reynolds' written question couldn't express his surprise. 'I didn't say brought in,' she countered. 'He used to fold all the packing up and keep it in his loft above the shop. Naturally there was a large amount, the books always came well wrapped. You reach the loft with a ladder from the yard. That evening, he went up and tipped everything out. I couldn't imagine what he was doing,' she went on. 'Such a cloud of dust. So thoughtless. I had to close the windows. I almost went to complain but there,' she gave an almost imperceptible shrug. 'I don't suppose he would have listened.'

'Then what?' Reynolds wrote.

'Later that night, I saw the flames,' she said. 'I was frightened at first. I knew at once the yard was on fire and I thought it might spread. When I looked out I saw him.'

'Who?' In his excitement Reynolds scribbled the word and had to reprint it.

'It was dark, mind you,' she said slowly, adding to the suspense, 'and the figure was coming and going through the back door, carrying things. I thought at first he was having a great bonfire and burning up all his rubbish at once, although it seemed an odd time to choose. That was before he left and the fire engine came. And then I read in the papers that it was arson and books had been burned.'

Reynolds sensed rather than saw her glance. 'Your books,'

she said, after a slight pause, adding surprisingly, 'I don't read much these days but when I do I like a good detective story. So I thought it very strange for yours to be the only ones burnt when I know he sells a lot.'

Reynolds turned the paper over to print sharply, 'Can you identify who you saw?'

'It was dark,' she repeated. 'Whoever it was left in a hurry, by the front door. I watched him go down the road past my house, then turn at the end. It leads to Badgewall Lane. It's the way Dr Sinclair always takes to go home. And to my mind he has a distinctive way of walking, like a heron flip-flapping along.'

She sat more upright than ever. 'And that's the second thing I had to tell.'

What she said was tantalizing, but not definite enough. Cursing this limited way of communication he wrote, 'Was the man you saw Dr Sinclair?' She didn't answer.

Trying a new tack, he wrote, 'Why didn't you speak before?'

She gave another glance. 'After the fire engine came and put out the fire,' this time her reply was succinct, 'I thought no more of it. The danger was past. All I'd lost was sleep and at my age I don't need much. It was none of my business what he did with his wrapping paper and books. It was only after I read about the murder in the quarry and then today, the finding of Rab Tremayne, I began to reconsider. There's more to this than meets the eye, I told myself. And, as you should know, things don't happen just by chance; there's always a link. That's what I like about your books,' she added, 'although you juggle with ideas, in the end you always look for links. You rely on them, not chance.'

With this last remark she looked at her watch, a dainty contraption hung on a chain about her neck. 'My, it's late,' she exclaimed. 'I must hurry home. No,' as Reynolds started to stand up, 'don't come with me. I'd rather go alone. I don't want anyone to think I've been, what's the phrase, "squealing" to the police.'

He started to say, then wrote, 'Thanks, most helpful. Would you make a statement?' But she had already gone before he'd written it, as silently as she had come, leaving him at the end of his most bewildering interview so far, as unexpected as it was full of surprise. For if she were correct, and he had no reason to doubt her word, then she was suggesting Dr Sinclair was an arsonist.

The significance of her claim took him back to Old Forge Cottage and through the rest of the long evening. Until it was too dark to see, he dug in his garden, weeding ruthlessly. Hard work was good for generating ideas but at the end of the session among his rose bushes, he still didn't know what to make of her evidence. Setting a fire by mistake, although stupid, didn't justify failure to report the fire or admit the cause. And what about the broken window? What about the burnt books? As Derrymore had pointed out in the beginning, they hadn't walked into the yard by themselves.

On the other hand, Sinclair had made no secret of his shaky financial position, and setting a fire to claim insurance was a well-known trick. It was also a criminal offence, although not quite on the same level as murder.

There was no way he could associate Sinclair with murder or manipulation of murder; they seemed so out of character. After all, the ex-professor lived alone and was an old bachelor who had no ties with any woman as far as Reynolds knew. By his own admission he was frightened of heights and, as Reynolds could testify, was so physically inept he couldn't even drive a nail in straight! He seemed too fastidious, 'other worldly' was the expression Reynolds himself had used, to steal a child's crown, or spill blood through a church, let alone leave drawings behind; crude, ugly drawings, at that.

Those crimes didn't match Sinclair's sophisticated and bookish mind. It was possible, of course – before he could formulate a counter argument, the last surprise of the day occurred.

Chapter 10

There was a great banging on his door. Dropping his papers he raced to open it. Derrymore staggered in, half carrying, half dragging, Sally Heyward. Blood was streaming from a gash over Derrymore's eye and, no longer in uniform, his white shirt front was splashed with red. Sally herself seemed unhurt until they brought her into the lighted room and put her on a sofa. Then the bruises round her neck showed vivid against her skin.

She was shaking violently, and after Reynolds had covered her with blankets, and padded Derrymore's cut, he reached for the phone.

The sergeant said thickly, 'No, wait. Listen.'

He held up his hand. There was no sound. 'Thank God for that,' he said. 'I was afraid he might have followed us.'

He added almost incoherently, 'Your car's all right. I left it in the street. But for God's sake don't move it; there's a madman on the loose. And don't call anyone until I tell you what happened.'

Resisting saying the obvious, that the cut needed stitches and Sally should see a doctor, Reynolds busied himself making hot drinks, lacing them liberally with brandy. It was Sally who spoke first.

'Why does Derry have a towel on his head?' she asked in a hoarse whisper as if still not aware of where she was. 'Like some eastern potentate.'

Speaking must have hurt, for she instinctively put a hand to her throat, until Derrymore turned to face her; then she whispered. 'He attacked you too. Oh God.'

She shuddered again. 'He came out of nowhere,' she continued in the same hoarse whisper. 'I didn't see him. It was his hands. I felt them, slimy, smooth.'

Probably wearing rubber gloves, Reynolds thought and a wave of rage engulfed him. This was no ordinary mugging. A potential murderer, gloved, lurking not moments away from his own front door! But he didn't say anything; better the would-be victims talked the experience out of their systems first.

Sally had put down the cup and was staring at Reynolds, her eyes large in a white face. 'I couldn't breathe. What stopped him was the leaves in the lane. It's dark under the trees there, and I slipped as I struggled. It threw him off balance. At that point Derrymore shouted. I suppose the man left me and went for him.'

Finish him off first, Reynolds thought, return for you later. He didn't say this aloud and again anger threatened. The attack seemed so cold and calculated – could it have been premeditated?

'But why was he there?' Sally was continuing, echoing Reynolds' thoughts. 'Was he waiting for us?' The questions sounded childlike, innocence caught out by evil.

'He couldn't have been expecting us. How could he have known who we were?'

Here Derrymore, who had recovered enough to take notice, interposed. 'I only stopped for a moment to let you out.'

He turned to Reynolds. 'I couldn't start the engine again,' he explained. 'Those posh cars are damned difficult, temperamental. You've got to humour them. But if I'd got it going I wouldn't have heard her.'

Here he too began to shake. After which reaction he straightened up and spoke more coherently. 'I drove to Truro, picked Sally up, drove back. When we got to the village we came in by the main road and went round the green.' His arms made circling motions. 'I dropped her off at the turn down there.' He made another circling gesture. 'She was going to my mam's while I brought the car back to you. Then I heard the sound.

'Not a scream,' he said, 'A cut-off moan. I knew instinctively something was wrong. I got out of the car and peered up the lane, shouting. It was surprisingly dark as Sally says, and I couldn't hear anything. Then something hit me.'

He started to shake his head at the memory, desisted as a throb of pain puckered his face. 'I was lucky, I suppose,' he blurted out after a pause. 'Just before the blow landed I ducked. Otherwise I'd have been brained.'

He managed a grin. 'Self-preservation. Intuition. My old CO would be proud.'

'And then?'

'I'm not sure. I know we struggled. I remember he tried another blow which I blocked.'

He frowned, trying to remember the details. 'I have the impression that if I hadn't been half-stunned, I could have held him,' he continued. 'He was tall but didn't seem that strong. Then he just slipped away, melted away in the dark. I should have followed. I wanted, well, I wanted to smash him. But I didn't know where Sally was. I was shouting and getting no answer and I was frightened that he'd cut round ahead of me to drag her off. I wasn't even sure she'd made the noise I heard, or what the hell was happening.'

He stared into space, reliving those moments when he went stumbling up the lane, calling out Sally's name and getting no answer, all the while cursing in a steady stream under his breath. Derrymore seldom swore; it too was proof, if nothing else, of the effect of this murderous attack.

'I finally guessed she must be on the ground,' he said. 'I

went down on my hands and knees and crawled. All I could feel was leaves. Finally I touched her foot. She was lying against the wall, sprawled where he must have shoved her. She didn't respond but was still breathing. So I dragged her back to the car, don't ask me how, I was terrified that the murderer was still somewhere in the vicinity and would attack again.' Once more the memory threatened to overwhelm him.

'Then what happened?' Reynolds' voice was curt, militarily precise.

Derrymore, responding automatically to it, again explained how he'd pushed Sally into the front seat and driven on to Old Forge Cottage. 'I didn't know where else to go,' he added simply. 'Mam would have had a heart attack if we'd showed up like this.'

'And I won't.' Reynolds tried a joke, was relieved to see an answering faint smile. 'And where exactly did this all happen?'

'In the Ope. You know, the little side alley that leads from your lane eventually into Badgewall Lane, and then to the library.'

Mention of these two places which had recently come to his attention had a strange effect on Reynolds. They made the danger so close, so personal, he almost felt it in his own house.

'Don't move,' he said, 'I'll be back.' Before they could stop him he had turned off the hall lights and was out the front door, moving stealthily among the bushes that led to the main gate. The long twilight had given way to darkness, without moon or stars, but the car's headlights had been left on, illuminating the lane as far as the bend. Nothing moved. A quiet village lane.

Both car doors were still open so he couldn't leave it as it was. Again nothing moved as he got in, although not before he'd checked the back seat. He slammed the doors and backed into the driveway, a little ashamed of his reaction. But if someone had been lurking, he would have attacked without warning.

Returning to the house he found the injured pair conferring with each other. 'Derry's cut needs seeing to.' Sally had regained her composure. 'And my throat feels like fire. But first we must phone Mazie with some excuse, she'll be worrying where we are.'

'I'll phone her later.' Reynolds took charge. 'Let's get to the emergency room. Then we'll deal with everything else. This'll have to be reported to the police, you know.'

Seeing their expression he tried another joke. 'Or rather since the police are represented here, we'll let the sergeant do the reporting.'

Again his joke worked. They both gave a feeble laugh. It was only when he'd seen them safely into hospital that it occurred to him perhaps he'd been too officious, taking matters into his own hands, so to speak. But he hadn't done so to impress. And after his long explanation, Derrymore had lapsed back into silence and sat holding his head with a strange look on his face, almost as if he were lost in some delusion, and nothing made sense.

Once assured there was no real danger, that Derrymore's concussion would probably prove to be mild and both victims only needed rest and overnight observation, he rang Nicholls, then Mazie.

Calming Mazie down took effort and needed all his skill, so sure she was that her Derry was already dead. After assuring her there was no need for her to come out at this time of night and he'd stop with a full account after his chat with headquarters, he added a warning, telling her to lock all doors and windows and open them to no one until an official policeman came round. He'd send someone she knew to sit with her until he got there. If the attack had been premeditated, he wasn't going to risk her being the next victim.

While Derrymore and Miss Heyward gave their separate statements to members of the team, who arrived with admirable promptness, Nicholls showed up in a rush to confer with Reynolds, taking over a hospital room placed at their disposal.

'Rum go,' Nicholls said, looking really worried. 'A one-off mugging?' He hesitated. 'Or are we talking more than that? Something serious?'

Reynolds chose his words with care. A lot depended on them. 'I think,' he said, 'you'll find Derrymore believes he was dealing with a killer. A mad killer. Who attacked him after trying to strangle Miss Heyward.'

Nicholls stared. 'Another killer?' he began, then, correcting himself, 'Not likely, is it, unless St Breddaford is suddenly swarming with them like a bee hive. Are we talking, then, of there being one murderer, who killed the couple at the quarry and possibly Rab Tremayne?'

His forehead wrinkled more than ever, giving him the look of a bloodhound, and his Midlands accent suddenly became very pronounced. 'That would put a very different slant to things.'

He felt for a chair and sat down heavily, the lines about his eyes deeply etched. 'For one, Dave Caddick must be in the clear. And so probably isTremayne. But,' here he brightened, 'if Derrymore stopped by chance to let his passenger out, could that mean the attack was accidental?'

When Reynolds pointed out that the man apparently had been armed with a stick, had been wandering in the lane wearing gloves, Nicholls swore to himself several times. The prospect of a second premeditated attempt at murder, even if the victims were accidental, cast its shadow over him. But all he said was, 'Makes things bloody difficult.'

Classic understatement. For a while he sat brooding. Then as if making up his mind, he straightened up and said briskly, 'Well that's that. We're stuck with it. The long haul I admit I've been hoping to avoid. So what's your opinion, where do we go from here?'

It was Reynolds' chance. He too sat down. 'Go over all the evidence again,' he said. 'Look for some clue that connects all the crimes, big and small. However unlikely, there has to be some link. Even if one man has master-minded the whole string of events, he will have left some calling card as it were, some individual trace to connect them.'

He thought for a moment that Nicholls would resist the idea. He saw the struggle, almost anticipated the objections: 'This is theory, not fact. You're twisting clues to fit preconceived ideas.' Instead, Nicholls reached for his case and slapped a handful of papers on the table. 'I thought that's what it would boil down to,' he said heavily. 'If I hadn't been so keen to get it over with and away I should have done the same thing myself, long ago.'

Along with the on-going files for the murders at the quarry, he had brought Derrymore's original notes for the first three events that had taken place before his arrival. Reynolds had not seen these before, of course, although he knew all the details by now. Together he and Nicholls began to piece them together, starting with the missing crown, over a month ago, still possibly not even to be considered a crime if Mrs Varcoe's fickle memory had been playing tricks.

Gravely, Nicholls began to recite the known facts, pausing only to ask, 'Could its value have played a part?' When told that its worth had never been considered until after its disappearance, he shrugged and continued with his litany.

'So far the only suspects,' he concluded, 'apart from the two feuding families, are a pack of schoolboys, who, a new addition this, dating from yesterday evening, were interviewed and cleared.'

Well done Derrymore, Reynolds thought, as Nicholls continued to explain that, according to the sergeant's recent testimony, the older boys who did the smoking had stopped going to the church hall months ago. Mrs Varcoe must have forgotten she'd spotted them at Christmas and ticked them off 'good and proper. As for the younger boys,' he quoted, 'they don't smoke. And none of them knows where the bookshop is. Whatever the hell all that means.'

He waited patiently while again Reynolds explained the source of this dubious piece of testimony, gained from Mrs Varcoe, during the visit to the vicar, then concluded, 'Only viable clue, a wretched drawing. A facsimile of which I understand was also found at the scene of the next two crimes but which, for various reasons, was destroyed . . .'

Reynolds' involuntary whistle cut him short. While he had been talking, Reynolds had picked up the drawing. He'd never seen it, either, and was curious. It was exactly as he had imagined, a crudely drawn circle of a face with round staring eyes and a large red smiling mouth. But something about the nose and eyes caught his attention. He stared at the drawing again, held it up to the light, and then without a word pushed it across to Nicholls, pointing at the offending lines.

'God,' Nicholls was equally startled, 'it's your initials. J.R. There, smack in the middle of the face. So what on earth does the "O" stand for?'

'My first name,' said Reynolds grimly, 'which I never use.'

And sure enough, there was the 'O' for the left eye. The line forming the eyebrow could be seen as the top of the 'J' the tail running down into a flared nostril on the left side, while the 'R' formed the bridge of the nose, the right nostril, and the round right eye.

Nicholls had jumped up and was striding round the room. 'Someone must know a lot about you,' he said. 'And the vicar admitted destroying the other? And the book fire circle was trampled over? If they were the same you know what this means? The link connecting them all is you.'

It wasn't pleasant hearing. And Reynolds had already begun to wonder if Derrymore had picked out the initials too, and if it was another thing he'd glossed over, as he had the information about Tremayne?

'There are another links,' he pointed out mildly, 'I was coming to them later. The phone calls, for example. One made to Caddick, earlier ones to Derrymore, and as learned today, one to Mrs Tamblin, the vicar's wife, made on the morning of the wedding. She's willing to help with voice identification, by the way, if that's possible.'

He thought for a moment before adding, 'There wasn't a phone call this time; I wonder why? Or who the real victim was? And there's another thing about that fire that I learned today.'

Nicholls was scarcely listening. 'And I've thought of something else,' he said. 'Did it strike you as strange that Derrymore was driving your car?'

A second time Reynolds was taken aback. He hadn't considered it.

'Derrymore was out of uniform,' Nicholls went on. 'You're very alike, you know. In the dark you could easily be mistaken for each other. And the young lady works for you, I believe. You could have been seen in each other's company.'

Against his will Reynolds remembered his last meeting with Sally, their coffee together, their leaving-taking on the green. His half joke about being so obvious didn't seem a joke at all now, if intended murder was involved.

'I'd say,' Nicholls' look was shrewd, 'that the smear campaign against you is nothing, despite the burning of your books and the use of them to involve poor Tremayne. So look out, old man, in some funny way you may be involved with everything as the personal target. But some mastermind behind it all? Some super-brain? For the moment the most I'll grant you is that it looks as if all the events certainly have a common thread. For the rest, I can only promise to keep our options open. At least, thank God, we've still some suspects left. We'll get back to the Barkers first thing. And we're still waiting for tests to ascertain exactly how Tremayne died.'

He gave a grin. It made him look younger. 'They told me your way of tackling crimes drove most people wild,' he said. 'Told me I might as well sit back and swing in the wind. Except,' and here he grinned again, 'they also warned that you were usually right. And if I could stand the course you'd turn up with the evidence eventually.'

So much for Miss Penwithen's praise! Reynolds had the grace to look abashed. But all in all, Nicholls' response had been fair. He couldn't complain. He looked at the inspector approvingly. That comment about Derrymore's appearance and the use of his own car had been sharp. Perhaps he had misjudged the inspector, perhaps Nicholls was more perceptive than he sometimes seemed. If so, the Devon and Cornwall Constabulary were lucky to have hired him and he hoped he'd stay. But if he believed that Reynolds could conjure up evidence out of straw, Reynolds had better get weaving. Although he hoped Miss Penwithen never heard of it.

'And now,' Nicholls went on briskly, 'about that fire.' He settled down to make what he could of Reynolds' unusual interview and the charges against Dr Sinclair, which he agreed should be immediately investigated, vague as they were, and most likely, as Reynolds had suggested, linked to some insurance fraud. All in, a good day's work. The two men eventually parted feeling satisfied, despite the setbacks and the savage interlude.

At the moment, Miss Penwithen herself was not thinking of her meeting with Reynolds. Hair plaited in its nightly pigtail down her back, her thin frame well wrapped in a fleecy nightgown, she was indulging in her favourite pastime, reading late at night in front of a fire.

Except for the lamp beside her chair the rest of the room was in darkness, and the flames from her wood fire cast cheerful shadows on the walls, crowded with mementos and pictures from her girlhood home. How often as a young girl had she sat upright in the same straight-backed chair, its tapestry seat and arms already shabby in those days, and now showing more signs of wear than her still swift needle could repair. In her old age, she sat in the same position as she had when she was young, a book open before her, and her mind gone from the everyday world into some wonderful make-believe.

As a girl most of her early reading material had been chosen by her father, and was, understandably, as dull and sedate as he was. The books came from the bookcases in his Victorian study, where he spent his days in dark grief for the death of her two brothers in the 1914–18 war – a state of mind which would eventually lose him his estate and her her home. But even as a girl she had acquired the delicious habit of reading late at night, when all around her were asleep – a delight only to be bettered by the more sinful pleasure of doing something that is forbidden and with books that were very far removed from her father's choice (ones her father certainly would not have approved of and may not even have known still existed, concealed behind the front rows in the abandoned and neglected library).

It was during this night-time indulgence that she acquired her taste for mysteries, mainly, she thought now, because they gave her active brain something substantial to work on. But before she had become bored with finding solutions halfway through the plot, the bad times had come. Then she had turned to more serious literature to help her cope with loss and humiliation and eventually the sheer struggle to survive in what she was always to think of as 'reduced circumstances'.

It was only in comparatively recent times that she had finally come to terms with the loss; and only in the last year or so reverted to her first love. Among the modern writers of detective stories she had discovered Reynolds, and his style had appealed to her, as did the fact of his living in the same village. Tonight she was not reading one of his books (although she had a new mystery from the library on her lap) but she had promised herself to save up to buy the next one when it came out.

She read quickly, turning the pages with her long thin fingers, her toes, poking through the holes of her old-fashioned carpet slippers, curling with excitement. In a little while when she had solved the mystery, she would go to bed.

She had become used to the little house with its old-fashioned furnishings, all worn and cracked but still substantial enough to 'see her through' as she termed it. Long before deafness had entombed her, she had learned to accept the cottage's defects, the narrow twisted staircase, the uneven floorboards that creaked, the back scullery with its smell of cat and milk and its window without a clasp, which banged when the wind was in the east.

There was no wind to make it bang tonight, and the creak along the narrow hall didn't come from settling timbers, nor was the shadow on the wall behind her from the fire she had even in summer, out of habit. So intent was she on her reading that the shadow had come up to her chair and reached its hands around her long aristocratic neck before she realized what it was – and by then it was too late.

And after she was dead, and her body, like a rag doll without stuffing, had been placed back in the chair with its hands arranged on its lap and its narrow feet set neatly side by side on the stool, the book she had been reading was retrieved from the floor where it had fallen in her death throes, and was replaced with another, the page opened at a passage encircled in red ink.

Chapter 11

That same Friday evening, life in the village had not come to a standstill, as it was to do the following morning when the news of the attack, and new murder, eventually filtered out. People sat at home, busy with DIY projects, watching television, even talking (or quarrelling) with each other – the sort of thing people normally do.

Art Newcomb was finishing his list of names for Reynolds. He had stayed late at the library and was pleased with the result. Not that he liked being involved in a police investigation; that was the last thing he wanted, but the truth was, in spite of his original opposition, he was secretly flattered by Reynolds' request.

Although well aware of the opposition to the ex-inspector's writings, he did not agree with it. When other libraries rang him up to borrow Reynolds' books from his shelves (which they frequently did on the inter-library lending system) he was always proud to point out that John (he always called Reynolds John) was a 'neighbour' here in St Breddaford, as if he knew him personally and lived next door.

Unlike Dr Sinclair, he wouldn't claim to be a book-lover but he did enjoy order and symmetry. Long rows of books, systematically catalogued, pleased his asthetic sense. If he had his way he probably would have been happier that they weren't ever taken off the shelves at all; he didn't like it when there were gaps.

Finally, he was a meticulous record-keeper and had a good memory; he could have repeated by heart the dates and times of all the requests for Reynolds' books and the names of the people who had borrowed them. Still, just to appear especially business like, he typed the list up on a computer and printed it out to impress the ex-inspector.

He enjoyed working in the evening, when the library was closed, when only a few pools of light lit up the polished tables and chairs in the reading 'nooks' he had installed, when in fact the place was empty of the public who, again to speak frankly, he could have well done without.

He knew they mainly had no taste, preferred cheap pulp stuff that didn't deserve the name of literature. But if people like Dr Sinclair kept Reynolds' books in their shops, and if Jen Murdock borrowed them, then there must be some good in them. And he liked what he called a 'good read' himself, when he was too tired to concentrate on anything heavy, and Reynolds' detective stories fitted his requirements better than anything else.

The computer gave one final green flicker. Putting the list into an envelope, sealing it, switching off the remaining lights before he left, he started down the alley towards Badgewall Lane, meaning to post it on his way home. It was only when he heard it drop into the box and was congratulating himself on a job well done, that it occurred to him for the first time that perhaps he had been foolish. Perhaps he should have consulted other people before acting so rashly; other people might not be so anxious to co-operate; if anything went wrong he would be blamed. The thought made him sweat and his mouth twitch.

Jen Murdock was busy on the phone. She loved the phone, especially to tell other people what to do. Dressed in a housecoat of gold satin brocade with a frilled collar, she lay on a sofa in her brightly coloured living room (of which she was so proud) and, circling her fingers over the chocolates in the Black Magic box, repeated, 'Well, that's what I told her,' before popping one into her mouth. She held the receiver away from her so she couldn't hear the voice bleating in reply, one of her committee members daring to argue.

When she'd finished chewing, 'It's no good shilly shallying,' she interrupted briskly. 'You've got to be decisive with that class of person.'

She made a distasteful grimace to herself as if to say, 'Of course I only speak from hearsay, thank God, I'm not one of them.'

'And how old are these May Queens anyway?' she went on without pausing. 'That young? Mere children. And how are they chosen? Ridiculous. As ridiculous as allowing Mrs Varcoe to run the procession. It should be done properly. And only older girls should take part.'

And when the committee member continued to protest that from time immemorial certain families, of long standing in the village, had the right to put forward their daughters, and wouldn't older girls change the nature of the ceremony, 'Of course they would change it,' she said. 'Besides, with older girls, the whole thing could be made much more of. Other villages could be invited to take part. The queen would be chosen for her looks or ability, for example. We could charge a fee; we could invite a celebrity to award the prize; we could vote for the winner.'

Anticipation of all these possibilities made her pause. Taking advantage of the silence, the committee member, in one last effort, pleaded that the whole thing would turn into a beauty contest. 'Why not?' Jen Murdock countered. 'What's wrong with beauty contests? I know all about them; and girls.'

And leaving the suggestion that at least she recognized what beauty was, being one herself, she put the phone down firmly, and chose another chocolate.

Pleased with herself she then made a second phone call, presumably to a man, for her voice sank to a whisper, and became more intimate. She even gave her throaty laugh, and when after a few more whispered moments asked, 'Your house or mine?' the joke must have been of long standing, because it caused an outburst of hilarity which seemed hardly justified.

When she hung up she busied herself making sure the cushions were nicely shaken, and the drinks cabinet opened invitingly. She didn't change, she was already dressed in the way that pleased most of her visitors.

Later, at another place, another phone call was made. It was strictly business but since it was intended for Reynolds and he wasn't there to receive it, it was recorded on his answering machine.

The call was long, the message crude. Its main thrust: that Reynolds had no place in the village and, if he knew what was good for him, he should leave while he could. It was punctuated by foul language and an ugly passage quoted from one of his early works. Among other things, he was reminded that he had originally been dismissed from the police force for drinking and womanizing, and as a writer of detective books was guilty of encouraging excessive violence.

'Like the previous calls then.'

Reynolds' comment was surprisingly restrained when he listened in the small hours of the morning, after his return from his promised visit to reassure Mazie. He ignored the references to his past career and cause of retirement, all false, and concentrated on the style of the message, and the way it was delivered. The disguised anonymous voice, the virulence, were typical. And there was a bright side. Vicious as the speaker was, she had left certain clues which this time might lead to discovery.

Firstly, there was a chance of tracing the call, which he reported immediately to the duty officer. Secondly, in spite of the usual distortion, this recording gave the best hope so far of identifying the voice, either by breaking down its exact nature electronically, or by allowing others who had received similar calls to make comparisons. Thirdly, here was the perfect example of gossip rampant, suggesting that perhaps Nicholls was right: the actual vendetta against him was personal, and more important than even he'd realized.

Eventually Dave Caddick, Mrs Tamblin and Sergeant Derrymore (when he recovered) all agreed the voice was similar to the one they'd heard. Mrs Tamblin was the most definite. She showed up first thing on the Saturday morning at the newly-established Incident Room (of all places, the same church hall where the troubles had begun). She did not come alone; she had her husband and her two large dogs in tow, and she was not in a good mood.

After she had agreed it was the same woman who had spoken to her, 'When are you going to catch her?' she asked eagerly. 'Just let me get my hands on her.' She turned fiercely on her husband who was tut-tutting in the background. 'I don't feel sorry for her, or forgiving, even if you think I should,' she cried. 'She almost ruined my daughter's wedding last week, and devastated me,' showing that the memory of her own recent breakdown still rankled as much as the actual atrocities in the church.

'You mean we'll have to continue with this protection caper,' she went on angrily, when told that the actual call couldn't be traced to any definite person or private number, having again come from a public telephone (this time from a kiosk outside a large shopping precinct). She gestured to the retrievers who had settled themselves in the sun. 'First time in my life I've needed a man and two dogs to escort me through the village. Everyone's terrified. And if that she-devil knows what's going on and is aiding and abetting it, then she's evil incarnate.'

And with that broadside she stalked away, husband and dogs hurrying to catch up with her. Staring after her, Nicholls shook his head. 'She's right about one thing,' he said. 'The whole village is in a state of shock. In fact I hear they're gathering on the green later this morning. Some sort of meeting. Asking us what we mean to do.'

He turned to Reynolds, who was looking grim himself. 'Under the circumstances, you'll do the honours, won't you?' he asked.

For once Reynolds refused. What circumstances, he thought? Surely he realizes that getting me to speak to them might be like waving a red rag to a bull. He voiced his opinion that explanations would come better from the head of the official team.

'Damn it,' Nicholls said, sounding worried. 'At least show your face. I was hoping to try and catch out anyone who was opposing you.' He gave a grin. 'No hard feelings,' he said. 'But if you're supposed to be at the bottom of the problems this might have been a good chance to see who thinks so.'

The grin didn't hide the fact that again he had been trying to use Reynolds. However, he didn't disguise his intentions. And the way he said afterwards, 'Well, if I have to address them, I'd rather be in bed alongside Derrymore,' was at least honest.

Derrymore was still in hospital, his condition feared more serious than had originally been thought and the result of further tests was awaited before he could be declared out of danger. This unexpected set-back sank the whole team into depression. It was seldom that one of their own was injured and they reacted angrily.

Since first light, they had been examining the Ope and surrounding lanes for clues, so far finding little except scuffle marks and splashes of blood, presumably Derrymore's. The stick, if that was the weapon, had gone, but there was no doubt they were determined to find it and the culprit, even if they had to search every lane for miles.

News of Derrymore's condition depressed the village too, while the detail that he had been hurt protecting a 'girl-friend' added to the shock. Rumours proliferated. Murder in a quarry was bad enough; attack on their own streets was unforgivable. And since by now everyone knew that Mazie Derrymore had had a police escort all night, they wanted to find out what was to be done along these lines to ensure the village's collective safety and catch the criminals.

But while the villagers mulled over the awful possibilities of more attacks, gathering in little groups for safety; while mothers planned to walk their children to and from school in convoy, and toddlers and pets were kept indoors, no one commented on Miss Penwithen's absence. It is doubtful if she were even missed. After all, a deaf old woman hasn't much to contribute to a village meeting, and even less to gain from it.

The meeting was important for public relations, and Reynolds had been right that the village deserved official reassurance. When authority, in the shape of a bland Inspector Nicholls, confronted the anger and fear of the crowd later that morning, he kept in the background, to listen and watch himself.

He found it difficult to believe that among the many well-known faces, one wore a mask, hiding a killer. And it was equally hard to judge which of the reactions he observed was genuine or not. Was the large man in farm clothes and muddy boots acting a part when he pointed out that protest was a waste of time. ('We'm Cornish, so forgotten. No one takes no notice of we.') Or the smaller man in a shabby suit, was he out of character screaming that he didn't want his wife and daughters molested? And what about the third, young, leather-jacketed, advocating that if the police couldn't catch the so-and-sos, why not go after them ourselves? With loaded shotguns – as if shooting pigeons.

It was only towards the end of the meeting, after the voice of authority had cautioned against panic, and suggested the best way to combat crime was to show restraint and firmness, that the murmurs began. It was impossible in the crush to say where they originated and there were certainly many present who were annoyed if not downright angered by their repetition. But the murmurs spread – and among the things said was that here again, if violence had erupted in a quiet village, the person responsible was the man who wrote the books, encouraging it. Nicholls needed all his skill and experience to quiet the crowd, finally relying on his officers to clear the green. And it was only after Reynolds himself had backed into a corner beside the bookshop, that the villagers dispersed.

The aftermath of this verbal attack, which later even Nicholls admitted he hadn't been expecting to be so pointed, made Reynolds realize how far things had gone. He told himself to pay no attention; he'd been on the rough edge of meetings many times in the past, but now he began to appreciate Derrymore's original concern over public feelings. Perhaps the sergeant had judged the village mood more accurately than Reynolds had given him credit for.

Here again, the recollection of his earlier statement to Derrymore came back to haunt him; he saw it for the foolishness it was. It was all very well to maintain blithely, as he had done, that criminals didn't read books – so therefore, by virtue of logic, his books couldn't be at fault. With hindsight, his claim not only sounded pompous; it was wrong. And since his unpopularity had now been demonstrated several times, even publicly, he should face up to that fact.

Although seldom bothered about his own position, previously he had always sensed he was liked in the village. People made him welcome, didn't intrude, respected his wish for privacy and yet were friendly when they met. He'd never thought before, until Nicholls had given him the idea, that his own safety might be at risk. Safety was something that didn't bother him much either, at least not in general terms, but now he could not avoid seeing that the animosity towards him was increasing.

For once his own taste for investigation began to falter. The thought that someone might eventually enact one of the actual crimes he'd written about, oppressed him more than he dared admit. 'Get out if you know what's good for you.' If that should ever happen the warning couldn't be more appropriate.

Besides, there were other pressing matters, personal matters, that he could use as an excuse to take himself off the case. Derrymore for one. He could plead Derrymore's condition and offer to stay with Mazie while she waited for news of her son. And there was Sally; he didn't know where she was although he'd been told that she would be released from hospital this morning. How was she coping with the trauma, could he be of help? It came to him how much he would like to see her and talk again. And finally, what he should have thought of first, it wasn't fair to put Nicholls under further strain by remaining – Derrymore had probably been right about that too.

He was roused from his reverie by Dr Sinclair who had come to the shop door, his hair flip-flapping more than usual. 'A rum show,' he said, pointing to the backs of the retreating villagers. 'Cornishmen and women on the rampage. Wonder of wonders. What ever's got into them?'

There was something in his voice suggesting a sneer, although Reynolds had never known him say anything derogatory about the village before. Resisting the temptation to reply with something equally sarcastic like 'Loyalty to their own,' or 'Fear of the unknown,' Reynolds said merely, 'You've not heard of the ructions in the Ope? I understand that's your usual route home.'

Sinclair frowned although Reynolds wasn't sure if the words 'your usual route', or 'I understand' (which he couldn't resist slipping in) had irritated the shop owner.

'I saw the police out gathering evidence, if that's what you mean,' Sinclair said finally, in a voice that sounded more hurt than offended. 'And I heard about the meeting. That's why I'm here; to make sure it didn't get out of hand and my new window got broken. I don't usually open on a weekend. If you ask me, which you haven't, I'd say you'd find as good clues hunting through your books as digging up lanes!'

His eyes glinted in the way he had when he'd scored one of his little jokes, but the smile was all innocence. 'Just jesting,' he hastened to add, with his usual show of affability. 'I don't believe what they've been saying about you and your writing. It's beyond me why so many people think the way they do. It must be infuriating.'

And he closed the door slowly, with a shake of his head at the stupidity of the world, as if happy to shut it out.

Back at the church hall there was also an air of calm, as if everything was on hold. Nicholls had gone to the quarry with some of the team so any discussion of Reynolds' leaving must wait until he returned. Most of the officers were engaged in what Reynolds thought of as 'routine work', although he admitted that computers and the internet provided information far quicker than in his day. And information needs to be quick, he thought; look at the way crimes spread, and the way things have speeded up, what's started one Saturday night finished the next, if we're lucky. The idea came to him that here in St Breddaford they had entered on a roller-coaster ride that was already spinning out of control, with no way to turn it off.

He watched for a while, the flickering lines of print and figures meaning nothing to him although presumably their operators were using them to gain facts that would all add up to clues. He had visits he could make, chief among them to Miss Penwithen, to clarify her statement. And there was Jen Murdock, and the Barker family. Computers couldn't explain people, unless the information was fed into them. He was wondering idly if in fact a book could be broken down into detail and analysed by computers, when an interruption drew his attention away.

Sally Heyward stood in the doorway, a basket in her hand. She wore a pale orange scarf around her neck and she spoke in the same throaty croak. But she seemed remarkably calm, and her message was encouraging. The tests on Derry had proved inconclusive and the scan had shown no permanent damage; the prognosis was more cheerful than it had been a few hours ago; he was definitely on the mend. In the meanwhile, she had come back to St Breddaford to run some errands for Mazie (still at the hospital) and had just looked in 'to tell you what's happened. Although I'm sure the hospital will pass on the information themselves.'

As she spoke, the murmur of good news began to spread through the line of officers manning the old-fashioned desks, commandeered for makeshift console tables. A cheer went up.

'I'm off to shop and so on,' Sally explained, when the noise died down. 'No, I'm better on my own. I can't always be living with protection. And in the daylight who'd hurt me? Or want to?'

She smiled, waved her hand and vanished, leaving Reynolds with a distinct uneasy feeling that was increased by her last remarks. 'I'm better on my own.' The words reminded him of someone. He moved to the door to watch her cross the green and disappear into Mr Abbot's butcher shop, half-tempted to follow, when another murmur ran through the hall.

This was caused by Nicholls' arrival; he was on a high, brimming with energy, pausing in the doorway, positively beaming. 'Just as you thought,' he shouted to Reynolds, 'Look at this.'

From behind his back, like an unexpected present, he produced a plastic bag. Everyone crowded round to peer as he held it out – a clear plastic bag containing what looked like a piece of old leather.

'Found in a roadside ditch, by God.' Nicholls' satisfaction was immense. 'About a mile beyond the stile. The sole of a boot, ripped off. Matching the prints you found by the same stile, and at the quarry edge. Just one boot so far, but it'll do for the present. And if it fits poor Rab, we'll find the other if we have to dredge every last inch of that pool.'

Reynolds nodded, but he was only half listening. All his concentration was fixed on the far side of the green. Sally had just emerged from the butcher's, had stopped for a moment as if to get her bearings, and was walking towards Sinclair's shop.

'And even better news.' Nicholls' triumph was infectious. 'They say Rab went in much earlier than the landslide. I'd wondered about that. If there's anything to the tale about three days before the body shows he came up too soon. This finding makes it about right. And his neck was broken first. With a cord. So it looks pretty positive that he was murdered as well.'

He took Reynolds' arm in the intimate way he had. 'What I don't understand was why it was important he had to be pushed off the quarry top? He'd have been found sooner or later. And there was all that stuff left in his house to incriminate him anyway.'

Reynolds had considered that problem too. He forced himself to answer. 'He may not have been meant to fall at all,' he began. 'The body may have slipped while the murderer was wrestling off the boots, something like that. One thing we can be sure of – it wasn't meant to have fallen into the water.'

He stopped. Sally had gone into the bookshop; he almost heard Sinclair's voice raised in greeting, although of course he was too far away to hear or see anything. A wave of panic, could it be premonition, shuddered through him; he felt the hairs stand up on the back of his neck.

He heard Nicholls say, 'What the hell's the matter?' He saw the consternation on Nicholls' face. Without a word he pushed past him out of the door, and began to run across the green. As in a nightmare his legs stood still and the thudding of his heart seemed to stop. Behind him he heard a shout as Nicholls pounded after him.

He reached the door, yanked it open. At first the shop seemed empty. Then he saw Sally and Sinclair standing in a corner. For a moment it seemed as if Sally was trapped by Sinclair's arm. But she moved, said something, smiled.

'Dr Sinclair was just offering to accompany me,' she said in the whisper that was beginning to sound more sexy then hoarse. 'My next mission.'

Sinclair too came forward, his hair flip-flapping. 'We were just chit-chatting,' he said. 'Books make such a welcome contrast to all these gruesome goings-on, don't you think? This young lady was just explaining she was off to see my neighbour . . .'

'With a note from Mazie,' Sally broke in. 'As she's deaf, Dr Sinclair's kindly volunteered to get her attention.'

She had come to the door and was trying to pass, staring up at Reynolds and behind him, Nicholls. 'My, a deputation,' she said, startled. And then, like Nicholls, 'What's wrong?'

Reynolds' heart had steadied, although the impression of impending horror didn't go away. He took Sally's arm. 'Then we'll all go with you,' he said. Nodding to Nicholls to follow, he let Sinclair lead the way.

'She won't hear us, of course.' Sinclair said with a shrug of his shoulders. 'You have to go round the back to get her attention. She's rigged up a special bell for her friends. I use it when we have to communicate.'

In single file they followed him as he took them down a little alley, past his yard (where the book-burning had begun, now swept clean) and through a gate into Miss Penwithen's garden.

The garden was small, the fence surrounding it half hidden by a low box hedge. The box bushes, the pocket-sized lawn, the straight flower beds, brimming with perennials, must have been modelled on some larger formal gardens attached to some formal mansion – by contrast, the cottage itself rose in homely levels, walls and roof dipping with age.

A great school bell hung beside the back door with a rope attached, its original bronze turned green. When Sinclair tugged at the rope the sound exploded inside their heads, so loud they cringed. They waited but there was no answer and when they pushed at the closed door, it swung open.

Sinclair looked puzzled, then alarmed. He hesitated, until a gesture made him stand aside to let Reynolds and Nicholls go first. Past the scullery, up the narrow steps, along the even narrower corridor, the four went in line. Horror stalked with them into the sitting room where Miss Penwithen still sat with the open book on her lap.

* * *

'But how the hell did you *guess*?'

When, after the ambulance had arrived and the body had been removed, when Sinclair, still in shock, had been sent home in a police car, and Sally, still remarkably untraumatized, had insisted on returning to Mazie at the hospital, Nicholls and Reynolds faced each other across the church hall.

Useless to say there was no reason; impossible to explain what he had felt. And equally impossible to put it down to intuition. How say that Sally's echo of Miss Penwithen's words had brought some sense of warning. Or had it been fear for Sally herself?

'I don't know,' Reynolds said. He felt sick. Trying to recover, 'But the same clues are all there,' he said. 'The lack of fingerprints; the strangulation. And the page torn from one of my books.'

He took it up, sealed now in plastic, and read the underlined words. ' "My next case revealed one of the most common causes of crime: jealousy. Of all things the world hates most to be put down by someone who believes he is superior." '

The only change was that the word 'he' had been crossed out and a 'she' substituted. Reynolds put the page down. He didn't need to read the rest of the paragraph, he could recite it by heart. ' "They say class distinctions are gone for ever now, but I recall when they played an interesting part in one of the most cruel investigations that I ever dealt with." '

The remainder of the chapter went on to recount some true episode from Reynolds' own experience, enlarged into fiction. But nothing could be as cruel as this senseless death here.

'Must be someone who knows my books inside out,' he continued, trying to gain composure. 'Someone who's obsessed with them. But there's still something wrong. When you think about it the passage sounds forced. As if the murderer had to think something up quickly.'

Nicholls was still watching him intently. 'But why her?' he said. 'A little, deaf lady who harmed no one.'

'The passage is meant to suggest that she felt herself superior,' Reynolds said. 'Put on airs.'

'And did she?'

'I don't think she herself felt anything either way.' Reynolds brought out his reply carefully. 'Mind you I only met her once but in my opinion she was superior, that's all there was to it.'

The memory of her upright carriage, her black rustling skirts, her faint scent of lavender returned to haunt him. 'It's possible that in her younger days,' he went on, 'before she became deaf, she might have been a real tartar. Maiden ladies who suffer reversals of fortune are likely to cling to their past glories as a bulwark against their present predicament. I saw no evidence of it. But she did talk to me in the church; and anyone could have seen us there. If she was killed before or after the attack on Derrymore (a substitute for me, as you suggested) the murderer may have made a spur-of-the-moment decision to get rid of both of us, killing off informer and informed at one swoop – a nice evening's work.'

It was a horrifying thought. 'I presume under the circumstances we'll have to check up on what Sinclair was doing last night,' Nicholls said at last. 'He seemed to know his way about Miss Penwithen's house – although as neighbours that makes sense. And if he'd done the murdering it seems unlikely he'd offer to take anyone to find the body. Of course,' brightening, 'he might have thought she was telling you about his setting the fire. We're still checking on his insurance, by the by, without getting anywhere. He hasn't even made a claim. I suppose it happened so recently, he might be still taking stock.'

'By all means,' Reynolds nodded. 'But whatever you do don't mention what Miss Penwithen said.'

Yet something in this analysis didn't feel right. He pulled himself together to find out what it was and discovered it in the words 'spur-of-the-moment decision'.

'I've been working on the assumption that all the incidents, including murder, have been preplanned,' he now said. 'In spite of the similarities, this breaks the pattern.'

As Nicholls looked at him, 'Not only in the trumped up passage,' he explained, 'possibly to hide some hidden reason, there are other differences. There was no advance anonymous phone call. The only one this time was made to me. That suggests that even the telephone accomplice didn't know what was going on.'

'And when news of that call comes out it may add to our problems,' Nicholls broke in, presumably thinking back to the scene on the green. 'Still, we have to soldier on. I'll never say again that country crime is boring,' he added in a rare burst of confession. 'I kept telling the wife I'd be back by the weekend, but it doesn't look like it now. And if the village was upset by the attack on Derrymore, God knows how they'll react to this.'

He rubbed his eyes, red with lack of sleep. Reynolds suddenly found himself liking Nicholls very much. As if aware of the other man's feelings, Nicholls sighed. 'I wonder how long Derry'll be out of action?' he said. 'Without him, we'll be at a loss for local help. Unless we can persuade you to carry on.'

He added quickly, as if afraid of Reynolds' answer, 'Don't leave me in the lurch. I'll never cope with this on my own, there's a fact. I'm swimming out of my depth as it is.'

All flattery, Reynolds told himself, all for effect. And yet he didn't really believe it this time. There was something about Nicholls' appeal that came straight from the heart.

It caught him on the raw, he didn't know what to answer. It was the opposite of what he himself had been about to suggest. 'Let's hold on that,' he said awkwardly. 'Hear me through first. I'm still trying to understand why, for a murderer who pre-plans so well, so many things are beginning to go wrong.'

'Rab Tremayne's body in the pool for one,' Nicholls broke in, following him intently. 'You were talking of it just now. When we were interrupted.'

'My guess,' Reynolds went on, 'I've no proof, is that whatever way Rab Tremayne fell into the water, his reappearance must be a shock to the murderer. He may not have known that a drowned body can surface; he may have assumed that the depth of the pool or Rab's heavy clothing would keep him submerged – in any case, Rab's drowning left him without an obvious suspect. So what does he do?'

Nicholls' face cleared. 'Caddick,' he shouted, 'he and his accomplice set up Caddick instead. Including hiding the wedge where no one except someone who worked at the sawmill could have known.'

It was Reynolds' turn to frown. 'A puzzler that,' he admitted, 'suggesting someone must have investigated the site beforehand.'

With every word he spoke he felt himself more deeply caught up in the investigation again. Nicholls' appeal had done its work. He couldn't back out now. 'We need to check on that aspect, by the way,' he added, 'see if anyone connected with the case has had dealings with the sawmill recently. After which, possibly another anonymous call to the authorities would have revealed the wedge's whereabouts, if it hadn't been found by accident.'

'And if the find hadn't already been made public.' Nicholls had the grace to look abashed.

'And establishing the time of Rab's death solves another puzzle – the timing of the anonymous call to Caddick,' Reynolds went on. 'It had to have been made after Rab fell into the pool otherwise it wasn't needed to ensure Caddick had a motive for murder. (Although why a man who's just been informed he's been cuckolded should automatically be expected to kill his rival beats me.) But even that still doesn't really explain why it was made in the first place.'

He glanced at Nicholls. 'The only explanation I can find,' he said, 'is that this second line of defence, as it were, was already prearranged, in case it was needed.'

Nicholls whistled. 'That's planning with vengeance,' he said. 'Never heard anything like it. But,' he added, with another of his shrewd looks, 'I'm beginning to see what you mean by your mastermind. Whoever plans this well must have an intelligence like a razor blade.'

This was most gratifying. Reynolds took it in his stride. 'And that brings me to what I'm beginning to think of as his biggest mistake,' he added. 'Overkill.'

Again Nicholls looked puzzled.

'The mastermind, as we've called him,' Reynolds explained, 'is cunning. We know he understands how to persuade, his woman accomplice for one, probably Rab Tremayne. We presume he has some knowledge of books, at least enough to hunt through mine for relevant passages, or again get someone to do so for him. He can plot and calculate in advance. But he's beginning to crack. He's not completely sure he's got it right. He doubles up. Take poor Tremayne again as an example. Not only the clues with the boots, but the clues at the house. And there's another mistake, by the by. Anyone who really knew Tremayne should have realized he couldn't read.'

'And why a woman accomplice?' Nicholls asked shrewdly. 'I'd have said that was a mistake right there. I understand there were calls made to Derrymore earlier,' he added, without expression, 'by the same woman. Why would a mastermind rely on her?'

Mention of Derrymore roused Reynolds' protective instincts although he didn't think Nicholls was probing for information. Tactfully ignoring the reference to the sergeant, 'Why not a woman?' he countered. 'It's usually women who are plagued by Peeping Toms and potential rapists, not men. But you may be right; our mastermind may have just been showing he could manipulate anyone.'

'So what does it all add up to?'

'If these last two events have come out of sequence,' Reynolds explained patiently, 'as I've said, were committed on the spur of the moment, they can't have been part of the masterplan. They are also mistakes, big ones. I mean from the murderer's point of view. He's acting out of character. And if I read him right, he'll know it. So, if he's really smart, his first move will be to lie low, regroup as it were and get his plan back on line. On the other hand,' he added even more emphatically, 'in my experience masterminds who are jolted out of complacency, who feel their competence or their intelligence are being questioned, are likely to make more mistakes. So we need to keep the pressure on.'

Nicholls smiled. 'Got you,' he said. He meant it in more senses than one. 'I have no quarrel with that. It's just a question now of waiting for the data to start clicking in and we'll catch him. Just give us time.'

He gave another rueful laugh. 'They told me you could pluck clues out of air,' he burst out, 'but not that you were bloody clairvoyant. How's a normal chap like me expected to follow that?' He laughed again, but the laugh was at himself.

It made Reynolds grin. 'I could always lend you my glass ball,' he joked, but in fact he still couldn't explain satisfactorily what had happened. And wasn't sure he wanted to. It might reveal too much about his own motives and wishes.

Chapter 12

This long talk with Nicholls was most satisfying, even if it meant that Reynolds felt obliged to stay on the case. And even if it meant that more than ever he was committed to finding proof for his theories. But the experience that morning had left him strangely drained. It was not until he'd again been to the hospital to ascertain that Derrymore was on the mend that a talk with Mazie cleared his mind.

Mazie was alone. Sally, with the same remarkable calm, had taken herself off for a few days, maintaining she was fine but needed 'time to think'. Or so Mazie said.

'I wanted her to stay at the cottage with me,' Mazie kept insisting. 'Imagine, if I hadn't given her that note, the poor soul wouldn't have been found. And all because my lemon cakes reminded her of home.'

A random string of non-sequiturs, worse than usual, indicative that Mazie herself wasn't 'fine'. Reynolds patted her hand and felt awkward. There was nothing he could say, but let grief run its course. After which, she wiped her eyes, begged his pardon, and pointed out that Derry was her flesh and blood, it was no wonder she'd been worried. His father had died young; it was wicked to think that in old age she'd be robbed of her Derry too, and him well short of thirty. And if Sally wasn't like a daughter, then she'd never have one.

Changing the subject Reynolds asked, 'What cakes?' To have something explained that was so everyday and simple, caused another pang.

Mazie had worked hard all her life. Even now, although

Derrymore didn't like it, she still cooked and sewed for people and Miss Penwithen had been one of her valued customers. The two ladies communicated by writing, and Mazie's note was only to explain why this week's cooking would be late. 'She'll never need them cakes now,' Mazie sobbed. 'She was a great lady. She'll be sorely missed. It doesn't seem right.'

Her opinion strengthened Reynolds' own. There was something particularly wrong in this senseless killing, a feeling that was reflected throughout the village. Even the fact that Miss Penwithen had been murdered seemed to pale beside the realization of what her loss meant.

'Last of the old family, last of her line,' were the expressions commonly used, as if the villagers were conscious they had witnessed the end of an era. If she had been arrogant, no one said so in Reynolds' hearing. But he heard enough of former days and the role of Penwithen Hall in village life, to wonder if the explanation for her death had some sense behind it after all, if only that perhaps the murderer had resented her place in St Breddaford's hierarchy. If that were true, it made her murder especially vicious, smacking of jealously and spite.

As it was, once pathology had finished with the frail little corpse, Miss Penwithen was eventually laid to rest with her ancestors, buried with all the solemnity that the church could command, with the awe and respect of a grieving congregation. Her death created a kind of vacuum, her burial marking a division between what afterwards Reynolds was to think of as preamble and conclusion.

For one thing the whole village sank into depression. People kept to themselves. No one strolled beside the stream or sat on the village green while the children played. A change in the weather added to the gloom. Instead of hot June sun, a steady drizzle persisted, turning even clothes and books damp. And the murderer was still at large and investigation was going nowhere.

To Reynolds, who loved heat and had almost enjoyed his days in the desert, this procession of grey skies and mist made him feel he was turning drab grey also, wallowing in mildew. Then too, although data poured in as Nicholls had promised, it seemed to lead to nothing but paperwork (which he detested and was never good at). His own inquiries about his books had come to an abrupt standstill. Although Art Newcomb's list reached him he scarcely took the trouble to read it through – no sense in trying to pinpoint hatred when he had been surrounded by it, for all to see. He put Jen Murdock and her dubious house and club on hold; if there were time he'd get back to them. He concentrated all his efforts to track down the murderer who had so disrupted village life.

Sally was still away, and he didn't like to ask too many questions, although Derrymore had dropped hints that she'd gone 'up north. Her parents are really well off, have a huge estate, I gather, but she never talks about it.' The one good thing was that in the evening he returned to his manuscript with relief. It appeared the only brightness in the darkness, and although the first burst of enthusiasm wasn't repeated, gradually the pages grew, hammered out line by line, a new experience in composition but one that kept him absorbed and brought consolation.

The official information itself was gleaned from a variety of sources and all in all provided good reading – but afforded few clues.

'The breaks just aren't coming when we need them.' After another fruitless day, Reynolds stretched wearily.

'It's like football.' Having recovered sufficiently to undertake light work, Derrymore had joined the others in the church hall. Now, looking sheepish, he explained.

'Sometimes even the better team can't score. They'll hit the bar, hit the post, hit the goal keeper and flatten him but the ball just won't go in the net. All that's needed is a little luck. And the weaker side suddenly gets it – and wins.' Since his return he had a lot of catching up to do, including the new light shed by the drawing. He admitted that he hadn't noticed anything odd about it, certainly not the initials, but if he had, would not have been surprised. At this stage, he might even have accepted it as natural. So much for any further sign of regret or apology!

'Well, Lady Luck, time to come our way. Although I've never believed much in you!' Reynolds picked up a bundle of papers. 'So far zero,' he said, disgusted, flicking through them. 'Take Rab Tremayne's bank account, for instance. No change in its regular transactions; they've been the same for years.'

He read the figures out. 'No one's held money back, and no one's given him any. If it was in cash there's nothing at his house and if he stowed it in one of his moorland hideaways, we're not likely to find it. But my guess is you were right. He didn't understand money's value and wouldn't want it anyway so that wasn't the bribe to persuade, or coerce, him into helping. But how in hell could someone live these days on an annual income of less than four hundred pounds?'

He tossed the record aside. 'No clothes, no water rates, apparently no taxes. Just bare essentials for which he makes regular withdrawals. A real hermit's life. And as we suspected no fingerprints anywhere in his house except his own, so no leads there.'

He picked up another batch of papers. 'Frank Barker. His fiddle about building his house: inconclusive, probably just shoving his weight around with the other councillors. His other women: inconclusive, all one-night stands until he meets Betty Caddick and is genuinely hit for six. His bank accounts: several, which looked promising at first. Instead, most held in common with Mrs B, whose spending, I have to agree, is remarkably modest for the wife of a rich man. In his own private account, which apparently she didn't know about, so more tears, no money in, but large sums out. Cash only. So, if he's not being paid but is paying someone, who's on the receiving end?'

'The girlfriend, that's what Eden suggested,' Derrymore interposed.

'What did Betty Caddick do with the money? She didn't have much with her when she died, and her joint account with her husband is minuscule. Sure, there were little gifts, brooches, necklaces, that sort of thing, but no cash. And if she stowed money away somewhere, we haven't found it.'

'Perhaps it'll turn up in another hollow tree!' In spite of all his mishaps, Derrymore was in surprisingly good humour. It was Reynolds who was growing testy. He didn't like this waiting, this cat and mouse game. Again he sensed the calm before the storm.

He went back to the papers. 'Eden's accounts: not yet available. His solicitor is making strong objections as he's not an "active suspect" whatever the hell that means. Your inquiries to the university, incomplete.'

He read out in a disgusted voice, 'The meeting of the English department, on May the such and such (the night of Barker's murder) confirmed as having taken place and having lasted roughly for three hours. But no exact time when it started and no proof that Eden actually was present. He could have been absent, he could have left early – you'd think university people would be more responsible.'

The next group of papers proved equally frustrating, the record of the interview with Dr Sinclair, undertaken by Nicholls. Repressing the thought that he might have done better to have carried it out himself (and only his squeamish conscience had stopped him; after all, he had already guessed that Sinclair felt piqued by his apparent neglect and he didn't want to add insult to injury by appearing to implicate the ex-professor in a murder inquiry) he went over the details.

Nicholls had a racy style, which was another surprise. And he could see the humour of the situation. Informally written as the report was, it brought that line of investigation to a dead end.

' "Admits he emptied his loft the same evening as the fire," ' Reynolds began to read aloud, ' "admits that the packing materials certainly fed the blaze. Swears he left for home once the stuff was stacked in the yard and it wasn't on fire then. Claims he'd asked the local refuse service to pick it up next morning so why on earth should he set fire to it? (Incidentally, said local refuse collectors verify this request). Says he never saw any so called 'smiley face'; the firemen may have. Firemen vague, but think 'someone' reported it so not much hope there. And according to ex-Inspector Reynolds, Miss Penwithen's testimony never clarified the real identity of the figure she saw leaving the shop by the front door, although she suggested it was Sinclair. In any case such hearsay evidence (pardon the pun) wouldn't stand up in court." '

'So much for that,' Derrymore began but Reynolds silenced him by continuing to read. ' "On the night of the quarry murders he was watching an opera on TV. *Orpheus*, one of his special favourites. (This information accompanied by renditions, out of tune, of some of the main arias). As for Miss Penwithen's murder and the attack in the Ope, swears he went to bed early and was asleep by nine o'clock. Also confirms that although he didn't see her often he was fond of her. Says they were friendly neighbours; in fact she'd given him some plants from her garden a few days earlier, which he was doing his best to cherish 'in the manner to which they were accustomed'. His little joke. (Also proved by said plants being in his living room, waiting for better weather to be tilled. My query, as I'm no gardener, how long can plants stay indoors without wilting?)

' "Says he could hardly not know about the bell, almost broke his eardrums when it rang, but he himself had seldom used that means to communicate. 'At least we never exchanged a cross word,' another joke. Conclusion: no sign of dislike, no motive, and (for ex-Inspector Reynolds' benefit) no mention made of Miss Penwithen's testimony." '

'Well that's the good doctor in the clear, I suppose.' Derrymore was brisk. 'Pity, though. I don't care for him much. He's got an old-maidish feel about him that I find irritating. What else?'

'Pages of testimony about the phone kiosks.' Reynolds riffled through them. 'No one remembers seeing anyone; as far as I can tell no one's ever used those particular call boxes. A conspiracy of silence? Or just sheer bad luck again.'

'Nicholls is keen to try a house-to-house inquiry through the village,' Derrymore reminded him. 'We might hit on some clue we hadn't spotted before.'

'And my guess is you'll end up in a worse mess than now,' Reynolds grunted. 'You'll get feed-back on a variety of personal grudges and not much else. No one in the village is doing serious talking. They're all afraid to.'

Derrymore looked at him sadly. 'You don't like us much these days, do you?' he burst out. 'Like Nicholls. He's convinced he can't get anywhere with us because we're so closely interwoven no outsider can find a way through. The same with Sally. She claims it's like trying to make a hole in a spider web. The faster one breaks the web, the faster the spider weaves.'

His reproach left a bitter taste. And he was right. As Reynolds went home after another unsuccessful day (this time at the sawmill, trying to trace where and how the wedge could have gone missing – if it had – and eventually, for lack of anything else, coming away with the foreman's recent order book, a last and forlorn attempt to link some suspect with the wedge's hiding place) he couldn't help thinking perhaps Derrymore was justified. His feelings towards the place he had so happily called home had changed.

There were several reasons for this and he was honest enough to admit them. Like Sinclair, he was disappointed to find not only arson but evil where he least expected it. Those two old bromides, peace and harmony – were they just figments of imagination, had they disappeared from rural Cornwall for ever? And had he been foolish, even sentimental, to hope for them? Then, too, the attack on him and his books had left him more vulnerable than he liked. Yet to distrust village life in general, to consider it all a mirage, wasn't fair either. It was only his own mood that made everything look so black. For most of all he was disappointed in himself. He had never met a case which seemed so difficult, where the criminal always seemed one step ahead, where the cleverness was so shrewd. And where his so-called ability to fashion evidence out of straw was so markedly absent.

As for Sally, if she had spoken to Derrymore openly of her feelings, in particular those she had hinted at to Reynolds over their afternoon coffee, had that caused a break in their relationship? Was that behind her leaving? In which case, Sally was 'free' as the saying goes. He blanked down the thought that it was equally possible after such a discussion the pair might have been drawn closer together. Instead, on his way home from the incident room, he had just made up his mind to ring and see how she was faring; after all over a week had passed, she might have returned, when a chance meeting with another woman again changed the course of events.

Later he was to think of it as the third coincidence. He was opening the gate to Old Forge Cottage when a woman hailed him out of the mist. 'Excuse me,' she said, 'but would you know where John Reynolds lives?'

Some instinct warned him to be careful. He leaned back against the gate so that she wouldn't see the name plate. 'What do you want him for?' he asked.

She had come up close to him by now, a tall young woman, her face fashionably painted, a scarf tied over blonde frizzy hair, her raincoat long and trailing. The smile she gave was artful as she said, 'My, aren't we all ultra-cautious these days. Nothing serious. I wasn't going to stab him. I'm just curious.'

She gave a girlish giggle, and, taking off her scarf with a coquettish shake of her head, like a horse getting rid of its bridle, said, 'You're going to laugh and say something like curiosity killed the cat, aren't you? Or point out it's only women who like poking at mysteries. But in fact it was a man, Art, who told me John lived hereabouts (he knows him well, he says). And since I'd ducked into the library, I thought, why not take a look now I'm in the neighbourhood.'

Her explanation was long-winded but funnily enough he believed her. 'John' he thought, irritated. So 'John' is on the celebrity tour. More like the notoriety line-up, I'd say. But what he asked was 'Who's Art?' with a twist to his voice that suggested sarcasm.

She reacted to it with another flirtatious toss of her hair. 'My, you don't say much,' she giggled, 'but when you do, you ask some leading questions.' She gave another giggle. 'Art Newcomb, the librarian. Said John's place, Old Forge Cottage, was down here somewhere but with this mist you can't see anything and all these lanes look alike.'

She looked at him through her eyelashes. 'And now I've gone and got all muddled, don't even know the way back to the green,' she simpered. 'So you'll have to take pity on a poor lost soul.'

Her way of speaking reminded him of someone. And the way she sidled, and peered up at him, like a village floozie, he thought, a second time irritated. Using books as an excuse. Again he was reminded of something, but before the thought could form she said, 'I'm Elsie, by the way. And you are . . . ?'

Immediately his mind jumped back to the first interview with Mrs Barker. Her friend, the one she'd been to the pictures with on the night of Barker's murder, was called Elsie too. It wasn't a common name, and mention of the library and librarian had suggested the link with books. At the time he'd suggested to Derrymore that they check on 'Elsie' but in the ensuing confusion, and given Derrymore's state of mind at the time, he doubted if anyone had.

'Don't you live next door to the Barkers?' he asked her, making an effort to be agreeable. 'Then I've heard of you.'

Instead of preening herself as he'd imagined, she looked alarmed. 'Whatever gives you the idea I know the Barkers?' she started to say, then, as if thinking better of it, 'Well, I do happen to live near them but . . .'

'Then I expect you remember the night Frank Barker was murdered,' he went on, with a knowing smile. 'I believe you and Mrs Barker were out together?'

She looked even more frightened. 'That's sheer guesswork,' she protested, followed more defiantly by, 'If we were, it was only because she asked for a lift. We're not intimate or anything, I mean I don't know her very well and I've never really spoken to Mr Barker. I knew nothing about his life.'

Her scrabble to disassociate herself from the Barkers was equally unpleasant. 'I thought you'd gone to the pictures together,' he interrupted her. 'Or that's what Mrs Barker said.'

'Then she's mistaken,' she snapped. 'We went to a meeting. The pictures was the week before, that new film that everyone's talking about but it was only there a few days.'

'I expect she was so upset she got muddled,' Reynolds cheerfully agreed. 'And what sort of meetings do you two ladies trip off to? Country gardens? Bridge?'

His change in tone relaxed her enough to give another little laugh. 'Books, actually,' she said, with a belated return to her more flirtatious way of speaking. 'But I still don't understand why . . .'

'Not Jen Murdock's group?' he broke in, surprised. 'You don't mean you were at Grange Manor the night of the murder?'

'Why not?' she countered. 'How were we to know what was happening somewhere else? It wasn't our regular evening anyway, but Art wanted to change. And then he didn't show up for some reason. And it's not so much fun, is it, when the men don't come?'

He ignored her. His mind was off on another tack. So if they'd all been at Jen Murdock's why hadn't someone mentioned it before? Why had Mrs Barker in particular taken such pains to cover it up? And, to parody an old rhyme, as Jen might have said, 'Where oh where had Art gone?' That was a leading question!

She was staring at him, her bewilderment growing. Any moment now she would ask, 'Why all these questions?' His guess that she genuinely didn't recognize him and had really been looking for his house out of curiosity seemed more and more plausible. 'When you see Art again,' he said, 'say John thanks him for the list. He'll know what I mean. And if you're looking for the way back to the green just follow your nose. You can't miss it.'

And before she could say anything else he went inside the garden, slammed the gate, and for all he knew left her staring foolishly at the name.

Inside his own house he switched on all the lights, and sat down in a bad temper. Silly idiot, he thought. But his anger that he and his house had become objects of idle female prying was soon forgotten in the new information he'd picked up. At once his mind reverted to the first interview with Mrs Barker and his suspicions were again aroused. She'd lied in saying that her son didn't know her troubles, and then lied again about where she'd been on the night of her husband's murder; had she told the truth about anything?

And Art Newcomb suddenly thrust into the foreground, that nervous little man with his nervous twitch. He too seemed the last person to be involved in a murder charge. But if it were true that the date of the meeting had been changed to suit him, and he hadn't appeared, was it to give Mrs Barker an alibi while he did some work for her? Some dirty work in the quarry, perhaps?

Finally, what did the woman mean by the hint that without the men 'it wasn't much fun'? Another sexual innuendo, what the vicar's wife had referred to by her oblique suggestion that some of the members should be ashamed? And she'd specifically mentioned Art Newcomb too. New clues, he wondered, or more red herrings? And somehow at the centre, Jen Murdock's name.

Jen seems involved with a lot of village activities, he thought: chairman of the May Day Committee, deep into church matters, focus of a circle whose nominal interest is books but whose real purpose may be something less educational. Again he remembered his puzzlement when he'd visited Grange Manor, and his intention to check up on Mrs Murdock's background, also put aside when his interest in her book club had given way to more pressing investigation.

Seriously unsettled now, he fiddled about the room, turning music on, turning it off, leafing through his writing and picking certain sections out. The house suddenly felt large and lonely, too big for one person. Like Sinclair he had claimed to be an old bachelor – but he wasn't a confirmed one. After his first marriage crashed, it was just the way things had turned out for him; he'd never met anyone else he really liked, or trusted. No wonder when he did she already had other suitors – or to be accurate, one other suitor, who happened to be his best friend.

And she hadn't been exactly fortunate in her choice of men. Her former lover had been selfish, greedy, a disappointed man who hadn't appreciated her. She too deserved better; he shouldn't add complications to her life. But the contrast between her and the woman who had accosted him in the lane was so great he couldn't put her out of his mind.

Finally, as if convincing himself to do something he shouldn't, he sat down long enough to make the phone call he had been thinking about all along.

He heard the number ring but no one answered. He let it ring several more times, was on the point of putting back the receiver when she picked it up. 'You're there.' He heard his voice at its most fatuous. 'How are things?'

When she didn't answer, 'I was wondering if you had any free time? I've several bits and pieces that need seeing to.'

'I'm sorry. I don't think I can.' The spring had gone from Sally's voice; she sounded low-spirited, even depressed.

'Are you all right?' he persisted. 'Is anything wrong?' She finally admitted that she had taken herself off to recover. It wasn't the attack on herself, she insisted. She hadn't minded that. It was the thought of that poor dead lady. 'If I hadn't brought the note,' she went on, just as Mazie had done, 'she might still be lying there.'

She hadn't actually seen the body then. Reynolds was relieved. He'd tried to shield her from that first sight and fortunately must have succeeded. But the sense of blame was very strong, as if somehow taking a note to Miss Penwithen was also the cause of her death, the type of illogical reasoning, he knew, that was shock-connected. He didn't argue with her, instead asked where she'd been, to hear her say something about 'home'.

'Outside of Manchester, actually,' she told him. 'And do you know I felt better when I'd been back in the city again. All those people, all those streets. I didn't feel claustrophobic as I used to. I felt safe.'

She said this as if expecting to be contradicted, and when he continued to listen without interrupting, 'So I've come back here simply to put things in order before I leave for good,' she went on. 'I meant to tell you earlier. But, well, there are still difficulties.'

It was the word she'd used before when speaking of Derrymore. She added almost defiantly, 'I've told him. Derry. I can't stay here. It's not just all this murder, and village gossip, and foul things happening. It's his work. He'll never be free of it.'

Reynolds felt a pang. He'd heard the same words, screamed at him over and over again by his ex-wife. Better to find out now before the relationship became too deep. But it was hard on Derrymore. And on her. Before he could stop himself he said, 'Isn't that running away?'

It was her turn not to reply. 'Look,' he said persuasively, 'you've had a shock. A series of shocks. They knock people off-kilter. Don't make a decision in a hurry that you may come to regret. Stay on a bit until the case is solved. Then you can both see things more clearly.'

He added gently, 'It will be solved, you know. And St Breddaford will revert back to normal. Village life won't seem so bad.' He might have been persuading himself.

After a while she sighed. 'I've given up my other jobs,' she said. 'They weren't paying me enough to live on anyway. I can't let my dad subsidize me.'

He started to say, 'That's why I rang . . .' She cut him off. 'And I can't expect you to either, Mr Reynolds, although you've been so kind. Bits and pieces won't pay my rent, I'm afraid.'

'There's a couple of chapters this time.' To his surprise he found he was arguing, pleading would have been a better word. 'In the last few days the gift of the gab has returned.'

He could feel her thinking. After a while she said, 'If I thought I could be helpful . . . one hates to be so useless. Impotent.'

She wasn't just speaking of her work for him. But he knew what she meant. She was echoing his own sense of frustration.

'Why don't you give some help with the case? Nothing difficult,' he suggested. As she began to protest, he elaborated. 'Nothing really connected. In fact it may be something right up your street.'

He was improvizing, thinking of things for her to do, although if he'd been asked why he wouldn't have known the answer. But an idea was forming, he began to enlarge on it.

'It was suggested as a sort of joke that if my books have been blamed, and if passages are taken from them, someone ought to read them through, searching for possible leads. I mean,' he was running out of ideas here, was waiting for her to refuse, 'it would be like researching a literature paper, if you'll forgive the comparison. All you'd have to do was read and underline. You could do that anywhere, even back in Manchester. But I wish you'd reconsider and do it here. And who knows, it might give us a real clue. I never read my own books through after they've been published,' he added, 'it would be too painful. I'd see too many flaws. But you might spot something significant. You're an astute critic.'

He could imagine her cheeks flaming as they did when anyone paid her a compliment. And her shining eyes. But all she said was, 'I'll think about it.' She gave a shaky laugh. 'Funnily enough, that's what Dr Sinclair and I were talking about that morning.'

Here her voice faltered a little on the words 'that morning'.

'The devil you were.' Reynolds was surprised enough to let out a real curse. When the idea had first been mentioned he'd thought Sinclair had been joking, at least he'd said so. What had he actually suggested to Sally?

She must have guessed the way his thoughts were going. 'I don't mean he spelled it out like you've just done,' she hastened to explain. 'It was only that when I asked about your books he laughed and asked if I were searching for evidence. In fact the reason for my going in was to order one of the earlier books I've not read. Then you and Inspector Nicholls burst – came into the shop. That's all there was to it.'

Again she fell silent as if reliving that moment. 'When I saw you together, I wondered what he'd been saying.' Reynolds couldn't help the comment. 'And after that he offered to take you next door?'

'It wasn't quite like that.' She recovered enough to laugh. 'You seem to be suggesting he was taking me to see his etchings! I think he was trying to be kind. He'd asked what I was doing in the village so early, and I told him I was helping Mazie. We didn't talk long,' she added. 'And if you want someone who's trained in analysing books, you ought to ask him. He'd be more used to it than I am.'

On the surface it was an interesting suggestion. But he didn't want Sinclair involved; he wasn't going to all this trouble to have Sally end up in some sort of scholastic partnership with Sinclair. He knew the thought was irrational but it bothered him. He wanted to get Sally involved with himself, on her own.

'I'll think about it.' In the end his reply was as hedged as hers. He hung up, in even worse indecision, not knowing if he had persuaded her to stay, not knowing if he should. And realizing belatedly that for the first time his concern for

Derrymore had been completely forgotten. Taking stock of what had happened, to his even greater surprise he suddenly felt happier than he had since Miss Penwithen's death.

Strangely enough at the same time Derrymore and Mazie were discussing the same subject. Or rather the central one – the possibility of Sally leaving Cornwall for good, and Derrymore's reaction.

'I don't think she means it.' Derrymore was unusually resilient. He and his mam were drinking their last tea of the evening before going to bed and in the firelight the plaster above his eye scarcely showed although it would be a while before the clipped hair filled in as thickly as before. 'She's only talking that way because she's nervous. She'll grow out of it.'

'She's not a child. You sound as if it's a dress she's got too big for.' Mazie's voice was sharp. 'And you can't say it's not important when Manchester's miles away. How are you to meet, for one thing? And when she's there she'll forget about you. And you will her.'

'No, I won't.' Derrymore sounded certain. 'It'll come right,' he said. 'Just wait and see.'

'Worse than your father, you big lummox.' Mazie couldn't conceal her impatience. 'Took a whiff of another suitor to make up his mind. You've got to get yourself almost killed, and her too, before you've had sense knocked into you. Well, it's knocked hers out. There's the problem. And what if she agrees but'll only have you if you resign from police work? Or,' she put her cup down and stared at him fiercely, 'suppose she won't live here?'

And when Derry didn't answer, 'Don't tell me you'd give it all up on her say so? Oh Derry, that would never do. St Breddaford's in your blood, it's part of you. They'd never get another to care about it as much as you do.'

Derrymore sat gazing into the fire much as he had done

on a previous evening which seemed years ago, so much had happened since. He didn't tell his mam that what she suggested was more than possible when his own unprofessional behaviour became the subject of an inquiry – as he was sure it was bound to be sooner or later. As for St Breddaford being in his blood – once he had thought so, not any more. The events of the last weeks had had a bigger effect on him than he liked to admit, and the fact that he had learned to hide his real feelings from Mazie was perhaps best proof how much he had changed. For it wasn't his profession, or even the course of the investigation which were gnawing at him, rather it was his relationship to Sally, about which he was much less carefree than he gave the impression.

Usually Derry wasn't what his mam'd call an 'introspective person'. He took things as they came. And from what he remembered of his father he thought his father had been the same. His mam might talk of 'knocking sense' in or out, but to his mind it was much more like having your eyes suddenly opened where you'd been blind before. It might seem odd to say that crawling through leaves in the dark with his head half split apart had opened his eyes, but that was the truth of it, no matter how unfortunate the result. For if he now accepted that Sally was the only woman for him he presumed other people would see things in the same light, especially Sally herself.

He hadn't argued with her about leaving, or tried to change her mind. If she wanted to go, he would follow; the solution was that simple. It wasn't until this precise moment, when his mother in her anxiety had pointed out what should have been obvious – you can't keep a woman who doesn't want to be kept – that for the first time doubts had come into his own head. Namely, if Sally didn't want him after all, who might she want instead?

The idea swept over him like a thunder-clap. He had never

known jealousy before, in fact had once laughed at it. Now he felt it like a bitterness, like a taste or smell that wouldn't go away. And having admitted he could be jealous was only the beginning. He had to find someone to pin his jealousy on. And of all the people he knew, only one man fitted the role, and that was Inspector Reynolds, whom he loved and admired.

The thought was terrible. Yet each time he thrust it down it rose in another guise. He remembered Reynolds' concern for Sally when the former case was over; he remembered her defence of the ex-inspector in this present one when the rumours against him began. 'I chatted up your bird.' It was lightly said, too lightly – it was Reynolds' idea of a joke, meaning nothing. He remembered how Reynolds had taken control of the situation after the attack, how the older man always was in control. Reynolds was successful, famous, all the things Derry wasn't – even his age might be attractive to a younger woman.

Rising to his feet he went the nightly rounds, put out the cat, locked the door. Forget it, he told himself, put it out of your mind or it'll drive you mad. Concentrate on Sally, that's all that matters. Like a thorn driven deep, suspicion festered, for all that he told himself he had forgotten it.

Chapter 13

Left with the problem of what to tell Derrymore, Reynolds determined to let sleeping dogs lie. If there was any telling to be done, Sally must do it. For the moment the new clues were all important – if they were clues, not red herrings – although next morning, he didn't enlarge on the exact way he'd obtained the information. A chance encounter, with a definite sexual tinge, made for a dubious source at the best of times. He only said he 'had another hunch' that they might lead to something, what that 'something' was he was still not sure. But while the team questioned Mrs Barker and Elsie (more hysterics, more denials, finally mutual agreement that the two ladies had gone together to Jen Murdock's) at Nicholls' suggestion he and Derrymore tackled Art Newcomb in his little office behind the main library.

In the interim Reynolds had studied Newcomb's list carefully. As he'd thought the names meant nothing, and threw no new light on the proceedings. It was not the listed names that mattered – it was the one name that had been omitted, the one that stood out like a sore thumb.

'I gather this list shows all the readers who recently have withdrawn Mr Reynolds' books?'

Derrymore's voice oozed sympathy. Newcomb batted his sandy eyelashes and agreed. He was seated behind his desk, nattily dressed in grey striped suit and guardsman tie, the epitome of competence, only his eyes gave him away. When Derrymore went further, inquiring if the whereabouts of all the books in the library was Newcomb's responsibility, weren't they public property, he actually bridled, much as Mrs Barker might have done.

'Of course,' he said. 'This is a public institution and we render service to the public. As for me,' again his eyes batted, 'I think of myself as the keeper of the books. Here like Little Bo Peep, to see they don't stray.'

His laugh was high and nervous. 'By and large my readers are very careful; not many books get lost.'

About to launch into a recital of the previous librarian's slackness, he was brought to a standstill by Derrymore's next question. 'What happened to the books Mrs Murdock took?'

His whole demeanour changed. 'Who says she took out any books?' he cried. 'Is she on my list?'

Pretending to flick through it, he repeated, 'If her name's not there the question's meaningless.'

'Only,' Derrymore's reply came fast, 'if the books she took were never charged out in the first place. In which case, they must have been taken illegally.'

He and Reynolds listened imperturbably as Newcomb began to babble. People he knew didn't act like that; not here in St Breddaford. When this failed to impress, he changed his tune, maintaining it wasn't his fault. He couldn't be in all places at once. If someone wanted to slip a book or two under his arm he couldn't stop them. And finally, with a slight attempt at belligerence, Mrs Murdock was a patroness of the library; were they suggesting that she stole books?

'Stole is a harsh word,' Derrymore agreed. 'A lot depends on the circumstances, doesn't it. She might have removed them by mistake. Or she might have asked your permission first.'

And when Art repeated he had no knowledge of Mrs Murdock's taking any books, they could check the computer for themselves, Derrymore's next logical observation, 'Then we'll have to take other measures to find out what books are missing,' caused him to crumble, his little gesture of defiance over.

Slouched lower at his desk, he looked positively miserable as Derrymore added, 'Suppose they've been removed for some illegal purpose?'

He threw this in at random, and was surprised at the result. Newcomb reared up. 'I've done nothing illegal,' he shouted, 'you can't pin anything on me.'

He turned to Reynolds, 'I've never blackened your works. To the contrary, I admire them. I said as much to . . .'

As if aware of what he was saying, he lapsed into silence.

'I think you're a member of a book club?' Deftly Derrymore changed the subject. 'Run by Mrs Murdock? Were Mr Reynolds' books part of the general reading? Or did she take them for her own use?'

No answer.

'And when was the last meeting of the club?'

Sulkily, 'A couple of weeks ago.'

'Not on a Tuesday evening? The last Tuesday in May? The evening that Mr Barker was murdered?'

'Maybe. I don't remember.'

'Even if the date was changed at your request?'

Newcomb gaped, his mouth opening and shutting like a fish.

'Who told you that?' finally he managed to gasp.

'Never mind. Is it true?'

'It might be.' A return to sulkiness.

'Then if the date of the meeting was changed,' Derrymore said as smooth as silk, 'specifically changed to a Tuesday night, why didn't you show up?'

At that Newcomb went to pieces. He sagged within his suit, his eyes watering and his mouth twitching so uncontrollably he had to put a hand to hide it. He started to say something, changed his mind, stuttered. At length he pulled himself together sufficiently to explain that he had had an unexpected visitor he couldn't let down. 'Mrs Barker wasn't that visitor by any chance?' Derrymore, unmoved by all the splutter, remained stern.

Newcomb went white. 'If you're trying to link me to the Barkers,' he cried, 'you're on the wrong track. I know Mrs Barker, of course, but we're not friends. Quite the opposite in fact. And why should I want to murder anyone? Frank Barker's path and mine have never crossed. As for his woman,' his mouth again began to twitch, 'that was his business.'

Seeing that Derrymore remained unimpressed, 'I have an alibi, I tell you,' he insisted. 'My visitor will vouch for me. We stayed in all evening. He came to talk to me about books for his new course.'

'And when did this visitor arrive, and more to the point, when did he leave?'

Again Newcomb gaped. 'W-w-when?' he stuttered, 'W-why does it matter? He came about half-past seven, I suppose. And left again round ten-thirty; we listened to the news first.'

He added desperately, 'Someone in my street will remember the car. It's fast and rather noisy.'

'Plenty of time afterwards to get up to the quarry,' Derrymore addressed Reynolds, who nodded. 'And perhaps,' he added, turning back to the now petrified librarian, 'your visitor took you there. Perhaps if you think hard enough you'll remember.'

A thought struck Reynolds. For the first time he interposed. 'This visitor,' he said, 'with the fast noisy car and the interest in books for a course he presumably is teaching, his name isn't Charles Eden, by any chance?'

And knew from the sudden silence he had struck gold.

'All right,' Newcomb said at last. 'I'm not denying it. But

he didn't want his mother to find out. She's terribly jealous of me as it is. She'd never forgive his coming to the village and not seeing her.'

He stared in front of him, his hands twiddling with his tie. 'Actually our friendship goes back a long while,' he continued at last. 'He's younger than me and when he was still at school he used to come to me for suggestions on books. He always says I put him on the road to success far more than any teacher he had, and from time to time he still asks my advice. He's a lecturer now, you know,' he added with a strange touch of pride. 'But he came and left about the times I said. He didn't take me to the quarry and I'm sure he didn't go there himself. He had no idea his step-father had been murdered; it was a terrible shock.'

As an explanation, it was well detailed; smoothly fabricated for an on-the-spot invention. And explained why Charles Eden's previous alibi for that same evening had never been satisfactory. On the other hand, as Derrymore again pointed out, there was still time to have gone to the quarry afterwards.

Several new lines of enquiry were opened by Newcomb's testimony. These included rechecking the exact start and finish of that elusive faculty meeting, and Eden's actual participation in it. More important, where had he gone after leaving Newcomb, and had he left alone?

Apart from these details, a case was building. Newcomb and Eden could have been working together, Newcomb acting as the local link. Living as he did in St Breddaford, a long-time resident, he had the opportunity to know Rab Tremayne and select him as scapegoat. He had the means to arrange the earlier incidents, including the book-burning. Eden, on the other hand, presumably would be the brains behind the schemes, masterminding the events. Eden had himself given a reason to kill his step-father and, as Reynolds and Derrymore had previously agreed, he was conceited enough to think he was cleverer than anyone else. Finally both men had the literary background to provide the relevant cut-out passages from Reynolds' books, an idea which certainly wouldn't occur to a non-bookish person, like Caddick, for example. Add to all of this the change of date for the book club meeting, and the fact that if the time fitted, a convenient alibi for Mrs Barker was also provided, if she were the woman accomplice who'd made the phone calls – the segments all slotted into place neatly: too neatly. For there were still some notable gaps, mainly who of the two men had prowled the streets looking for a victim? And who had a reason to kill Miss Penwithen?

'This is a serious matter.' Becoming suitably ponderous, Derrymore turned to the stricken librarian. 'You realize we have to ask you to accompany us down to the incident room?' He went through the usual ritual of formal warning, finally suggesting himself that Newcomb might want to contact his solicitor. Newcomb, in a state of terror, had become tongue-tied, the twitch so pronounced he could no longer speak.

After he had been led away, and after Nicholls had given instructions to bring Mrs Barker and her son in for questioning, Reynolds and Derrymore discussed with the chief inspector what their next move should be. By common consent a visit to Jen Murdock was imperative, and as they drove to Grange Manor, through the continuing drizzle and mist, Reynolds filled Derrymore in with details of his previous visit (which he had never discussed with him before, and which he now found embarrassing. At the time it had been a part of his own personal investigations, forced on him really by the disagreement between them.).

'Keep your eyes open,' was his final suggestion. 'See if you can pin her down to facts and figures. She's a hard nut to crack.'

'We'll crack her.' Derrymore was in rare good humour. He

grinned at Reynolds. 'What I've heard and seen of her I don't like at all. And Sally actually saw her with the books!'

He mentioned the name openly. 'She's staying on, by the by,' he went on, as if aware that Reynolds knew about her earlier decision to leave. 'I gather you've had a little chat and suggested something for her to while away the time.'

Taken at face value the comment seemed harmless, but for a moment Reynolds wondered. I suppose you think I'm doing her a favour, he thought, but I've too much respect for her to talk down to her. The truth is, modern women don't like being told what to do and how to do it, as little as they like being stuck at home cooking and cleaning and idolizing their partners, things I've had to learn from hard experience.

About to give Derrymore this advice he stopped himself in time. Was it only his conscience that made him glance at the sergeant self-consciously? But as Derrymore continued to steer his way through the fog with something like his old dogged determination, the subject dropped and he thought no more of it.

They reached Grange Manor and parked, the police car looking suitably battered and insignificant beside the Mercedes. 'Wouldn't mind one of these,' Derrymore said, giving it an approving pat, although the thought of his driving it made Reynolds shiver. Together they walked past the flowerpots whose contents had finally given up the ghost and rang the doorbell. And as they previously had arranged, Derrymore spoke first when Mrs Murdock appeared.

This time she didn't hurry and presumably hadn't been looking out of some window. Or, if she had, she didn't like what she saw. The contrast with Reynolds' last visit when she had originally been so gracious was especially marked. 'Ah Sergeant,' she now said coldly when he introduced himself, 'I've seen you hanging about the village. And Mr Reynolds I know of old.'

The implication that Derrymore was some insignificant street urchin must have gratified her sense of superiority. She smiled in her artificial way, and led them into her living room, with a toss of her head that suggested they should be grateful she was taking them seriously. Bathed in red light, the room looked appropriate for some Yuletide festivity, an impression enhanced by the fog outside which seemed to have filtered through the red curtains. Again there was a smell of incense, stronger than ever, and a row of little candles was still smoking on the coffee table – more than before Reynolds felt uneasy as if something was off balance.

Derrymore had scarcely mentioned the book club when she opened the attack, her voice as brittle as her smile. 'Don't tell me you're a reader too,' she interrupted, the sarcasm just showing. 'And don't tell me you want to join our club. If you do, ask Mr Reynolds. He was here a few days ago, angling for information I didn't have to give.'

As if hoping this revelation might cause trouble she enlarged on it. 'I didn't know a private citizen was permitted to badger another private citizen under cover of the law. And I didn't know that an ex-police officer had the right to harass me by virtue of his previous position. You have that to answer for, Sergeant. That's your area of authority. Or should be. My lawyer tells me that a private book club is just that, private, and my house is sacrosanct. Unless we've become more of a police state than he and I like to believe. Or unless you have a real reason for hounding me.'

End of first skirmish; a rattling of sabers and a series of scarcely veiled threats. Victory hers. Whereupon, having seized the initiative and succeeded in making both men ill-at-ease, she attacked again. 'And don't tell me that the innocent doings of my friends are important to your great investigations. We meet to drink coffee, talk books and laugh. For a lonely woman, a stranger in your midst, far from her real home, my little club's been a life-line.'

Lonely stranger, my eye, Reynolds thought. That's a nice exaggeration. But as an appeal to sympathy it works. End of second skirmish. Victory again hers.

Derrymore waited patiently. 'Yes ma'am,' he said when she paused for breath, 'and can you verify if the date of your last meeting was changed?'

'Changed?' she said, her eyes darting to Reynolds. 'Whatever gave you that idea? And why on earth,' recovering, 'does it matter? We could meet every day of the week if we liked.'

Derrymore nodded. 'Of course,' he said soothingly. 'But it's one specific change which concerns us. The last Tuesday in May. We've reason to suppose the librarian, Mr Newcomb, requested it. Did he give a reason?'

'Oh Art.' She dismissed him with a wave of her hand. She smiled again. 'He's so precise,' she said. 'Likes things cut and dried. He said originally we needed one more session to round out the series. I didn't mind. I said . . .'

'Why didn't he come?'

For the first time the smile flickered. 'Didn't he?' Her reply was careless. 'Who says?'

'He does, for one. And presumably so will his visitor.'

Before she could recover, 'We are talking of a murder here,' he said. 'A murder that happened that same night. The widow of the murdered man spent the evening with you. When did she arrive? Did she stay to the end? Could she have left and returned?'

'Ah, murder,' Jen Murdock's expression changed to one of a pious solicitude. 'Dreadful,' she said. 'And to think Mrs Barker was amusing herself with us at the same time as . . .'

'What time did the meeting start?'

'Six,' she said, 'six-thirty. We aren't tied to time. People come when they can.'

'And end?'

'Again no set time, ten, ten-thirty, sometimes eleven if it was a good discussion. I think we left very late that night.'

'Did Mrs Barker, or anyone else, leave early?'

'Well now, Sergeant,' Jen purred, 'I don't keep my guests under constant observation, you know. But as I believe she came with her next-door-neighbour, perhaps she could tell you better than I when they arrived and left.'

She looked at him defiantly, as if to say, 'Make what you will of that.' Her lack of co-operation caught Derrymore on the raw. 'And what about those guests?' He slapped his notebook firmly down between the candles. 'You must have some recollection of who else was here.'

He waited patiently, like drawing blood from stone, he admitted later, while she hemmed and hawed, as he eventually compiled a list of names that meant nothing to Reynolds and were strangers even to him.

He folded his notebook away. 'And while we're at it,' he barked, 'how many books did you remove from the library on . . . ?' He named the day, the same that she'd been seen by Sally. 'All written by Mr Reynolds.'

For once she was caught off guard. When she began to bluster, 'It can be verified,' he added.

'Art Newcomb is a sneak,' she cried with a vicious snap. 'You know of course he's gay. And you know his history? He wasn't a librarian all his life; oh no. What he won't tell you was he was just a simple primary school teacher. Who was dismissed for indecency with one of his boys. So whatever he says I wouldn't believe him.'

Derrymore kept his temper. 'We're also interested,' he said, 'in the smear campaign against Mr Reynolds. And that was the reason for Mr Reynolds' first visit. A private citizen,' he emphasized the word, 'has the right to protect himself against slander.'

'Slander is a criminal offence,' he continued, when she didn't react.

'Don't talk to me of slander,' she shouted, her eyes flashing. 'I think I'm being slandered here. You've hinted that I've removed books from the library for illegal purposes; you've hinted that my book club is involved in illegal acts. And you're suggesting I'm at the back of it because I started my little club. Well,' with an effort calming down, 'if some of those who feel left out have made complaints, that's sheer jealousy. I think we've been a benefit to people here. Heaven knows what anyone with a love of culture did in this benighted place until I came and stirred things up. And,' the smile was back but cold, 'if that's all you have to ask then I'll let my lawyer answer the rest of your questions.'

'Whew!' When they were outside and the door firmly shut, Derrymore wiped his forehead before putting on his helmet. 'A real tough nut,' he confirmed. 'I see what you mean. And don't tell me she hasn't picked up a lot of dirty gossip since she's been here. And that room,' he wrinkled his nose, 'what a stink! I can't think what it looks and smells like.'

'Ye Gods.' Reynolds was startled. I can, he thought. Derrymore's observation suddenly made clear what he'd been searching for. Of course! A brothel! It was just he hadn't expected such a setting for it in this part of the world. In any urban venue Jen Murdock would make the perfect madame! No wonder the vicar's wife had been shocked; no wonder Elsie was suddenly into books!

When Derrymore added as innocently, 'And that stuff about Newcomb, where did she dig that up? Never a word breathed about it before as far as I know. And I don't see it's relevant.'

'It may explain his bond with Charles Eden. Or have been used as a means for Eden to get him involved.'

'I didn't think of that,' Derrymore admitted. 'But I agree

with you she must be hiding something. And her so-called "guests", where did she round them up, I wonder? Not one from the village there that night as far as I can see, except Mrs Barker and Elsie.'

They had come to the car now, and he stopped to stare around him. 'And where did she get all her cash? That Mercedes for example. And the house and gardens. Vicar Tamblin's right, she could buy the whole Varcoe family out. So why was she so set to get Mrs Varcoe into trouble?'

'Desire to meddle. Mischief-making. You name it.' Reynolds let his disgust show. He suddenly saw why even a good-natured man like the vicar could be infuriated by her behaviour. 'She's managed to worm her way into every aspect of village life and take advantage of what she finds. So I think,' he added, 'we ought to check on Jen Murdock's background, as I meant to do earlier. She may have verified the change of date (and vilified Newcomb into the bargain) but she's cleverly fudged over exact times and people present. If Mrs Barker, or anyone else, left to make that phone call to Caddick from a public phone box, she's not saying. In my experience such unhelpful behaviour has only one purpose – to protect herself.'

Here Derrymore broke in. 'I think I know what it is!' he pronounced, with a satisfied grin. 'My guess is we've found the source of the rumours against you. If anyone's capable of starting them, she is. But I still don't see why she went to all that effort to pick on you.'

'The same as before, to make trouble.' Reynolds answered absently; he was thinking of something else. 'There's still too much that's not been clarified,' he concluded. 'Namely, is a smear campaign all she's involved in? What about the crimes themselves? We need to find a lever to force her to talk. Someone who uses village gossip in such a fashion is more than a trouble maker, she's dangerous.'

'And I never saw what she saw, or even looked for it.' Derrymore couldn't hide his chagrin. 'I thought I knew almost everyone in the village,' he burst out. 'I prided myself on knowing them. She's found out secrets I never even guessed at.'

He lapsed into silence while Reynolds tried to console him, suggesting first that Jen Murdock's friends must by default all be new to the region, and that it was this very influx of new people that had itself altered village life. It didn't occur to him until later that he too could be classified as one of them, as could Sally. And that, like some thoughtless developer with no regard for the natural environment, they might have contributed unwittingly to the alteration, even though they both regretted it as much as the sergeant did.

When they had gone, and Jen Murdock had made sure there was no trace of them, even going to the gate to check, she scurried back into the house, her high heels tapping. Reaching the safety of her living room she sank down on the sofa, kicked her shoes off and dialled the familiar number.

At first no one answered. When at last the phone was picked up, the voice on the other end was not exactly friendly. It listened in heavy silence while she ambled on about her recent visitors, and her cleverness in stalling any further enquiries, until even through her self-absorption she must have sensed the disapproval.

'But what else could I do?' Her question was tremulously truculent. 'I didn't know what else to say. That possibility had never been discussed before.' She held the phone away as the voice now asked for details which she didn't want to give; the abuse that accompanied them shocked even her although she knew how to use foul language as well as anyone. But it didn't really worry her. She knew it was occasioned by irrational fear. When it was over, 'Now then,' she cooed, forcing herself to sound natural, 'let's talk it over like the good friends we are. Your house or mine?' And she gave her little giggle.

Chapter 14

Sally Heyward had spent a strange day, first in her own flat in Truro where she started to unpack what she called her 'bits and bobs', already put in boxes to be taken back to her parents' house. That they would be lost among her parents' belongings, as she herself felt lost in the same palatial quarters, hadn't seemed to matter earlier. Now it became an added inducement to stay in the little niche which she had made for herself. Besides, she kept reminding herself, she still liked Truro. With its cathedral and close, it reminded her of Trollope's nineteenth-century ecclesiastical city, and its cobbled streets, lined with boutiques, made window-shopping fun. She could always stay on in Truro, find a better job, start another life again. Today she fought down all the negative feelings that told her she was as out of place in this Cornish environment as a fish out of water.

In spite of her misgivings and in spite of the weather, she actually enjoyed the ride to St Breddaford. The first glimpse through the rain of the funny steepled church on the village green, with the stream beside it, gave her an unexpected sense of homecoming. But she probably wouldn't have remained in Cornwall, hadn't even told Derry that she was planning this visit to his village, if it hadn't been for Reynolds' suggestion the evening before. That had given her a purpose, so that now, standing in the alley behind Miss Penwithen's cottage, she could admit what she really wanted.

She had never heard of Miss Penwithen until the murder, although she had often admired the neat front garden and the uneven thatched roof of her cottage, and the lost opportunity of knowing the elderly lady had inexplicably saddened her as if some special gift had been wrenched away.

She couldn't put into words why she felt this way, but if she had given Reynolds the impression that she hadn't seen Miss Penwithen's body, that was only because she knew he'd tried to protect her from the sight. She had seen. And the image of that old lady, upright, dignified, facing death with such outward stoicism, was imprinted on Sally's mind, and, somehow, had become mingled with the wish to make amends for the manner of her death – hence Sally's special interest in Reynolds' offer.

And there was another reason, equally inexplicable. She had begun to dream of Miss Penwithen. In the beginning, the dream had always been the same, the figure too far away to be really identifiable, the face hidden. But since her return to Cornwall, a few days ago, it had begun to move swiftly towards her, through what she had come to recognize as some garden, not the cottage one, something larger but equally well known and loved. Still too far off to allow the features to be distinguished clearly, still surrounded by mist and rain (which in reality surrounded Sally when she woke) Miss Penwithen seemed about to ask Sally for something. And today Sally had come to find out what it was.

Seeing the cottage again made her more certain than ever that she had been drawn there deliberately – by the thought of the cottage being left desolate, perhaps. Or the wishes of its owner! And as she tried to remember how it had been when she had stood there less than two weeks past, the four of them staring, not yet knowing what lay behind the closed windows and doors, she fought with the suggestion, absurd in itself, that she held the key to Miss Penwithen's death, that if she rang that great bell the door would open and Miss Penwithen would be standing there . . .

'Well, well.' A jovial voice made her jump. 'Miss Heyward, back at the scene of the crime.' And as she tried to steady herself against the gate, 'Don't tell me you're into detecting too, I didn't know it was catching.'

Dr Sinclair was beaming at her across the fence that divided his yard from Miss Penwithen's back garden. He was wearing his flapping raincoat and his hair lay in damp streaks. He took off his spectacles to rub them dry. 'And are you tempted to look inside,' he said, in his pedantic joking way, 'still searching for clues? Although, mark you, the police have been more than thorough. Even questioned me. But then as I told them, the poor old soul wasn't easy to talk to, and I think I did my bit as a neighbour. And she never objected to a thing I said.'

He gave his whinnying laugh but she didn't respond. It would be a long while before she could laugh about Miss Penwithen and her deafness. Perhaps he sensed it. 'Sorry,' he said, his own smile fading. 'Didn't mean to sound callous. But if you'd like a peek inside, I expect it could be arranged.'

He fumbled ineffectively in his pockets, pulling out a boyish clutter of handkerchiefs, string, wrapping paper and twine before eventually finding what he must have been looking for because he waved a screwdriver at her. 'The police have locked everything up, of course,' he explained, 'but there's a wonky back window. I tried to fix it for her once, but never did a good job. This should get it open. I meant to tell the police about it, but it went out of my head. Absent-minded professor, that's my name.'

He twinkled at her. 'But there's another saying you may have heard of. By one of our lesser poets. Seize the moment, says he. Enjoy the chance, that sort of thing. I've just shut the shop to arrange some things up here in the loft, hence the screwdriver. And I'm at your disposal, if you want to visit now.'

For a moment she was tempted. And he saw it in her eyes. He made a move towards his gate that led to the alley, swinging the screwdriver by its handle. A neighbour unexpectedly looming out of the mist and, having recognized Sinclair, stopping him to talk, brought Sally back to common sense. Feeling ashamed of what might seem morbid curiosity she moved away from the cottage gate, and, brushing past the two men, went back down the alley. She didn't want to be seen as an intruder; she didn't want to come upon Miss Penwithen's ghost in anyone else's company. She wanted to meet her on her own.

She had reached the main street and was hesitating over what to do next when there was a rattle of the shop door and Dr Sinclair's head poked out. 'I thought you'd gone,' he said. 'It was only Alf Bantree complaining that the police had questioned him as well, and all this inquisition was bad for his heart. "My dear sir," says I, "in cases like this everyone is suspect. We're all on the hook until they find the real culprit. It's like being searched at airports, we say it's inconvenient but we'd rather the inconvenience than be killed by terrorists." '

He laughed. 'Unfortunately the allusion was lost, as he's never flown, and doesn't trust planes either. And now, if you've a moment, I've found those books you wanted.'

He made no more mention of visiting Miss Penwithen's cottage, and Sally stifled the urge to bring the subject up (although she longed to ask if he knew what would happen to the place, were there relatives to inherit?) Instead she followed him inside the shop and waited while he rummaged beneath the counter, coming up with a paper package.

He waved aside her request to pay. 'No, no,' he said with old-fashioned gallantry, 'They're not for sale. On the best of advice I've removed all Mr Reynolds' books from the shelves until the troubles blow over. These happen to come from my own little stock at home, although you may be the last person ever to want to read them. If you were in the square you'd have seen how unpopular they were.'

He regarded her for a moment, then said, 'What's he like? To work for, I mean. As a professor of literature it's always interested me how writers set about their task.'

Again resisting temptation, this time to say that although Reynolds' productivity had been at a low ebb it was beginning to pick up again, instead she thanked him and started to leave when he stopped her. 'If you're wanting somewhere warm to sit and read,' he said persuasively, 'you're welcome to a chair and table here. As I explained to Mr Reynolds, I've even got the American coffee machine to go with them, as one of their magazines suggests. I've heard that the library is closed today. They've taken Newcomb off to interrogate.'

Taken aback by this news, for the library was her next stop, and surprised, because she had heard no mention of the librarian as a possible suspect, she hesitated for a moment before accepting. Under such pressing hospitality, and in view of his generous gift, she felt it would be bad manners to refuse. She let him place the chair and table with fussy precision, then, when he had equally fussed with the coffee machine, sat down and opened the first book, sipping as she read.

Perhaps the American magazine was right. Several people came in to browse, and stayed to buy books. Dr Sinclair was busier than she had imagined. Not that she paid much attention, what she was reading fascinated her. Usually her own taste didn't run to detective stories, and since working for Reynolds she had sensed even his disappointment in his current work. These earlier books were authoritative, full of energy, the style sparkling, the subject-matter gripping. I'm beginning to sound like the blurb for one of his covers, she thought, but I can understand now why he's become so popular without pandering to popular taste. So engrossed did she become the morning passed without her being aware of it and when she next looked up it was with an unexpected sense of pleasure, and the feeling that at last she had been usefully employed.

This pleasure was to be dispelled by Sinclair. 'That's not the way to research a book,' he said disapprovingly, disappointment showing. 'You need note cards, pencils, paper. Here, I'll give you some. Make a list of the ideas that appear in every chapter. Or in every incident. Reynolds has even helped you in these early books by using chapter headings, so you can leaf through them quickly, looking for ones that fit.'

She was startled. She hadn't said anything to him about the purpose of her reading. She could only presume that he had guessed, or that, for a college professor, it was the correct way to read and enjoy a book. But she didn't much enjoy being lectured to like a student for her shortcomings. Refusing the offer of supplies and thanking him for his advice she caught the bus home and sat reading all afternoon and through the following day. And thus came up with a revolutionary idea that was to stun everyone.

While she was kept occupied the team were interviewing their new suspects. Until now, dissatisfaction with the way the investigation had been going had sunk the church hall into depression. A sort of damp smog enveloped them, a combination of cigarette smoke and wet wool, over which the stench of ancient oil lamps (discovered in one of the many cupboards and lit to keep warm) hung, almost tangibly. Even the house to house search which Nicholls had instigated, had brought no new leads, as Reynolds had predicted, except the re-emergence of two life-long feuds and a complaint about a loud car. 'Bloody thing woke the baby twice' (which was eventually to substantiate Eden's arrival and departure, alone).

This atmosphere of continuing gloom lightened

considerably with the arrival of Art Newcomb, although he himself sank even further into silence with every mention of book club, Charles Eden and Jen Murdock.

Mrs Barker arrived in a squad car, her protests heralding her arrival. But they were nothing compared with those later expressed by her son and his lawyer. 'My client wishes to inform you that he is here under protest.' 'My client has nothing to say about that matter.' 'My client finds this whole investigation repulsive.' The lawyer's familiar responses went their rounds until Art Newcomb's name was mentioned.

Then Charles Eden leapt to his feet. 'What's he doing here?' he shouted, followed by, 'I don't know him. He's nothing to me.' He didn't even have the decency to acknowledge his inconsistency when it was pointed out. In fact his disavowal of friendship faltered only when Art Newcomb's version of their meeting on the night of the first murder was related. At that both Charles Eden and Mrs Barker reacted violently.

The son capitulated first. After contemptuously dismissing the idea of any visit to Art Newcomb – why would he visit a librarian to get help with his teaching, for God's sake? – he must have become aware of the advantages of confession: namely a water-tight alibi. Without a word of explanation for his change of tune, he now claimed to have driven to St Breddaford after his faculty meeting (the hours of which meeting at last officially and firmly were identified as between four and six, giving him and his car plenty of time to make the journey by half-past seven).

'I stayed with Newcomb well into the night,' Charles Eden proceeded to protest. 'Too late to go to any quarry. I don't know even know where it is. And as I stopped on the way home for a meal I certainly didn't return to it later.'

Naming the place as an all-night eatery which he swore he patronized regularly, made them take this seriously enough to arrange a visit to the establishment.

As for Mrs Barker, her howl of anguish on hearing of her son's visit was to become legendary even to officers hardened to all varieties of emotional outburst. Its gist, when they could make sense of what she was saying, was that Charles couldn't have ignored her in favour of Newcomb. Charles would never come to the village without seeing her first. Charles had promised never to meet that scum Newcomb again – all of which was proof of the underlying maternal jealousy that Newcomb had warned about, to say nothing of his downplay of Mrs Barker's dislike of him.

'Not my boy, not my son.' Eventually Mrs Barker wept. By then it was commonly admitted what the real reason behind the visit was, and the nature of the friendship – a subject which a lady of Mrs Barker's background and age couldn't be expected to accept, or discuss. 'If Charles was tired or depressed (weak excuses Eden himself trotted out to put himself in a more acceptable light) he should have stayed a few days with me as he usually did when work got him down. Why did he have to hurt me when he knows how much I mind?'

The question was rhetorical. Remembering a previous discussion – it seemed a life-time before – of whether Eden really cared for his mother, here's proof, Reynolds thought, from her side at least, that he doesn't care much at all. And another question apparently was as unanswerable, put now to Charles Eden after his bank account was opened to police scrutiny – where did the large sums showing up each month come from? Cash payments, perhaps, but from whose pocket?

These and other leads took most of the working day and night and brought them still without solution to the Friday; another week wasted. But probe as they might, the team could get no further forward with proving the two men's complicity in the murders, even Newcomb finding his voice to protest vehemently that he was innocent, had never met Rab Tremayne and never been in the quarry. As for the other crimes, neither men could be linked to them, although Eden swore if he'd had a chance he'd not only have tossed the blasted crown into the river, he'd have followed it with the kids who had scratched the paint on his car. His last retort, that he was a teacher of literature, not some wretched artist, was equally decisive.

The real downer, after this day and night of frantic activity, was the doubt, finally confirmed on the Friday morning, of the legality of holding the suspects any longer. The first disappointment, to universal surprise, was that the all-night transport cafe, for large lorries, did confirm Eden's arrival on the Tuesday evening. He reached it about eleven and he was alone. His stay, to eat and talk with one of the chefs whom he knew, lasted well into the small hours, long after the time of the murder in the quarry, as was confirmed by said chef, a tall pimply youth with a beautiful profile.

The second, equally damaging, was that neither man had been in St Breddaford the weekend of the Tamblin wedding and neither had returned until the day after the book-burning, Newcomb having gone to stay with cousins close to Salisbury; Eden having alibis galore to prove he was at his university post. The third disappointment was that both men had firm excuses for the night of Miss Penwithen's murder, Newcomb attending a librarians' seminar, and Eden actually teaching one of his courses at the university.

These new facts were more than a downer, they brought the line of investigation to a skidding halt. Add to them the independent statements of both Mrs Barker and Elsie that neither had left the other's side throughout the evening, even staying together after their return home, drinking coffee or 'something stronger' at Elsie's house (where as a young divorcee, newly parted from a weak but wealthy husband, Elsie lectured Mrs Barker on the advantages of legal separation).

Even the ingenious suggestion from one of the team that Mrs Barker could have made a recording of the message (thus explaining the background static as well as freeing her from making the call in person at a specific time) failed to break the Barkers' story. They departed, their lawyer muttering about false arrest and lawsuits; Newcomb followed them, and the investigation was stuck.

'Under the circumstances, better let them go.' Nicholls' tone was weary. 'We can always round them up again if need be. But where does that leave us? Damn well in the soup.'

He was stating the obvious. Even the few other new avenues of investigation were proving difficult. Chief among them, the tracing of Mrs Murdock's past had so far ended in failure. Murky it might be, but she had disguised the trail thoroughly. And a possible line of inquiry, Daisy Abbot, the butcher's niece who 'did' for Mrs Murdock, added nothing new except, as Mazie had suggested, a long complaint about the work. Since Daisy only came the morning after the meeting to clean up she couldn't speak for what happened on the night itself – except what they did to the furniture with wet glasses, and the sheets she had to wash, no one would believe.

Better luck had accompanied the search for Murdock's 'guests'. Most were traced from the list she had given Derrymore, and as he and Reynolds had assumed, they were newcomers to the area – in spite of Jen's claim to be of benefit to St Breddaford, few village participants seemed to have stayed the course, except for the luckless librarian, Mrs Barker and Elsie.

What the vicar's wife really thought of the club, and whether its real purpose had been carefully disguised when she turned up, was one of those side issues carefully glossed over.

For they did begin to discover what the book club really

was, or rather what it was not. To start with, most of the regular 'guests' seemed unlikely to be interested in reading, were what might be called a 'nouveau riche clique' from the neighbouring countryside who had become friends mainly because they all originated from similar backgrounds, far removed from village life. They were in fact all members of the new breed of countryfolk who descend upon Cornwall in their thousands, rich enough to gentrify it to their standards and transform it back to familiar city ways.

Once convinced that the investigation had to do with murder, not their own private peccadillos, they fell over themselves to be helpful. Conversely, as their sexual lives were not the investigating team's priority, the exact nature of Mrs M's club was shelved for the time being (albeit when the murder was solved, questions would certainly be raised about its operating so freely within parish boundaries).

Apart from admitting they had met at Grange Manor on the specific Tuesday, not their regular night, to enjoy a 'social evening' (without identifying what that meant) in reality Mrs Murdock's group had nothing new to contribute either. They hardly knew Mrs Barker ('A right old bore'; 'Talks only about her son'; 'Don't know why the old biddy comes') but were sure she wouldn't have left early. 'She always hangs on to the end, wouldn't miss a moment. Gives her a little thrill, I suppose,' the kindest observation. Art Newcomb, a village librarian, was scarcely worth their notice; if anything he was described as a hanger-on, Jen's handy-man, although eunuch was closer to their meaning, they had at least categorized him correctly. They didn't know or care why he had changed the date of the meeting and were as indifferent to whether he came or not. Elsie, on the other hand, equally not surprisingly, was termed a 'good sort' and 'fun'.

It was at this low-point that Sally Heyward's revelation made its maximum impact. By now it was Friday evening.

She rang from her flat, asking for both Derrymore and Reynolds, excitement just showing in her voice. Suggesting that it would be better if they met in person, she was perhaps surprised at their alacrity in offering to come at once. They didn't have to tell her they were so despondent, they jumped at any possibility, no matter how tenuous.

The hour was late; but they were there within the promised time having speeded most of the way in Reynolds' car. Her flat was on the outskirts of the city in a block that had been built in the concrete and glass style of the sixties and hadn't worn well. It was not the sort of place Reynolds had imagined her living, but from the shabby exterior he assumed the main advantage was the cheap rent.

She let them in with a wan smile. 'You must be hard up for ideas,' she started to say, then realizing they weren't in a joking mood, led them into her sitting room where she had made an attempt to tidy up prior to their arrival, pushing the half-emptied boxes into her bedroom, and preparing a large pot of coffee. Only the straggle of papers on a low table suggested how hard she had been working.

In spite of the urgency of their mission, Reynolds found time to be surprised too at the appearance of her flat. The way she had carefully re-arranged her meager possessions, the hints of good taste on a limited budget, had an effect on him. Standing aside so she and Derrymore could greet each other in whatever private way they chose, he found himself fingering a cracked porcelain cup, looking for whatever quality had attracted her. Derrymore had suggested her parents were wealthy, and from his own past he identified with this attempt to live on her own, making her own way, probably in spite of opposition. It became another, unspoken, bond between them.

'I may be wrong,' she now said as the two men squeezed themselves onto a tiny sofa, 'but I've gone over it several times.' Taking up a list she pushed it before them and then sat back watching their faces as they studied it.

The list contained five sets of quotations, the first two already found in Rab Tremayne's and Miss Penwithen's cottages. The next three Reynolds had difficulty identifying, finally confessing with a sheepish grin that he never remembered what he had written unless there was something specific to jog his memory, could she elucidate. Before she could say anything, Derrymore, who had been looking a little left out, broke in to ask if she was predicting three more murders, hadn't they had enough?

His manner was stiff again, his expression showing that he disapproved of this whole venture, but Sally refused to be intimidated. 'No,' she said stoutly, 'I don't predict anything.' Then, addressing Reynolds directly, 'What I did first,' she explained, 'was skim through all your books I could find, looking for crimes that fitted a rural environment. Many of the stories were obviously irrelevant, those dealing with financial scandals, or international gun-running, or even city gang warfare (which I found intriguing. You must fill in the details sometime). But as I read,' here she leaned forward and gazed at her listeners intently, 'I found that the crimes fitted into certain patterns. And when I went back to the first two quotations, I think I found what they both had in common. So I looked for the same thing in others, and came up with this list.'

'The quotations may not be right,' she added. 'I put them in for identification. And of course, if one wanted to and knew the books well enough, one could probably find a quotation somewhere to fit any situation. I looked only for the pattern. And all these five I've listed have the same one. A sexual background. A twisted sexual motive. Usually caused by a woman.'

As Derrymore gave a snort between disgust and disbelief,

'It's not a thing to be proud of,' she insisted. 'But I've read that the number of crimes committed by women is rising. And when you think of it, all the incidents that have happened so far in St Breddaford have had a strange sexual tinge. And think of the drawings. I believe they were supposed to be grotesque. Then there's the children's crown. I always thought it strange that it should have disappeared. But if you consider that all May Day festivities were connected originally with pagan fertility rites and even the crowning of a child queen may have originated in some virgin sacrifice, you can see the connection. The horrible despoilation of the church decorated for a wedding is part of the same thing, the virgin bride ravished. A bride who's accused, by the by, in an anonymous phone call to her mother, of being "wild", I think the expression was. Of having too many lovers I suppose. And then the murder in the quarry – illegal lovers caught in the very act.'

Reynolds looked at her with growing respect. He had always known she was intelligent, but this analysis matched anything he'd ever met. 'What about Rab Tremayne's murder? And Miss Penwithen's death? What about the book-burning?' His questions, abrupt as they were, paid her the compliment of dealing with her as an equal.

'I thought of those too.'

Sally's answer was as brusque, her grey eyes still fixed on Reynolds. 'The book-burning is a one off; I can't fit that in except as an obvious attempt to point up your books. But Miss Penwithen must have been part of the pattern, an elderly maiden lady, you can see for yourself how that might fit. And if Rab Tremayne was persuaded to help with the first murder, could it have been a woman who did the persuading?'

Again Reynolds stared at her. 'By God,' he said, 'that's the one thing we never thought of. But,' the idea was growing on him, 'it might work.'

Derrymore could stand the discussion no longer. He rose to his feet, looking taller than ever in the low-ceilinged room. 'It's all guess work,' he said loudly, as if trying to drown Sally out. 'It's nothing like that at all. And you shouldn't be talking about these things.'

If he hadn't been so genuinely upset they might have laughed. As it was Reynolds tried to calm him down, gently explaining that it wasn't Miss Heyward's own fixation, she was merely quoting from anthropological references to give her theory some sort of credibility. 'All those big words don't hide the nastiness,' Derrymore said, doggedly. 'And saying Rab Tremayne was tempted by a woman, what sort of woman would do that to him?'

They were all silent then, until Derrymore put their probable thoughts into words by adding, 'My mam was good to Rab. Like a mother, I'd say. He worshipped her, mind you.' As if aware of what he was saying he too fell silent.

'A woman.' Reynolds reverted to the starting premise. 'With some sexual perversion. Whose motive was to attack and kill out of some illusion that dominated her private world.'

He wasn't shocked by the idea, certainly not disconcerted at discussing it with the pretty young woman who had come up with it on her own, and, what was more, had given it some credence with her thoughtful comparisons. But he was also cautious. He'd been so sure the mastermind was a man he'd never considered the other possibility. Now that he was forced into doing so, it made sense in many ways. The overkill for example, the prissy attention to minor details, even the grotesque smiley faces, they had the hallmarks of feminine ways of thought – and he wasn't just being a male chauvinist here. And even if he had to admit they had been looking for the wrong person from the beginning, well, he could accept he'd made a mistake, as long as they found the right one eventually. But a woman, with a woman accomplice to do the telephoning – or even doing the phone calls herself, took some getting used to.

For one thing she would have had to be a strong woman, both physically as well as mentally. Immediately his thought reverted to Mrs Barker. He could see her easily in the guise of accomplice, but as the mastermind?

And some of the crimes must have been committed by men. Suppose the woman, whoever she was, used men to do her work for her – a real reversal of roles. He thought of Tremayne, even of Newcomb and then the attacker in the Ope. He was about to ask Derrymore if he was sure that had been a man, when Sally gave a nervous laugh. 'You know,' she said to Derrymore, 'right from the beginning I made a joke about being sure it was a man. Remember?'

But Derrymore didn't want to be reminded. He was still too upset to answer. He must have known he'd made a fool of himself, and having no way to retrieve himself from an awkward situation, he maintained a sulky silence. Sally looked at him much as his mother might have done, smiling over his bent shoulders at Reynolds. 'So you think there may be something in it?' she asked. Before he could reply she went on, 'Because if you do, there's another thing I haven't told you.'

And so revealed the end of the incident outside the library, involving the woman with her bag full of books, and her flood of vicious remarks.

And by then even Derrymore was sufficiently interested to sit up and take notice.

At the same time another exchange was taking place. Art Newcomb, suitably chastised, having been released, had regained the shelter of his house where, free from prying eyes, he could begin the task of rebuilding what he was to call his shattered life. But first he had other things more important on his mind, and the phone call he put through was one of them.

'I didn't know what to do. Or say, when he asked.'

Like Jen Murdock, his voice was whiny, full of self-pity, and he used some of the same excuses. 'I thought you'd said we shouldn't draw attention to ourselves. I tried to keep things on a level key. I'd no idea they'd be so thorough. And I'd no idea Charles would show up, out of the blue like that. I hadn't seen him in ages, I swear. I didn't think my not attending the meeting would be so important. I did just what you said otherwise.'

'Didn't know, didn't think,' The voice on the other end remained calm but there was something about its icy condemnation that chilled the blood. 'You should have thought of all that before.'

And as Art, once more frantic to redeem himself, began to stutter, 'We put you in a position of trust,' the voice pointed out. 'We don't like being disappointed. Remember, we kept faith with you. No one knew about you until you gave yourself away.'

And with that the line went dead, leaving Art still stuttering. Only when he realized no one was listening did he hang up and, after pacing back and forth for several moments, scurry upstairs to pack.

Jumping at any sudden noise, throwing clothes in a suitcase at random and then in panic unpacking them, gradually he abandoned any hope of escape. No matter where he went he was sure the rumours would follow. That had been part of the bargain, spelled out so there could be no mistake, although never in so many words.

'Keep faith with us.' What did that mean if not, in effect, a bargain. 'Keep faith with us, help us, and in return we hide your secrets, cover your past, prevent it becoming public knowledge to ruin you.'

Instead of running, then, he should stand firm. Cling to the one hope of refuge that he was sure of. Show that you are a man not a mouse, he told himself, repeating this advice again and again, trusting that he would in fact be man enough to go through with it.

Later that same evening, he crept from his home and began the trek to that refuge.

It wasn't late. Rain still fell in scattered drifts and tattered clouds raced across the sky, and the village seemed deserted. His route, through woods and fields, was roundabout; he had been told to take it in emergencies, in case of being followed. He went this way now (although he was sure there was no need; no one would follow him on an evening like this) because he wanted to prove he was still a loyal disciple and could be trusted to obey orders.

He was no hiker at the best of times and soon the path became a quagmire, a nightmare of sounds and shadows. Walking turned to running and then to full flight against whatever terrors his guilty conscience had conjured up. It is easy to imagine his relief when he reached his destination: his sigh, signalling the return to normality; his pause to let his racing heart slow down and his facial tick steady. Even his social smile, put on as the front door opened, managed a certain charm – until a gasp of returning horror kept it fixed, at the sight of the unexpected figure standing before him.

Chapter 15

'You're bloody well serious!'

A furious Derrymore faced Reynolds, arms akimbo, head jutting forward into the rain, as if, Reynolds thought, he's about to bowl me over in typical wrestling style. It was later the same night; Reynolds and he had just left Sally's flat, where, after his first outburst, during the ensuing conversation the sergeant had remained conspicuously quiet. Now, having re-parked the car to give a view of front and side doors of the flat, Reynolds had just told him they would be staying on watch the rest of the night, and at first thought it was this order that helped Derrymore recover his voice.

They were standing out on the street as the sergeant continued angrily, 'You really think it's Murdock, as if I wouldn't know the feel of a woman if she attacked me! As if a woman like that would be capable of such an attack.' His vehemence made Reynolds wonder. Here again was a different side of the man he was used to dealing with.

True, Derrymore's voice was thick with disbelief, as if the arguments in favour of a case against Murdock had all boiled up into a great surge of resentment. The more Reynolds pressed her knowledge of people in the district, the more he highlighted her undeniable penchant for causing trouble and produced her circle of 'guests' as possible unexplored accomplices, the more the sergeant opposed him. Even quoting Murdock's love of books (which Reynolds himself had at first so scornfully doubted) caused resistance. But Reynolds himself could be as stubborn.

As he glared at Derrymore, for the first time he noted the other's clenched fists. Reynolds had never seen Derrymore so belligerent. About to remind the sergeant of an occasion when he himself had taken his assailant for a man, when if he hadn't had enough sense left to stop fighting against the cord that was strangling him and used his remaining strength to fall back on top of the strangler he wouldn't be here today, he held his tongue. The woman in that case had certainly been young, a terrorist trained to kill since childhood, not a forty-year-old in high heels – although one thing both might have had in common was anger, as venomous as it was deep.

Earlier Reynolds had decided that Derrymore had turned against the idea of Murdock as a suspect because he really respected women too much to believe them capable of such evil. It was the same sort of reasoning which made him disapprove of Sally's suggestion. He, on the other hand, had focused immediately on Murdock's irrational hatred, pointing out that they'd seen it themselves in action against Mrs Varcoe, arguing that even if Jen Murdock wasn't built like an Amazon and hadn't been trained in martial combat, unbridled hatred alone was a time bomb waiting to go off. He was about to insist that ignoring the warning was like burying your head in sand when something about Derrymore's stance and look brought Mazie's earlier warnings flooding back. Especially when Derrymore now snarled, 'And if Murdock's dangerous, you've landed Sally in a mess with your stupid suggestions.'

It made Reynolds take a step backwards. The last thing he wanted was a fight with his partner. And as Derrymore continued to bombard him with a series of furious questions he was faced with the problem of extricating himself from a situation that was growing more difficult by the minute.

'You really think Sally's in danger? You think our so-called "female" attacker was after her? How can you pretend to out-smart a "mastermind" with all these cockeyed precautions? That's about as stupid as your theories always are.'

With each of these furious attacks, Derrymore took a threatening step forward, his fists still clenched, forcing Reynolds to retreat still further. 'If Sally's in danger now, it's all your fault.'

Ye Gods, Reynolds thought, as insult followed insult, I believe he's jealous. Never mind if there's some justification for Derrymore's reaction, it's just what I need at the moment, a partner who a second time is letting his own emotions get the better of his professional detachment. He almost groaned in frustration.

Yet even as the depth of Derrymore's feelings surprised him, he struggled for some way to calm the younger man. Prospect of a brawl that would be sure to drawn attention, one way or the other, two members of the force in some ignominious quarrel over a young woman who might not care for either of them, was as ludicrous as it was likely to end in disaster – he was probably no match for Derrymore if it came to fisticuffs, might have to resort to real violence to subdue him.

It was at this stage that a trivial incident, so trivial to be also ludicrous, saved the situation. There was a clink, a sound of footsteps. Both men froze as a pale figure loomed out of the pre-dawn shadows. That it was only the milkman, leaving a line of bottles at the trade side door, brought them both back to their senses. When he had gone, whistling cheerfully but not without a curious glance or two in their direction, rather shamefacedly they climbed back into the car, where they sat in silence, the only noise the wipers occasionally clearing the windscreen.

Derrymore finally broke the impasse, as he so often did, to ask, 'So what's our next move?' His question was not factual this time. What he really was saying was that by going along with Sally's theories, encouraging her, the pair of you have forced my hand. It's put me in an awkward position. But the awkwardness wasn't all on his side. Although he might not know it yet, his unspoken accusation had some root in fact. Fortunately Reynolds was sufficiently in control of himself to have the sense not to admit it at the moment.

For Reynolds, this was no time for breast-beating or tearful confession. 'Let Sally sleep now,' was his abrupt advice. 'As soon as it's day, we persuade her to listen to reason. Then we go after our new suspects. Sally does need protection,' he added as once more Derrymore began to protest. 'If her theory's right (and as far as I'm concerned it's close enough not to quibble) she's already been singled out for attention. And you and I can't always be around; we've work to do.'

As Derrymore subsided, 'And there's no sense in bringing her back to the village,' the ex-inspector finished firmly, 'even though I know Mazie would be glad to have her. That'd be like using a tethered goat to attract attention.'

It was a chilly comparison, reminding both men of Reynolds' earlier talk of tigers. In fact, as Reynolds now went on to explain, seeking in this way to defuse the situation, the most frightening animal encounter he'd ever heard about was with a tigress which had attacked a young girl close to the victim's village. Somehow the girl had managed to get away. 'That night,' Reynolds went on, 'while she and her family were celebrating her good luck the tigress entered the village. It circled every hut, chose the one where the girl and her sister were cowering, broke in through the walls and snatched her away. So don't tell me tigresses, animal or human, can be distracted easily. As killers I've found they have one objective – that's to kill.'

An even more chilly observation.

By now it was past six on a Saturday morning. City life was beginning to stir. 'Time to be moving,' he said. 'Let's call a truce. We need to. We've got to work together, if this case is ever to be closed. After it,' he tried a grin, 'you can take as many swipes at me as you like. But for the moment it's business as usual. For both of us.'

Derrymore wasn't smiling. Letting that thought sink in, 'Get on the blower to Nicholls,' Reynolds next ordered briskly. 'Tell him what's happened. He can deal with the loose ends. Tell him that when we've settled Sally, we'll tackle Murdock ourselves.'

He swung himself out of the car. 'I'll do the settling,' he told Derrymore grimly. 'Remember what happened once before because we didn't act soon enough.' Not giving Derrymore chance to argue, he left him to reflect on that earlier incident in their partnership when they had hesitated too long. It should be sufficient a reminder to make any jealous suitor put his own feelings on hold.

Sally was already up, or perhaps she hadn't gone to bed either. She was looking none the worse for her lack of sleep as she let him in, but she was puzzled. 'What's the matter?' she started to say. 'Something's happened.'

Her awareness was alarming, coming too close to the truth. He shook his head. But when she changed her question to, 'What's brought you back then?' Reynolds' answer was abrupt. 'To knock sense into you, if I have to,' he said. 'We went over the reasons last night.'

She said, 'I'm not afraid.'

'The more fool you,' he finished bluntly. 'I am. At the moment, I'm afraid for every man, woman, and child in St Breddaford. But I'm afraid most of all for you. So either you get a police escort, or you go into hiding. Your choice.'

'And if I still don't agree?'

He eyed her. 'Well,' he said at last, 'you may not like the idea but Derry and I together are more than you can handle. I'll have you arrested for resisting a police officer. You can sue me afterwards from your police cell.' He added as she glared at him, speechless. 'At least you'll have an afterwards to do it in.'

He saw her anger at his high-handed methods, and for a moment thought he'd lost her. Then good sense came to the rescue. 'All right, you win,' she said, with her quick laugh. 'I don't fancy a police cell at the moment. And I suppose you've done the dirty work because you want to spare Derry getting in my bad books. Or,' she added as shrewdly, 'because you thought he'd be too soft and would back down if I said no. If you can stay on duty all night (don't bother to deny it, I saw you from the window) I'm not going to be stupid and ignore your kindness again. In fact,' and here surprisingly her eyes glistened although she was too proud to wipe them, 'I'll elect to stay indoors in my own place, thank you, with a policeman on guard if you say so. And I'll keep on with my reading. Who knows, I may come up with some other ideas.'

He heard her with relief, but what he was also hearing were the silent words that accompanied her unshed tears. They gave her away as if she'd said out loud, 'I've never met men who cared for me before.' It struck him with a pang again how true this was, and how true also Derrymore had been in accusing him of involving her in danger, no matter how unwittingly. Still feeling admiration for what he called her 'pluck', he said, 'Better still, finish my new manuscript for me. I have a feeling you'd be doing me a favour.'

She looked at him quickly. 'Oh no,' she said, with her wide generous smile, 'that's for you to do. But I have a suspicion that the next you write will be what you call a "real one", without any help from me.'

She held out her hand. 'A promise then,' she said as she laid it in his. It was brown and firm, small within his own. Once more he caught the look in her grey eyes as she glanced up at him. But all she said was, 'Remember, I always keep my promises.'

Back at the car, he would have given anything for a moment's privacy to analyse that look – and track down the meaning of that last statement which could have been mere confirmation of his recommendation, or a warning of deeper things. But to herself or him? And the brief little show of emotion earlier, so quickly over he hadn't had a moment to comment on it or use it to get through her guard . . . what was he to make of that?

With Derrymore in the car beside him, it seemed unfair to think of her at all. If he'd warned Derrymore to keep his personal feelings on hold so he should himself. Except all his training was to do just that – it was the characteristic that his ex-wife had hated most, and the one that had helped him live through her betrayal and treachery.

Giving himself a mental shake he turned to his partner and began the business of detection. And having, with Nicholls' permission, instructed the local policeman (who arrived with admirable promptness) to let no one in or out of Sally's flat, they left with a squeal of tires and a spurt of speed that set the car rocking, not Reynolds' usual style of driving, causing even Derrymore to brace himself.

Awakened abruptly from a good night's sleep, Nicholls was not as enamoured by their change of tactics as he might have been. Reynolds had the feeling that tolerance was running short. Calmly then, all the while driving as fast as he could along the narrow roads, he began to lay out the possible case against Jen Murdock, as discussed by him and Sally the previous night. After which, reverting to more mundane details, he pointed out too that of course they were still working on conjecture and had no proof. The last thing they wanted was to startle any suspect off; he and Derrymore would be the souls of tact when they handled Jen; for the moment they would focus merely on her 'social activities' while the team rounded up and grilled those so-called 'guests' again.

'And if you have another go at the Barkers, mother and son, you might be able to break their resistance,' he added persuasively. 'The same for Art Newcomb. As far as I know, no one's queried their exact relationship with Murdock, or, more to the point, linked her specifically with the crimes. The worst we've suspected her of is running some sort of sex parlour which served Mrs Barker with an alibi for her husband's death. And, dear God, for having started some smear campaign against me. She must be laughing up her sleeve.'

At that point Nicholls' howl of exasperation could be heard. 'Enough,' he begged. 'I understand. I accept. Get on with it. But if your sleuthing instincts are off target, remember we'll look a right set of fools, pounding after a middle-aged woman, more at home at a gossipy coffee morning than a killing frenzy.' At which Derrymore could scarcely repress a self-satisfied smile. Refraining from saying, 'I told you you'd gone too far this time,' he sat back and waited smugly to be proved right.

The early downpour had given Grange Manor a forlorn look and although the Mercedes was still parked alongside the waterlogged pots, no one answered the door. They tried peering through the downstairs windows but the red curtains were drawn, and the rear premises were securely locked and equally silent.

Baffled, they were about to leave, when a call from the team put Derrymore on full alert. Mrs Barker and son had been rounded up again, no trouble finding them, although their lawyer was screaming. Eden had actually been obliging enough to spend the night with his mother thus saving them the expense of dragging him back from his place of work. The bad news was that Newcomb was missing. His car was in the driveway but when they went to the house they found the front door unlocked. Inside there was evidence of preparations for departure, a suitcase on the bed, clothes tossed about at random, but still no sign of Newcomb. He must have done a flit on foot. Last night, by the looks of it. They were already checking on the trains and buses – what was happening their end?

Looking suitably chastened Derrymore passed on this news to Reynolds. Without the all-clear to continue Reynolds took the law into his own hands. Using a convenient paving stone he smashed a window, then climbed in.

Inside, everything looked normal, the sitting room tidy although the curtains were still drawn. The kitchen showed evidence of an evening meal, pots and dishes were left dirty by the sink and there was a half-eaten casserole on the table. Upstairs, however, none of the beds had been slept in, and although a dress was slung carelessly over a chair there was no sign of packing. One strange thing; there were many bedrooms which presumably in a single woman's house might not have been necessary. Each was completely furnished and, moreover, had a feel about it that could only be called 'used'. When Derrymore silently pointed to what looked like a whip and chains, their real function was made all too apparent. But where was Mrs Murdock, the Madame of this strange establishment?

'Done a flit too, possibly a combined job.' Reynolds' brisk tone hid his fury and concern. He was so sure he had her; even if only to shake the truth out of her. On the loose, God knows where she would turn up next. And Newcomb as her accomplice . . . 'What if Newcomb arrives here first?' he hazarded a guess. 'On foot. Persuades her to go with him. What about a taxi? Check the telephone, see if you get anywhere with that. See what times the trains leave.'

Back and forth went the inquiries, the lines buzzed. Before there was any agreement on what direction to take, two other pieces of evidence showed up.

The first was the finding of Jen Murdock's handbag, stuffed full of cash. It had fallen behind one of the chairs, and lay with its contents spilled over the carpet. The second was a passport, in the name of Lily Hanson, but bearing Jen Murdock's photo. And whatever else that meant no one in their right mind did a flit leaving passport and money behind.

'And look at the way the dress has been tossed aside.' Reynolds came back to the main bedroom, the one with the pink roses on the wallpaper and the pink frilly bedspread. 'Almost as if it's been thrown down in a hurry. Jen Murdock's too neat to have left it like that. So what's happened to her?'

Leaving the search of the house until later, they moved into the garden. Grange Manor might have been much altered and diminished over the years but the grounds were still extensive, and beyond the paved formal area there were stretches of woodland leading to a small stream that eventually fell into the sea several miles away. This part of the estate had been let run wild and the undergrowth was thick, in places so dense it resembled a jungle. Even in the rain it retained the faint purple sheen of massed bluebells, past their prime yet in these shaded areas still vaguely visible. If their search hadn't been so urgent they could have paused to enjoy the view. As it was the place was too much for two men on their own. It was only after they had been joined by others of the team, that they came upon their other major find – a figure huddled under a fallen tree trunk.

It must have been dragged there in a hurry for a trail of wet crushed ferns showed clearly on the house side of the tree and no attempt had been made to hide the body. It lay on its side, face down in the wet leaves and from the state of its suit had been there all night. And when later it was turned on its back, the thin red line around the lolling neck was horridly familiar. As was the look in the staring eyes, suggesting that Art Newcomb had died in a state of extreme terror.

After that the search for the missing woman intensified.

Nothing showed up throughout that long wet Saturday and it was not until early dawn, Sunday morning, that her whereabouts was discovered. It was a day of unexpected sun after so much rain and by now they had exhausted all leads at airports and ferries. Their search had brought them to the end of the property where, to their surprise, a wooden pagoda of Edwardian design sagged drunkenly beside the stream. From its rotting steps, beyond the last line of fencing and across several fields, these was a tantalizing glimpse of blue sea cupped between two high hills. Against the new fence which surrounded the outer perimeter, Jen Murdock was propped like a rag doll. She too must have been dragged there, but more time had been spent on 'arranging' her than had been given poor Newcomb.

She had been dead several days. Her brocaded gold housecoat was sadly stained by now, her feet stuck out in front of her with her high-heeled shoes still on them. But the shoes were perched askew on the wrong feet, and her make-up had been so thickly plastered on that, even after so much rain, the eyes still looked out from black circles and the round of her mouth was still ruby red like a grotesque parody of the smiley face in the drawings. A red line encircled her throat and on her lolling head the missing crown was set. Finally, as a last insult, a card had been pinned to her chest. They could just make out the stained words where the red ink had run. 'Thus perish all whores.' Its message was perhaps not so original as the ones they'd become used to, but nevertheless uncompromising.

'So where and when was she killed?' Reynolds' first thought after the horror sank in was that somewhere there must be signs of a struggle, two victims strangled, garotted rather, within hours of each other. This question was followed by a host of others. 'Why did Newcomb come here? Could he have killed her first, then later been murdered himself? In the same way, not likely.' And of course, most important of all, 'Who, in God's name has done these killings?'

The 'why' was more clear. 'As self-protection, most probably,' was Nicholls' logical pronouncement. 'Either because the murderer believed both had given away too much already, or the actual police inquiries had brought discovery too close.'

'Or,' Reynolds had recovered enough to explore other possibilities, 'they might have always been potential victims; it's only the time of execution that has been put forward. The homosexual and the whore, another bizarre coupling. And what was their real part in this whole affair?'

That too was a leading question – their link to the murderer. Their very deaths proved they must be linked in some fashion. But the murderer had left no visible clues. If the librarian had been killed on the Friday evening, as was now established, he must have come to Grange Manor after Jen Murdock was dead, her murder timed to the Thursday evening, perhaps after the meal she had prepared – there were dishes and cutlery for two people left in the sink.

And if there was no sign of a struggle, no sign of other crime such as robbery, it had to be assumed she knew the murderer, perhaps had been expecting him – hence the casserole and dishes.

The manner of death suggested similarities with the other murders. As before there were no fingerprints, no murder weapon, just the red marks around the neck. Strangest of all, after Murdock had been killed the murderer had known enough about her to strip off the dress she was wearing and exchange it for a housecoat. Reynolds had been right to think Jen herself would have been more careful how she left her clothes. And the mockery of the shoes, the exaggerated smiling face – suddenly Sally Heyward's analysis of sexual perversion again made sense.

Suspicion fell upon Murdock's 'guests'. With her true name to help them the team soon were able to trace her past. As had been suspected she had run a successful 'call girl' operation from London, had 'retired' probably to run a similar establishment in the country, with an essential difference. Apparently now relying on volunteers, she had culled her 'girls' from the ranks of young and bored wives, or divorcees, like Elsie; while the men, equally bored and rich, were more than ready to join in anything which helped fill their spare time.

As Nicholls and his team hammered these truths out, Reynolds concentrated on scouring the house and grounds again looking for other clues. 'There has to be a clue somewhere,' was his only excuse. 'No one, however smart, can continue to act under pressure without leaving some trace. That's all we need, one little trace to give us the connection.'

And he found not one but two eventually, beside the rotting pagoda where Jen Murdock's body had been so contemptuously laid out.

Reynolds and Derrymore had returned there to stand on its ruined steps and wonder why it had been built so far from anywhere, a real lover's retreat. Inside they had even found shreds of silk and net fabric at the windows, and the decaying remains of chairs and cushions. It was difficult to imagine the former inhabitants of the manor trekking all this way with their gramophones and picnic hampers, or more likely having their servants do the trekking, to lie on these cushions in what must have seemed like a tree house, in the breaks between the music listening to the sound of the stream and through the net curtains watching the far off blue sea.

'There's been an old road through here.' Derrymore's observation brought them back to earth. He had been leaning on the balcony, shading his eyes, when some unusual marks attracted his attention. Probably the rain had blurred them previously; now the unexpected sun caught on the edges of the indentations. 'Look, beyond the fence,' he shouted excitedly. 'And by gum, it's been used recently! See there, and there.'

Scrambling over the fence they could see what looked like the verge of a road, just visible under the splatter of mud and long-fallen leaves. Following it for a few yards to a bend they found even plainer evidence of fresh car tracks in the mud. If a car had come here that explained perhaps another puzzle: how Jen Murdock's body had been taken to this spot so far from the house. It also raised another possibility: that she might have been killed anywhere and merely her garments retrieved from her bedroom – again proof that she and her murderer knew each other well. But tire marks can be matched with cars! About to ring up the team on his mobile phone Derrymore was stopped by Reynolds who was still balanced astride the fence.

'This fencing,' he said slowly, as if he couldn't believe his eyes. 'What do you know about it?'

Derrymore stared at him as if he were mad. 'Fencing, sir?' he asked. 'Well, it's expensive for one thing. Must have cost the earth. It's newish, several years old, I'd say. Probably put in when Mrs Murdock bought the house. Why all the interest?'

'The name. Read the name out.' And as Derrymore obediently did both men suddenly stared at each other, their minds functioning at last as a team again. 'Stageways Sawmills, that's where Caddick works.'

'And where someone must have gone to find a place to hide the wedge.'

Reynolds swung himself off, excitement rising. 'I got a list of customers from them, remember,' he told the startled sergeant. 'But it only went a few months back. I should have asked for all their records. Although who would have thought anyone could have been so thorough as to plan a murder and its aftermath five years or more ago.'

That thought cooled his triumph. 'Come on, old son,' he added more soberly. 'There's work to do. With a little bit of luck this time we may have nailed the bastards.'

Reynolds had earlier been given the day-to-day accounts that the sawmill used to complete its orders for fences, gates, even rough-hewn garden furniture. Now, once more installed in the stuffy little office where the foreman, summoned from his Sunday lunch, usually worked, he asked for the books where the exact orders and payments were recorded.

This wasn't so difficult as he'd feared. The sawmill had only started making fencing about five years ago, and there had been few orders at first. One had been for a couple who wanted a vast amount quickly.

'Funny pair.'

The foreman's assessment after all this time suggested that he had found them difficult customers. 'The man seemed less interested in the proceedings than in wandering through the fir trees.' He jerked with his thumb. 'Had a row with Caddick who told him to bugger off. While the wife, who for some reason didn't want us to deliver, kicked up a tantrum, insisting on an independent carrier which she arranged herself.'

Reynolds' expectation, which had begun to sink at the prospect of more complications, soared to even greater heights at the next words. 'A very forceful lady. From somewhere near St Breddaford. Here's her name, a Mrs Sinclair. Know her?'

His voice trailed away as did Derrymore's first objection that Sinclair wasn't married. 'Of course he isn't.' Reynolds was on his feet and out the door. 'Come on.' He took the yard at a stride and had the engine started before Derrymore managed to jump inside the car. They spun past the startled manager and made for the road.

'You mean they know each other?' Derrymore was still trying to comprehend.

'More like knew each other from the start. Murdock comes here first and Sinclair follows.'

Reynolds drove at a corner, rounded it with a squeal of tires, pushed past a farm vehicle on a hill crest and dived down into the valley. 'Sinclair can't have known she gave his name,' he said. 'If he did, he was a fool to have allowed it. Another mistake. A real one. By God, it's come home to haunt him, hasn't it just. And if I'm right we've caught the tiger at last.'

He was right and wrong. They had the identity of the tiger but they hadn't caught him. When they got to his house Sinclair too was gone.

Chapter 16

Sinclair had gone, taking his car with him. Several neighbours (attracted by the police activity) confirmed having heard it splutter out one evening from the garage where he kept it behind the house. It was an old 'banger', they didn't know why he kept it, he only used it once a week or so, preferring to walk everywhere with his long-legged stride. This would have been at least three nights ago. Yes, it was Thursday because he had brought it back that evening and had spent the next day in his shop. On the Friday evening he had gone out in it again, early, and hadn't returned since. No, they hadn't thought much of it, and no, they hadn't seen anyone with him; as far as they knew no one ever visited the house. And they certainly had no idea of where he'd gone; he wasn't the sort of person of whom you asked questions. 'Kept to himself, a real quiet gentleman,' was the common verdict.

Reconstructing his movements the police came up with this scenario. Thursday was the day Reynolds and Derrymore had questioned Mrs Murdock. That evening Sinclair had presumably gone to Grange Manor, perhaps on her suggestion – her telephone calls showed she had rung his number at the shop and there was the meal waiting. He had killed her then, after eating what was in reality a 'last dinner'; had had time afterwards, or, since he may have returned early the next evening, perhaps had waited until then to arrange her body. On Friday he had spent his day as normal in his shop, had returned again to the manor, and after killing

Newcomb, who may or may not have been expected, had driven off, thus giving himself a good day and a half lead. (And as Reynolds now recalled, since he never opened his shop at the weekend he wasn't likely to have been missed until the following Monday or later.)

Setting up new checks on roads out of Cornwall, and reinstating the previous ones at airports and ferry points to prevent his leaving the country (although given the age and state of his car, it was felt he couldn't have got far without being spotted) Nicholls turned out everyone to search for positive clues to his whereabouts, hoping along the way to find some record of his criminal activity.

The nature of the understanding between him and Jen Murdock, and Newcomb, the motivations behind their actions, were still obscure – and the exact relationship between a bachelor scholar and a whore, whom no one even guessed had been acquainted, underscored the difficulties. Yet, knowing in part the sort of man Sinclair was, Reynolds was convinced he would have kept an accounting of his actions somewhere. Call it a hunch, he knew it was part of Sinclair's scholarly background. He almost heard Sinclair's mocking laugh as he polished his spectacles, quoting as was his habit, 'Seek and ye shall find.'

Reynolds had no idea what form this accounting would take; he couldn't say exactly what he was looking for and it said a great deal for his reputation that Nicholls went along with him, even offering to have every piece of furniture, every book, every bit of paper taken out and searched.

They started with the house, combed through it, a modest place in one of the ugly new estates that surrounded St Breddaford, built in the heydays of the eighties and regretted ever since. Reynolds remembered Sinclair's scornful dismissal of it as not up to the taste and standard of his own home. It was neat but somehow had an unlived-in look, nothing personal on display except a few books and a collection of withered plants (presumably given him by Miss Penwithen). They found files in plenty, stacked and sorted in different coloured folders, labelled in neat, clear printing, not the usual scholarly scrawl, confirming Reynolds' assessment of the man's character. But nothing more incriminating than bank and tax statements, the former detailing the small payments from his pension that he had complained about, the latter always paid on time and properly documented. And nowhere any scrap of evidence that he had claimed or intended to claim insurance for the burnt books – an oversight, or a deliberate ploy?

Sinclair was a hoarder. He kept everything, from bills for food and wine going back to his university tenure, to out-of-date laundry lists. And then there were the letters, vast quantities of them, also arranged in chronological order, an on-going correspondence with former students (again Reynolds remembered Sinclair's pride in their keeping in touch). Such precise attention to long-gone details, such meticulous logging of every facet of his life, convinced Reynolds anew he was on the right track. If Sinclair were involved, somewhere he would have kept a record of events, catalogued as neatly. And if not in his house, then certainly in the bookshop, among the books where his real heart and mind were fixed.

Abandoning their part in the house search he and Derrymore took half the team to tackle the shop, not before facing a barrage of questions from the local press and TV who had been alerted to the new murders and were instructed to follow every police move.

'What exactly are you looking for?' 'Why aren't you out searching for clues at the murder site?' 'Does this mean the murderer's found?'

The questions came fast and furious, bordering on the

hostile. Tempted to tell the media to bugger off and leave well alone, Reynolds curbed his temper long enough to suggest that police work would go faster if they weren't forced to answer silly questions. Inspector Nicholls was actually in charge of the case. Nicholls would hold a conference in due course (here Nicholls shuddered at the thought) and yes, he himself had been asked to work on the case contrary perhaps to public opinion . . . At that, a faint cheer went up, a voice shouted, 'Good for you!' One solitary voice of approbation, perhaps, the one voice in the wilderness, but it gave Reynolds heart. Two more murders were bad enough, he didn't want them laid on his conscience. But without Jen Murdock to keep gossip boiling, and without Sinclair to stir it up, perhaps it would die down altogether . . . a more pleasant prospect.

The shop was as tidy as the house, not a book or paper out of place, the coffee cups, sugar pot and milk jug laid out in readiness for potential customers, proof perhaps that again Sinclair had acted on impulse. Or as Nicholls had suggested, had been driven to murder by the recklessness of his accomplice, or by fears that the police net was closing in and he would be implicated, despite all his careful planning. It was only when Reynolds had climbed into the infamous loft, surprisingly still stuffed with wrapping paper, that he found what he was to call the last coincidence.

There was less wrapping than a cursory glance suggested, as if it had been spread about deliberately to look more than it was. And if Miss Penwithen was right and Sinclair had emptied it prior to the fire, what was he hiding underneath? Getting rid of it was a nuisance, until again he remembered Miss Penwithen's description of how the fire had been started. Carefully examining each scrap of paper first, he had the loft gradually emptied by the simple means that Sinclair himself had used – tipping the contents down the ladder into the yard beneath.

As the first pieces of cardboard and wrapping floated earthwards, a local reporter, a real wag, who had stationed himself beside the corner of the cordoned-off alley, spotted it and shouted his comments to his fellow villagers, crowding behind him, 'Do they expect to find the doctor rolled inside, like Ali Baba?' the most printable.

This witticism roused a howl of laughter; impossible to explain that it wasn't Sinclair they were looking for, but what they hoped Sinclair had left behind. Gritting their teeth they endured the laughter and continued with their search. Laughter was at least as good an antidote to shock as depression, and they could afford to be laughed at if only Reynolds' last hunch was right.

And after the loft was empty and the old floorboards swept clean, in places actually lifted where the wood looked worn, they found what they were looking for. It was tucked behind the rafters which came down to the floor at one side, and if they had known where it was they could have reached it easily without all the extra work. As it was, the discovery came as they were on the point of giving up – and if nothing else, finding it vindicated Reynolds' tenacity.

It consisted of a series of black leather notebooks, arranged in chronological order, again dating back to Sinclair's university days. Each book dealt with a separate year, stamped on the cover, like some journal or old-fashioned memoir. The covers themselves were well worn but clean; no dust or cobwebs on them; they must have been consulted frequently. Inside, they found an extraordinary record, all compiled in the same precise way and written in the same precise printing.

The whole could have formed work sheets for a play or novel, such as Reynolds himself sometimes kept. To

Reynolds, the word 'dossier' fitted better, a clandestine account of innocent people's secrets. Starting with his own students, perhaps even in the beginning listing their characteristics as a way to help him understand them, over the years Sinclair had honed this skill to compile a devastating account of the movements and behaviour of a great many people, focused deliberately on things no one would want anyone else to know.

The last books concerned St Breddaford, and were arranged alphabetically. Here Sinclair had found his real inspiration. With deadly accuracy he noted the weaknesses and foibles of his neighbours, amassed gossip and collected information about the villagers as carefully as any police investigation would, from the most important to the least, from the Alsops' little daughter, June, (over whose expected May Day crowning the Varcoes had been so bitter) to Matty Tamblin's boyfriends, and her mother's indulgence towards them. Derrymore's name was there, several pages devoted to him and his mother, but he got off lightly compared with Frank Barker (whose domineering nature apparently rankled). Jen Murdock, under her real name of Lily Hanson, was worth half a book, the police could call off their search into her background, their work had been done for them.

As Reynolds had surmised, Sinclair and Murdock had known each other for a long time. He had been a regular client at her London establishment, where he was far enough away from his usual haunts to avoid fear of recognition. He catalogued carefully, with scholarly detachment, his own growing dependence on her for gratifications of his sexual needs which he failed to find in normal relationships, and when she moved to Grange Manor and suggested he come too, he did.

For her part she liked what she called his 'keeping tabs' on people; spying and voyeurism were part of her trade. And as she grew older, he listed as detachedly her growing obsession with her fading looks, and the effect it had. 'Nothing surpasses the anger of a fallen beauty,' he wrote. 'It is easy for a beautiful woman who is no longer beautiful, to hate. Envy consumes her; it eats and twists her into a caricature of herself.'

Likewise the details of Art Newcomb's criminal record with all its nasty innuendos were meticulously recorded – along with his almost puppy-like attachment to Jen Murdock, who amused herself with him, as she was to amuse herself with Rab Tremayne. In short here was a source book for every piece of village scandal, true or false, for the last few years, enough material to set a dozen or more feuds flaring – since Sinclair's retirement to St Breddaford he must have devoted hours to the task.

Ironically, it was one which in the right hands might even have had some literary value, the internal workings of a village and its environment as appeared personally to the author who now lived there. Except the personal touch was lacking. As time passed, the records degenerated into a cruel and ruthless list, whose only function was to cause harm in as cruel and ruthless a way as possible, when the time was deemed right – and whose author's own ability to collect and analyse began to reveal a precision bordering on obsession itself.

But when had the time been deemed right? Even here, motivation was lacking. In the few instances where Sinclair did feel himself wronged (by Frank Barker, for example, whose bank had refused him a loan; by Miss Penwithen, whose gift of plants was construed as lady-of-the-manor patronage) these incidents were recorded with the same mild disinterest that Reynolds had noted previously (although the fact that the perpetrators had themselves become eventual victims was bound to be important in any legal case). About to point this out and to suggest that another search should be started for what he felt must also be hidden somewhere – that is, a record of the exact details of what had been done and why and how, Reynolds was suddenly silenced. For in one instance only had Sinclair allowed his true feelings to pour out. And that concerned Reynolds himself.

'My dear life.' Derrymore, who'd happened to pick up this section first, was clearly taken aback. He put the volume down and unconsciously wiped his hands on his trousers, as if all this deliberate cataloguing of village gossip made him feel dirty.

'He's certainly got you to a T as far as description goes,' he went on, trying with clumsy tact to pass over the relevant pages. 'But only on the surface, like. Most of what he says is so contorted it's as if he's talking about someone else. And guess why he hates you – because you're successful with your writing and he's not!'

Derrymore might take that in his stride, but for Reynolds it was a strange and bitter blow. He had been fond of the professor; now he admitted he had secretly been pleased that Sinclair, a university professor of literature no less, had liked his books enough to stock them in his shop (although on thinking their discussions over, he saw that Sinclair had never actually said he liked the books, merely insisted that they served to attract customers). It now appeared that until he had come to the village, Sinclair had not even known about Reynolds' writings, detective fiction being beneath his notice. Once made aware of them, and their author, he was affronted.

The catalogue of grievances was long. Reynolds had not shown him the respect he should; Reynolds had not frequented the shop or been drawn into Sinclair's sphere of influence; he had not even had the decency to thank Sinclair for stocking his works.

In these secret notes, Reynolds' books, Reynolds himself, all became the butt for Sinclair's sarcasms. The novels were scrutinized with scathing criticism; somehow, the method not revealed, details of Reynolds' personal life were raked up; his failed marriage, his retirement from the force, all were spelled out in grotesque and inaccurate hyperbole that didn't disguise the mockery – although it revealed the real fount of the smear campaign against the ex-inspector. It also showed who had the real knowledge to pick out those apt quotations.

Nothing was glossed over, even the first meeting after the fire when Sinclair recorded with glee his little comments to throw Reynolds off his trail. His remarks, 'I hate heights,' and 'I'm hopeless with my hands,' had apparently amused him so much he mentioned them several times. He was so sure that he had given the impression of an artistically inclined wimp that he gloated over his actual physical prowess; he was a good hill-hiker, proud of his endurance; he was a good shot, he owned a handgun.

And he noted with equal glee the slip he had made that Reynolds had not noticed, the mentioning of Caddick as a suspect, for example, when Caddick's name hadn't yet been released – Reynolds wasn't so clever a policeman as he boasted, look at the way he had come begging for clues, pretending to take him out to lunch as a favour; look at the way he had gone off at a tangent about shoplifters . . . Here was obsession turned to madness.

There was one interesting anomaly. With that bitter irony which Reynolds had noticed in the doctor on other occasions, Sinclair seemed to take delight in goading himself as well. How is it, he asked repeatedly, that a man like myself, devoted to literature as I am, a professor of English, can be bettered in my own field by an ex-policemen without sensibility or education, a mere hack who panders to public taste? And what's more, makes a fortune out of it, while I have to live on a pittance, all that I'm worth after my years of hard labour devoted to learning. The bitterness was acute, as well as the sense of failure.

But it wasn't only Reynolds and his writings that came in for condemnation. So did Reynolds' friends and acquaintances, such as Derrymore (his 'toady' Sinclair called him); and Nicholls (his 'puppet'). And his women. Among the real and invented was Sally Heyward.

Sally's background had been scrupulously researched and her former relationship with her notorious lover made much of. The meeting with Murdock at the library (where Sally was noted as 'hanging about indeterminately, as if waiting for someone, or as if making up her mind' – another shrewd guess) was recounted in all its sordid detail, as was the chance encounter with Reynolds himself. Their parting on the village green was given more than its share of unsavoury and vulgar colouring, as if Sinclair, like some old woman, had been peeping from behind lace curtains, although it must actually have been from his shop's bow window that he'd done his spying. All this made uncomfortable reading, but true to their agreement, Derrymore made nothing of it. What he thought of it, Reynolds hated to imagine!

The last entry, only a couple of days ago, was devoted entirely to Sally. It told how Sinclair had almost 'caught the little bitch. Had her hooked as she stood outside Penwithen's empty cottage, obviously dying to go inside – and I'd have helped her in more senses than one, if Bantree hadn't wobbled into the picture.'

It was that account that sent Reynolds and Derrymore leaping for the phone.

In the course of the last hours, Reynolds hadn't had much time to think of Sally, and presumably Derrymore hadn't either. There certainly had been no moment for light telephone calls or friendly visits, and for what it was worth, their 'pax' had remained in effect, simply because they had been so preoccupied. If Derrymore had thought anything it must have been with relief that at least she was safe from Jen Murdock. And if now, because of her exposure to Sinclair's hate and envy she appeared at risk once more, he should have congratulated Reynolds for having the foresight to keep her under police protection – a generous gesture to a rival he could afford – until he and Reynolds heard with sinking feeling, that following the news of Jen Murdock's death, Sally's police escort had been withdrawn that morning. 'No need to keep him on,' the local police station reported cheerfully, 'seeing she'm dead and gone.'

They were right in one way. But hopelessly, woefully, wrong in another. Jen Murdock might be dead; Robert Sinclair was on the run. And had taken Sally Heyward with him. A message on the table in her flat showed that he had been there, and why. And the passage, ripped from Reynolds' book, was a quotation from one of those cases which the ex-inspector had most dreaded from the start.

Sally had found the first police officer pleasant company and in his way considerate. While he lounged on the sofa, reading a sports magazine, she had prepared a meal, got on with the rearranging of her flat, and finally returned to her reading of Reynolds' books, more for pleasure than work now.

Her job was done. And by and large she was gratified with the result. Reynolds at least had seen what she was driving at. Warming to the thought of his approval, she almost felt Miss Penwithen's as well. She had done her bit to help the old lady; she felt Miss Penwithen would have agreed with her conclusions and wouldn't have shied away from them.

As for Derrymore and his reaction, it was much as she

expected. Not that she blamed him, it was the way he was; it was part of the old-fashioned ideas that she liked him for. Or had liked him. Here was the crux of the dilemma that she still couldn't solve and which had led her to blurt out her final indiscretion.

But saying one kept promises was easy compared with the actual keeping. Derry for example wouldn't see the difficulty. He wasn't a complicated man; it would never cross his mind that once you had shown your attachment to a person, it could change.

When they had first met her previous experience had left her jaded and suspicious. Derry's being the opposite had seemed a life-line. And Mazie had seemed the mother she'd always wanted, not a brittle lady of fashion, too busy to bother with a growing daughter. It hadn't yet occurred to her she might be lucky, that there might be men who could be honest and yet her equal. Derry's own simplicity was the healing agent which enabled her to see this – another complication which he wouldn't understand, but which she now knew Reynolds would.

She didn't mean to use Derry and his mam. That was the last thing she wanted; she recoiled in horror from the idea. But she couldn't be flustered into pretending she was something she knew she wasn't; or smothered by protection. That wasn't right either, for anyone.

The first officer was replaced with a second and then a third, each of them young enough to be her brother and presumably good at their work. Nothing dramatic happened; she slept or did not sleep that night, bothered by these personal thoughts which occupied her much more than any fear of her own safety. For the first time, she didn't dream. She woke in the morning to the smell of breakfast and coffee. 'Comes with the job,' the third told her with a wink. She fiddled through the Sunday morning and was quietly preparing to go mad if she couldn't escape into the open, away from her own thoughts, when the call from headquarters released her and her guardian from the same imprisonment.

After his departure she had immediately gone out. Quite uncharacteristically, for once using money which her parents sent regularly (out of pride she always refused to accept their cheques, but because she could not stop them arriving, she had given up protesting and kept them stuffed in a drawer) she indulged herself with what her mother would call 'a wild spree' of grocery shopping, as much as was possible on Sunday afternoon, with the idea, only partly formed, of inviting Reynolds to come for a victory dinner. Laden with food parcels she had returned to her flat to find a familiar figure standing on the doorstep.

'My, my,' Sinclair said, his eyes sparkling with fun. 'We've been busy. Let me help you in.' And without giving her the chance to ask how he had known where to find her or wonder why he was there he had taken the packages from her and followed her inside. 'Very nice too,' he had commented as she invited him to sit down and rather crossly (for he was the last person she wanted to entertain) offered him tea. 'And busy with your investigations still, I see.'

He leaned forward to turn over the books he himself had given her, riffling through the pages. As he did so, the list she had originally made to give Reynolds fluttered to the floor. He picked it up and surveyed it, his mouth pursed. 'Ah me,' he said with almost a sigh, 'I thought you were intelligent. You can always tell an intelligent woman,' he went on. 'Among my students I suppose I could count them on one hand. But they all had something in common. They were inquisitive. It's that familiar little feminine vice that gave them their extra spark. I was right in sensing it in you. And now if you don't mind, we'll be leaving.'

Before she could ask what he meant, or jump up, he had come towards her. 'Don't disappoint me,' he said, his voice scarcely changing but something about his eyes behind the spectacles making her cold. 'After my compliments you wouldn't want to act out of character, would you? We'll just go quietly together, no fuss, no noise.'

The glint of the gun was unexpected. She couldn't picture him with such a weapon. And his grip was surprisingly strong as he wound the cord about her wrists, unexpectedly deft and quick.

The light shone through the black hairs on the back of his hands. She suddenly thought of the twine that he had tipped so innocently out of his pockets when he had emptied them; she remembered the hands about her neck in the darkness of the lane and felt herself go limp as she had then, as if in a nightmare when she could neither move nor scream.

'That's it,' he said, as if he felt her reaction. He had jerked her close to him and was already tying the gag through her mouth, yanking it tight with a vicious knot. 'Escaped me then, didn't you, you little flirt. And escaped me again outside Miss Penwithen's house. Almost had you then, if that fool Alf Bantree hadn't broken the attraction. But got you now, haven't I? Caught good and proper,' he added, as he pulled her towards the door. 'Let's take a ride together where no one can find us. My car awaits.' And he gave his little laugh.

She tried to resist him then, breaking from the dream-like trance to kick and struggle. To no avail. He let her fight herself, like a fish on a line, holding the end of the cord away from himself. And when she was exhausted, with the gun jammed against her ribs, he said 'But before we go we'll leave a little something to let your two lovers quarrel over its meaning.'

And he ripped out the page he had chosen and laid it on top of the other papers. 'From *The Sacred Tree*,' he told her.

'Remember it. It should fit very well, don't you think?'

And saw from the expression in her eyes that she did indeed remember, had just finished reading the book, the story of the hostage and what had been done to him at the end.

Chapter 17

The police were soon on their track. By Sunday evening they had traced Sinclair's car to Truro, the old grey Ford with the rusting bodywork and damaged exhaust pipe parked outside Sally's flat that afternoon (to the anger of the woman next door, whose parking place it was).

And if he had come to Truro expressly to get her, this suggested he might have been in the city, under cover somewhere, since Friday, when he had killed Newcomb, perhaps had already been there when Reynolds and Derrymore had arrived. Seeing them on guard later he may have driven away to wait for them to leave (incidentally suggesting that Reynolds' instinct had been right, and his talk of hunting tigers, in retrospect, horribly significant).

Early on Monday they had Sinclair's hiding place. His picture in the papers and on TV alerted his unsuspecting hosts at the small bed and breakfast he'd stayed at. He'd phoned first thing Saturday morning, they explained, arriving soon afterwards, from up-country he said, touring Cornwall on holiday. He had even asked if he could put his car in their garage to see to its brakes – as good a way as any of keeping it out of sight, as smooth and cool as if this too had been planned. He'd stayed one night, leaving early on the Sunday morning, apparently then parking for several hours close to the river (legitimate but secluded). He must have spent all day Saturday and Sunday watching Sally's flat, had followed her on foot when she finally left, and only returned with his car as she returned.

Clever, collected. In control. The mastermind. Proof that if in the past anyone had been guilty of excessive overkill, he wasn't to blame. Yet, as Reynolds had once pointed out, under pressure even the most orderly minds may make mistakes. In the wastebin of his cramped rented room were found the bits and pieces of his stay, the small bottle of whisky, empty; the crumbs and wrappers of store-bought food; the crushed Sunday paper with the first revelations of the murder at Grange Manor – and at the bottom, a stained and blotched map. Of the moors. With the site of poor Tremayne's cottage marked in red.

By now the gap between hunted and hunters had narrowed; they must be only a few hours behind. Yet in those hours was all the time in the world for the victim to play the part that Sinclair intended her to play. It was with the same growing feeling of dread that Reynolds led the team towards the cottage, to find it empty. But they were on the right track, Sinclair's car was parked nearby; he and his prisoner had been there.

Besides the pale orange scarf snagged on a wire fence and identified by Derrymore as Sally's, the two used mugs and plates, the only dishes owned by Tremayne (although whether Sally had actually eaten or drunk from them was doubtful) Sinclair had left one last thing: the missing book in which Reynolds was sure he must have kept all the notations of the crimes.

It was like the others, the covers black leather. It was even labelled, the writing small and neat, the scholarly diary of all the events that had rocked St Breddaford this past month. But it was empty. The inside pages had been ripped away.

Reynolds had seized it eagerly. He'd banked on its existence; it would vindicate him and provide the last of the missing clues. Finding it worthless was a bitter disappointment; he could imagine only too well Sinclair's satisfied smile.

He had hidden the fear that it might also tell him what Sinclair had already done with Sally, or what he planned to do. As he hurled it to the floor in disgust Derrymore broke in, 'But what the devil does it matter? What's important is where he's gone now. Why doesn't he contact us direct and tell us where Sally is?'

He didn't seem to have grasped the situation thoroughly, for he went on to say, 'If she's his hostage, what's he waiting for?'

He fingered the scarf, drawing it over and over through his big hands, turning on Reynolds and Nicholls as if they were the enemy. 'Why the hell isn't he using her to bargain with?'

The words died on his lips. He seemed to read the answer at last in their silence. 'You mean,' he brought out, 'Sinclair doesn't want to get away. He left that map deliberately for us to find. Just as he left his car and this book and scarf. He wants to be found. And her with him.'

And again silence was his answer.

His outburst was natural. The long-drawn-out search had been hard on him and he had taken the map as the one bright light. It had been hard to creep up on the cottage, hoping to find her there. When he spotted the car and the scarf he'd paid no attention to Reynolds' instructions, had bolted forward.

'Sinclair's mad,' he now said, quiet himself. 'Flaming mad.' It was as if this made things better. At least it showed what they were dealing with. Once more he turned to Reynolds. 'So how are we to stop him? In this fog they could be anywhere.'

His voice choked, as if the fog had come into the house and was smothering him.

The other members of the team had all crowded into the room by now after searching the sheds and surrounding fields, without success. The cottage suddenly was overwhelmed by people, all its private secretiveness spilled open under their inquisitive eyes. But perhaps it had already been spoiled; the previous police search had ruthlessly stripped it bare of all its quaint and unexpected charm.

'Don't be too hasty.' Reynolds made himself answer logically, although he had to steel himself not to push everyone outside. The sense of being overwhelmed, of being suffocated, was so intense that like Derrymore he felt the fog was smothering him. 'Get out,' he wanted to snarl.

He had already anticipated Derrymore's reaction, but being older, could hold his anger and disappointment in check. Besides, as Sally's 'official' friend Derrymore had the right to show his feelings. Reynolds had no rights at all. He also had one extra piece of knowledge carried with him like a hidden knife-wound: among those present he alone knew what outcome was intended, had known it from the moment he'd read the ripped-out page in Sally's flat. For all his claiming he didn't remember what he'd written after it was finished, he remembered this.

If they didn't catch Sinclair it was more than possible he would act out his part from the book, scene by scene. The knowledge sickened Reynolds; it was enough to paralyze him. But he had learned never to give up trying until every trick has been played. And a criminal who bases his crime on some previous one cripples his own initiative, in that the end is known before it actually happens. Life doesn't have to mirror fiction, he told himself. If only there's a clue to where Sinclair has taken his victim. He had to think of Sally impersonally as 'the victim'. He could deal with that.

'If he's mad,' he now said slowly, thinking things through, 'we don't have much control. He'll do what he wants to do in his own way and time. Kill her gradually, then himself. That's what happened in the book.'

He stared at his listeners. 'The book I wrote,' he told them. '*The Sacred Tree*. The one I'm responsible for. The one he's copying. But he may not be mad enough to do it straight away. He may want to savour his joke first. His own writings tell us he likes jokes.'

He picked up the empty cover and struck his hand upon it. 'My guess is he's testing us, seeing if we're capable of finding his hiding place.'

He was trying to sound convincing, raising their spirits and his. 'If he's deliberately led us here, then it's possible he'll keep to the moors. He's left his car; he has to go on foot. Although it won't be easy, not in this fog, not with a prisoner in tow, he's already boasted of his experience in hill hiking. But,' he paused for effect, 'he can't squat long in the open. He'll have to go under cover.'

They were listening, even Derrymore. And speaking in this professional way brought them all back on line. 'My guess is he's found some den or shelter among the rocks or tors; otherwise the moor is open land. Being the sort of man he is he may have already equipped the site. And the most likely person to have told him where to go is Rab himself. I think he's pried enough out of Tremayne to discover where he went.'

He could see hope now in all the eyes watching him. 'I may be wrong,' he wanted to shout, 'don't expect the impossible, I'm not a miracle-maker.' Men who had seen him conjure up Miss Penwithen's death from nowhere expected miracles.

Exasperated, he turned back to Derrymore. 'Think,' he said. 'Those places Rab Tremayne used to go to, do you remember where they are?'

Derrymore shook his head. 'No,' he said, 'I told you I never went with him. I only know he used certain places for certain reasons, to find certain things and . . .'

'What things?'

'Well,' Derrymore was trying to concentrate. 'Sometimes

he trapped rabbits. Or caught pheasants in the Duchy estates. And,' he spoke quickly now, stumbling over words, 'he picked berries, worts and so on, except they're found everywhere. But my mam might know. He used to bring her presents.'

Mazie had been listening to the radio. She sat without moving, her hair unbrushed and her clothes dragged on anyhow so she didn't even know her cardigan was inside out. When neighbours came to the door to commiserate or offer comfort, she didn't open it. It was as if a coldness had overwhelmed her, she felt she would never get warm again.

It had been bad enough when Derry and Sally had been attacked, and Miss Penwithen killed. Next to the day her husband had died that had been the worst. But the effect on her had been intensified by Sally's reaction. If Sally had been so upset then what would she feel about Cornwall now? Surely she would have nothing more to do with St Breddaford, with Mazie or with Derry. And if her kidnapper was what they said, a madman, would she even survive to feel anything?

She had no tears left. She had been to Chapel yesterday as she always did, but for once in her life she had no prayers. God seemed to have deserted her. Like old man Tremayne, she thought, I have gone into the wilderness and left all that I believed behind. If God spared my Derry when he was so ill in hospital, I did not ask for his life to have hers taken instead.

When Derry rang her, a strained voice, old, almost as he would sound when he reached her age, she hardly recognized him. He spoke of gifts. She could think of none. Rab Tremayne was dead too, all were dead or dying. God took; He no longer gave.

'Mazie.' It was Reynolds speaking. 'Help us. What sort of presents did Rab give you? Could you tell where they came from?'

She heard him talking in the soothing way she always associated with him, the sort of voice that inspires confidence and suggests all will be well. It loosened her tongue. 'Eggs,' she said, 'wrapped in fern. Flowers.'

She forced herself to think back to happier days when the world moved in its ordered seasons and there were no dreadful secrets. 'Iris,' she said, 'and violets. And once, something special, wild orchids that grow only in one place.'

She heard the excitement, contained yet urgent. 'On Grey Tor,' she said, 'the southern side. In a dell beneath the rocks. My husband took me there before we were married. Rab shouldn't have picked them, I suppose, but he must have remembered me speaking of them.'

In Rab's cottage, Reynolds was beckoning for a map, was spreading it, was stabbing at the contours that indicated the steep cliffs of the tor. As the crow flies not far from where they were, due east in fact. Much longer by road. A pile of rocks, a small speck on the map, but wild, remote. And the only lead they had.

Even on clear days moorland can be treacherous; there are unexpected bogs and gullies, steep dips and sudden ravines. And then there are the tors themselves, outcrops of granite that dominate the landscape, now all hidden in dense mist. If Sinclair hadn't killed Sally already and if Reynolds' theory held, Grey Tor was as remote a site as any. In this weather it would be a devil to reach. As they converged upon it, a convoy of rattling cars as close behind each other as they could along the fog-bound roads, Reynolds too tried to pray that he was right, and they had made the right choice. And more importantly, that Sinclair, who had led them deliberately to Rab's hut, would not anticipate their tracking him so soon.

In the cars intercoms buzzed as Nicholls called in more reinforcements from further afield; there was talk of helicopters if the fog lifted, but for the moment Reynolds had vetoed that idea. He didn't want to scare Sinclair into breaking his pre-planned routine. He sensed that would be disaster.

Sally's parents had arrived, her father rich enough to pay any ransom price if his daughter could be saved. They all knew now it wasn't ransom money Sinclair wanted. He had gone beyond hostage-taking into some fantasy world of his own making.

They passed through the villages which bordered the east edge of the moor, where police had already searched every house and farm in case Sinclair had hidden there. The moors in general had been cordoned off after the finding of Sinclair's map, not only to prevent him from breaking out but, as importantly, to prevent hikers or farmers wandering into his path – although in these worsening conditions there were few who would venture out.

Reynolds could have told them these efforts were a waste of time. They might flush Sinclair out on foot; he wouldn't stir from his den otherwise. He would let them dig him out, delight in it, waiting to the last moment when they were upon him to do what he had to do. It was all part of his predetermined plan.

So the onus would be on them to find him, without much help from any modern equipment, in fog that thickened by the moment, patches of it so dense it streamed through their hands like strands of smoke. The odds were stacked against them, in his favour; how he must be chuckling over that.

In Reynolds' book, the killer had hidden himself and his victim in the same way. Except his lair had been in a maze of sordid city streets. They had ringed the killer then, moved inwards street by street. He had always been one step ahead, leaving his frightful evidence behind as lure. First the lopped off ear, then the finger, then the entire right hand . . . Even with all the help of modern tracking devices, cars, metropolitan policemen trained to deal with the complexities of modern living, they had not caught him until it was too late.

To Reynolds, newly appointed to his position on the force, the messages had seemed to ask for help for the murderer as well as the victim. Stop me, he thought they pleaded. But that was when he was young and inexperienced. Since then he had come to accept that men who are mad are often mad only in one separate part of themselves; in everything else they function as normal. Like stricken tigers, their killing instincts are sharpened by physical, or in their case, mental impairment.

Nicholls and Derrymore had listened to Reynolds' reasoning and Nicholls at least accepted it. He had taken the responsibility for ordering in the special team; his forehead wrinkled more than ever with worry, he had helped formulate the plan of campaign, ill at ease himself in this rural hinterland which held more terrors for him than any urban slum. He was a practical man, however, and knew when to cut his losses. If their search didn't end in success today he would give up. Again, that was something else on Reynolds' mind.

Derry was another matter. What he felt when Reynolds openly accepted responsibility for the effects of his book was impossible to judge. Perhaps he felt justified in his original condemnation of Reynolds, and in his subsequent disapproval of Reynolds asking Sally to decode Sinclair's use of his books. After Derry's initial outcry he kept his thoughts to himself. But he had asked to be a member of the assault team, insisted on it, partly because as he himself said simply, 'I'm trained for it,' which was true. But there were other reasons and although he did not mention them Reynolds sensed them from his looks and subsequent behaviour.

Not that he said anything untoward; to the contrary he seemed to have shrunk into his clothes, as if energy had drained out of him. But the quietness with which he stared out, his vacant expression, not exactly hostile but rather indifferent to all that was going on around him, indicated the strain he was under.

His attitude worried Reynolds. He guessed that like Sally, Derrymore needed to be doing something; he couldn't sit idly by and let others take over. But for once he had lost faith in Derrymore's judgement. He would have preferred to leave Derry behind, safely out of the way. If he was right, and God help him, he hoped that he was not, he didn't want Derrymore to see what he feared would be seen. And if he was wrong he still wasn't sure how Derrymore would react under pressure. He accepted without question that Derrymore would not spare him, would have the right to hound him unmercifully. Yet remembering Derrymore's break from cover at the cottage, he was afraid for him. He didn't want Derrymore in danger too, for Mazie's sake as much as Derrymore's own. And if he felt the responsibility of Derrymore's anguish he didn't want to be held responsible for his death.

Funnily enough he never thought of himself in the same light. It didn't occur to him, for example, that he too might break. He was too old for that; life had made him too hard. However deeply he felt, even in this most terrible situation, he had not lost the ability to put his personal and private feelings to one side when he had to. Some people might call that a virtue, he thought bitterly, but it had never brought him thanks before and had always cost him dear in the end.

They had reached the section of the road where it petered out into grass and heather, and parked beside the other cars, manned by the special squad. There weren't many of them, a mere dozen or so, but they were the best, used to the most gruelling conditions; this pile of rocks would be child's play – if they could find them! All were armed except himself. As a civilian he didn't have a gun. He noted how Derrymore cradled his, checking and rechecking it endlessly, as if already Sinclair was in his sights. Or possibly Reynolds; again the ex-inspector couldn't help remembering Mazie's warnings.

The new arrivals had spread maps on the front of their cars, prior to studying them. These had been rustled up from some village shop which saw its whole season's stock vanish in an instant. Dividing into three small groups, each under a separate leader, they now began to move off, swinging over fences and down narrow lanes to take various routes to the tor, where they would meet before making a united assault on what they assumed was Sinclair's stronghold. What would happen after that, how Derrymore would take the result, hung in the balance. They still had a few hours of light but in this mist neither day nor night really mattered.

Nicholls went with one section; Reynolds another, keeping Derrymore with him. As they came out on the moors free of a plantation of fir trees which had blocked their direct approach, more for the sergeant's benefit than anyone's, again he ordered everyone to stay close to his neighbour. If they became separated they were to wait or make their way downhill. Only in an emergency were they to use their hand-sets – their quarry might hear them. In any case communication might be limited, the intervening rock face probably would cause too much interference. And their quarry was dangerous. Remember, he could creep up behind in this mist and throttle as he had done before – he most likely had a gun himself. His anxiety for Derrymore spilled over in these unnecessary instructions. The men he had with him were experts; they knew what to expect.

Much of the time everything was hidden by the same dull grey fog that had shrouded Cornwall for the past weeks; gorse bushes loomed up out of it in strange distorted shapes and under the fir trees the branches had dripped with it. It was a long while since he had run like this over boggy ground, soaked within seconds, larded with mud. It told on him. His knees and back ached; he felt his whole body shake with fatigue. Less than a yard away the stolid form of Derrymore moved resolutely forward, sometimes in view, sometimes gone as the fog dipped and swirled, thick in the hollows, thinning in the open so that he could just glimpse the other two shadowy figures. Behind and beside him he heard their stifled grunts; a stone slipped, there was a muttered curse.

On higher ground he felt better. There were rocks here, and the fog seemed lighter. Occasionally it swirled away to reveal the base of the tor. The six of them moved more slowly now, searching every rock as they went, but the dell, as Mazie had described it, a sort of cleft on the southern edge, was only accessible from the top of the tor.

The three groups were to meet just below the top, approaching the crest from three sides. Reynolds glanced at his watch and its illuminated dial surprised him. He had thought they had been too slow yet only a quarter of an hour had passed.

One of his companions came up behind him, startling him with a whisper. 'There's an open gap to our left sir, no one's covering it.'

Damn, he thought. One of the other teams must have moved too far off course. A gap was the last thing they wanted. 'Spread out,' he whispered back. 'Reform. We'll wait here until you've made contact.'

It was tempting to use the handset, but he was afraid. Sinclair might have a listening device; he was clever enough to have thought of that. As Reynolds had suggested earlier the likelihood that this hideout had been prepared weeks ago seemed more and more probable. Of course Sinclair couldn't have planned on fog; hidden by it he might feel more secure. Hopefully he would forget that it gave his enemies cover too, enabling them to approach without being seen, but he doubted it.

Reynolds was alone now, the other men had gone. Even Derrymore had disappeared. He leant forward, listening. No one, just the silent drifting of fog. It's going wrong, he thought, fighting panic. They've spread too far, too thin. Again he fingered the handset.

A figure moved below him, he tried to attract its attention but it slid out of sight and hearing. He waited. When he checked his watch, conversely now time seemed to have raced ahead. His group should have made contact with the others by now; should have returned so they could all move forward together, closing on the fixed rendezvous. Had they misunderstood and gone on, leaving him behind? And where in hell was Derrymore?

It was at that moment three things happened at once. Somewhere below him a gun went off. It reverberated among the rocks like thunder. At the same time, in a high angle of the tor above him, to his left, the setting sun shone out of the fog onto its cragged face and outlined a sheep's track that twisted and turned towards the top. Then, while the mist swirled back again, he heard as clearly as if it had come from mere feet away, a cut-off moan, the sound that Derrymore had described.

Like some weird bird's cry it spun out of the fog, and died away, so that as he started up he couldn't even remember from which direction it had come. God, he thought again.

He began to crawl now as Derrymore had done in the lane, feeling about him as he made his way as best he could towards the tor and the direction of the sheep's track. Rocks and gorse tore at his clothes, the mist mingled with the sweat that dripped off his face. He sensed the solid substance of the rock face before he felt it, and heaved himself up against it, panting, glad for a moment to have something at his back.

Now was the time to use his handset, but all he got was crackle. He must be too close to the rocks to be heard or hear any reply. Setting his compass by that brief shaft of sun he found he should turn right again towards the rendezvous spot, but he couldn't leave without finding the source of that cut-off moan. Feeling about him like a blind man he went left. And where the track began, a mere opening in the rocks and furze, he came upon the body.

He knew without looking who it was. Even on his side Derrymore had the appearance of a fallen giant. And he was alive. As Reynolds reached him he stirred, coughed, put one hand to his throat, held the other close to his chest.

'Came at me from behind,' he croaked, much as Sally had done. 'Caught me off guard, like. But that gunshot must have startled him because he didn't pull tight enough. What were they firing at?'

There was something about his speech that reminded Reynolds of how disoriented he had sounded after the attack in the lane. He was worried. Another blow to the head could be serious but there was no time for worry. Every second gave Sinclair a chance of regaining his lair, if he had any reason to go back. Otherwise he might try to slip through after all. Reynolds thought of the blockade around the bottom of the tor and wondered if it would hold.

'Which way did he go?' he panted.

Helping Derrymore stand so the sergeant could gulp at air in great heaving breaths he repeated the question. But for the moment Derrymore could only wave one hand aimlessly above his head – the other was sprained or broken at the wrist where he had fallen heavily.

He made a snap decision. 'Stay here,' he said. 'Hold this track. If you have to, use your gun. Keep trying on the blower to bring up help. I'm going after him.'

It was the wrong thing to say. With his one good hand Derrymore grabbed the front of his jacket, holding on so tight he almost ripped it open. 'No you aren't,' he croaked. 'You've been in charge too long. She's my girl. I'll save her.'

For a moment the two hung together, Reynolds with his back to the rock. All Derrymore had to do was smash him against it, beating his brains out in the bargain; all Reynolds had to do was put weight to bear on that shattered wrist.

It was all too dramatic for his practical self. 'Don't be a fool, man,' he heard himself say cooly. 'It's bad enough as it is. We've flushed him out too soon, if he's heard the gunfire, and caught you. He knows we're coming. Let me go. I . . .'

'No.' Even without his proper voice Derrymore was determined. 'We go together. I'll keep up with you. You shan't fault me for that.'

Reynolds didn't stop to argue. Shaking himself loose, he started up the sheep track, hearing Derrymore flounder behind him. The grass was soaked underfoot, the track steep and slippery. For every two steps up he slid one back; he had to snatch at heather roots and hope they would hold. Fighting his way, like skiing uphill on ice, he reached the top exhausted. But still Derrymore kept up with him. And there was no sign of Sinclair.

They turned right now, ran along the rocks, making by instinct for the south. The rocks were slippery too, flat slabs of granite, worn into shape by centuries of weather, piled on each other like children's blocks. When they came to the place where Mazie had described the dell, they crouched again and listened.

There was no noise in front or behind and as far as they knew they hadn't passed anyone. But Sinclair must have come ahead of them, unless he had run along the base of the cliff where he might be caught by the others. Again there was no time to check.

The dell or cleft looked dark and ominous. Mazie herself had described it as an opening beneath the rocks, but she hadn't been there herself in years and was quoting from memory. It didn't look promising as a hideout, the opening appeared too shallow. But now they were committed they had no choice but to go on.

Reynolds went first, easing his way down by bracing himself on both arms. He stopped himself from again suggesting Derrymore remain behind. If Derrymore insisted he couldn't prevent him. It was his right to come. He had scarcely moved a few yards down when his feet slipped and he hung in air; the rocks had curved unexpectedly inwards and he was dangling over space. 'Careful,' he whispered, flailing for a foothold, and when he found it, pausing to catch Derrymore's boots and set his feet in the right place.

They were standing on a narrow ledge with the rock they had been on jutting out over them in a sloping overhang like a porch roof. Behind them, backing under the rock itself, an equally narrow entrance led into a sort of cave. In fine weather there would have been a view of all the moors beneath and around them, perhaps stretching to the sea.

As they stood peering into the darkness they heard a thread of sound. Feeling for the torch Reynolds switched it on and shone it in cautiously. It picked out the walls, lined with moss, and the dead bracken flooring, raked into piles. There were boxes too, a cardboard carton upturned for a table with the same sort of jam pot on it that was in Rab's cottage. And stretched behind some more boxes in a far corner, gagged and bound, the figure of a woman.

Reynolds reached her at a bound, his knife out. While Derrymore still stood in the doorway, he cut through the twine, cradling her head against him. Under his breath he heard his voice muttering words of encouragement and relief, endearments he had long ago forgotten.

Sally was so cramped she couldn't stand. All she could whisper when the gag was removed was, 'I knew you'd come.' From the way she spoke he could tell what she too had been anticipating. It was the hardest blow of all.

'Are you OK?' Derrymore came lumbering forward. His face was filthy and his tunic torn and he held his damaged arm close to him, but his smile was dazzling. 'In a trice, we'll have you safely home,' he began, when Sinclair's voice cut through his happiness.

'How nice,' Sinclair said. He dropped onto the slab by the cave entrance, landing neatly on his feet, no flapping raincoat today, his hair bound back into a skier's band.

'Just what the doctor ordered.'

His laugh was excited, high-pitched without mirth. 'I don't mean your medical practitioner,' he said and giggled again. 'I mean your old doctor of literature. It's quite a treat, isn't it,' he went on, 'the last of the classic forms. The eternal triangle. The two males fighting for the same woman. Traditional. Going back to the time of Arthur and Guinivere and Lancelot. And which of you two gentlemen is Lancelot?'

He looked at them quizzically in the feeble light, a torch in his own hand. 'My, you do look alike, no wonder I mistook you in the dark,' he added as Sally said softly, 'Watch for his gun.'

'Oh yes,' he said, 'I have a gun. You didn't count on that, did you Mr Clever ex-Inspector? You never imagined I could climb or shoot. Well, here's a coincidence. You won't be armed, I'm sure. And your side-kick here can't use his gun, not with a broken arm.' And with a sudden vicious swipe he aimed a blow at Derrymore's wrist which he must have seen him holding, at the same time drawing out his weapon and firing it.

In the split second between Sinclair aiming a blow at Derrymore and pressing the trigger, Reynolds leapt forward.

He felt the flash as the gun went off and seared his face. The smack of the bullet on the ceiling above showered him with granite splinters. Then he was on top of Sinclair, fighting to pin him down, and Sinclair was writhing like a snake with a broken back, across the rock slab.

They were both on the edge, he felt the void beneath. Sinclair was clinging to him now, wrapping himself around him, dragging him over. He made one last effort to break free, clung to the rock and felt Sinclair slip from his grasp. There was a long sigh and the sound of falling stones. And for a while he himself lay on the edge, struggling to get his breath.

When he stumbled to his feet and looked into the cave his first thought was for Sally, his second for Derrymore. They were both together, side by side, staring at him from the rear of the cave. While he had dived towards Sinclair, Derrymore had thrown himself at Sally, shielding her with his body.

And for the longest while they remained staring, the three of them together.

Chapter 18

All murder cases leave various odd ends to clear up, after the criminals are caught or suitably punished, and this was no exception. First, Reynolds and Derrymore were not left long in doubt about their companions; heavy boots were heard scraping on the rocks overhead and their own shouts brought the rest of the team swinging down onto the ledge, and crowding into the cave.

'My God,' Nicholls shouted when he saw them. 'They managed it on their own. Damn sheep got among us, hence the shots. And where's our villain?'

He called for a flare and peered into the cleft at the twisted body, spread-eagled below. 'Serve him right,' he said.

The flares also revealed Mazie's 'dell'. The word had conjured up something poetic, not this crack of grass trapped between high rocks. Whether orchids still grew there no one knew, but daylight revealed the extent of Tremayne's eyrie; from his cave he could see over miles of rolling moors to the border with Devon. If he had been taught by rote where to go for things he needed, he must have come here just to appreciate the beauty. And again that made as good an elegy to him as anything else.

More flares were lit, ropes were suspended, supplies broken open, toasts drunk. Tremayne's hideout was denuded of its secrets as Sinclair's occupation of it became fully revealed. Adding to what he had seized from Tremayne, Sinclair had had the foresight to equip it well, including, as Reynolds had suspected, a radio receiver.

Derrymore, his arm tied into a makeshift cast, sat on a box, not saying much. Commended for his bravery and, when Sally had been taken down to the village inn, ragged about his lover-like instincts, he took all of this good-natured joshing with remarkable aplomb.

Sally showed the same calm as in an earlier ordeal. Apart from cuts and bruises she wasn't hurt and was whisked out of the cave so quickly there wasn't time for her to say much. Before she went she did express her thanks to the men crowding round her. It was a general thanks but her gaze picked out the two who had really rescued her.

Her parents were waiting to take her away and for a while she went north with them again. But she wouldn't stay permanently although they continued to urge her, their way of making amends, she supposed, like the monthly cheques, for years of benign neglect. 'I'm in Cornwall for good,' she said.

Nicholls was understandably jubilant. A successful conclusion in dramatic circumstances, his reputation assured, once back in the village, along with the whole rescue team, he enjoyed the hospitality of the inn and basked in glory. In the midst of the celebrations he didn't neglect to express his appreciation of the special forces and, more to the point, of the local policemen for their fine co-operation.

'A job well done,' he repeated, and meant, his Midlands accent never stronger. 'A real Cornish flourish to a remarkable ending.'

He saved his serious accolades in private for Derrymore and Reynolds, especially Reynolds. In a more sober moment he admitted that Reynolds had saved the situation, more than once. 'Saved my bacon too,' he insisted. 'I'm grateful.' His handshake was the start of a lasting friendship.

As for Reynolds himself, after making certain Sally was safe, he turned his attention to the remaining details, insisting on being one of those who swung down to examine Sinclair's body. It seemed fitting to him that the doctor's life should have ended like the first of his murder victims, in a rock fall which broke his neck as he had broken so many others. But he felt a sort of sadness when he looked at him – what a waste, he thought, all that intelligence run to seed.

There were several reasons for Reynolds effacing himself during the immediate flurry after Sally's rescue. When he'd seen Sally, still alive, he'd been startled into showing his true feelings – but Derrymore had offered his life without thinking, whereas Reynolds downplayed his own similar action as simply professional conduct. As Derry himself would say, it made you think.

Not wanting to intrude on his friend while all these confusing thoughts were still churning, not knowing either how to cope with his own unaccustomed emotions, Reynolds therefore felt it prudent to withdraw from the limelight. It was only later he thought, my God, the doctor of literature had the last laugh after all. Derrymore may be too young for the role of Arthur, but damned if I don't feel as guilty as Lancelot.

He decided there would be time for personal settlement later. It would wait. Then too, he still was so relieved at the way things had turned out, so grateful Sinclair hadn't actually carried out his intentions, the festivities were almost an anticlimax. Or at least more than he deserved.

Last, and by no means least, having viewed the body in silence, he took the liberty of going through the pockets. He'd been afraid that Sinclair might have tossed the missing pages away but he should have known that even in these last frantic hours the doctor was too careful, or too conceited, to destroy anything he'd written.

The pages were a little the worse for wear, mashed into a wad – Sinclair's memorial to himself and the events he had set in motion. They contained all the evidence Nicholls and his team could ever hope for, the step-by-step confession of a descent into abuse and evil and death.

Actually Sinclair and Jen Murdock had started it together as a kind of joke, a way of using Sinclair's knowledge of people by turning it against them. His notes and observations had already helped Jen tighten her hold on village affairs; now it amused them to toy with the secret knowledge which gave them such advantage over what they termed contemptuously 'simple' people – Rab Tremayne a prime example.

They had planned for a long while, not perhaps as long as five years, but certainly Matty's wedding had given them the first firm date. And the murder in the quarry was to be their *piece de resistance*, their big chance.

Originally Jen picked the victims. She chose Matty because the vicar's daughter was young and popular with men. (For Jen, all those boyfriends Derrymore had laughed at were like red rags to a bull, reminding her of her own failing powers.) Then too Jen felt left out and ignored by the vicar and his snobby parishioners, of whom she selected Frank Barker as another example – as good a reason as any to make him the ultimate target, catching him and his vulgar little mistress in as vulgar and grotesque a way as possible.

It was difficult to say at first who was the leader, who the accomplice, Sinclair's thoughts and hers complemented each other so well. Again both Reynolds and Sally had been correct in their proportioning of blame – except that Jen Murdock had the strongest sense of being owed something, of being 'wronged'. Sally had been wholly right in her judgement of the twisted sexual motivation which lay at the back of her behaviour.

The stealing of the crown, for example, was Jen's idea. (As were the first and subsequent drawings. The use of Reynolds' initials was Sinclair's own wry touch.) Jen had watched the little girls practising and in a sudden fit of spite, decided to ruin their fun, hitting on the idea of using Tremayne to do the stealing. Alternatively frightening and rewarding him (the manner of the reward never detailed; even Sinclair found it too bestial) she persuaded him to remove the crown from the cupboard when everyone had gone home. (Sinclair's meticulous description of how she had afterwards danced round her sitting room with it perched on her head showed her at her most depraved.) Jen herself viewed the incident as a kind of justified vengeance, as shown by her hounding of poor Mrs Varcoe afterwards.

But it was Sinclair who first noted the link to the maiden virgin ritual which Sally had detected and the darker aspect now began to interest him also.

With the same cruel attention to detail he recorded how Rab had stolen the blood to desecrate the church. He listed the visits they made to Rab's cottage, the food they gave him, the equally sickening way they wormed themselves into his affection until he showed them everything, laying all his little secrets and hiding places bare. Equally without emotion Sinclair described Rab's puzzlement and distress when he discovered what he was supposed to do with the blood, finally refusing to enter the church at all so that Sinclair had to sling the stuff about himself.

The earlier discovery that Reynolds lived in the village only gave an extra dimension to the fun. At Sinclair's suggestion, Jen now set up the book club to campaign against his writings. The use of the same club for a sex-ring was her later suggestion, although Sinclair went along with it. It had the sort of twisted ambience he now began to delight in, although he never attended, preferring seeing her alone, both for his own pleasure and as a precaution. Even from the beginning he was cautious, never trusting anyone.

Who first thought of making the crimes fit the criminal, as

it were, was not clear; it was a game they both enjoyed. The idea of using quotations from the books and setting fire to them was all Sinclair's (although she had insisted he leave the 'smiley face' as their trade-mark). And with the murder came the first glimpse of difficulty – Jen's insistence on what Reynolds had called 'overkill'. She made no secret of her fear that Sinclair's methods were too intellectual for her taste; no one would understand them; she opted for the boot prints and Rab's dead body as more obvious clues.

By now Rab had become a burden too. Since his act of defiance he had to be got rid of. And since Caddick's behaviour at the sawmill had long rankled, and since Caddick was the wronged husband, here was extra incentive to draw him in, in case something else went wrong. When Rab's body fell accidentally into the water, she had Caddick ready to step literally into his shoes.

After this, their ways began to divide. As impartially, Sinclair described how Jen preened herself on the fact that everything had been her idea and she wanted recognition for it. He meanwhile, latching on to the 'mastermind' theory that began to dominate the news, took the credit naturally for himself. She devoted more time to her club, where Art Newcomb had become her second Rab Tremayne, her docile 'handy man' as the 'guests' had called him; Sinclair spent his free hours planning more crimes (luckily for the villagers, only Miss Penwithen's was achieved; he had a long list, including Mazie's name).

Although Jen approved of Miss Penwithen's murder, it and the failure of the attack on Derrymore and Sally Heyward troubled her. She'd not been consulted and became offended. She began to suspect that Sinclair was interested in the younger woman. When she accused him of this, he denied it, there was a scene, the first of many, all listed unemotionally with exact dates and times. Their friendship continued on the surface, but Reynolds had again been right – the idea of her death coupled with Art Newcomb's had begun to appeal to him. It would show another version of the sexual twist that had begun to interest him. It would show who was the 'mastermind'.

Finally his obsession with Sally Heyward. Whether in the end he would have carried out the dreadful sequence of events as described in Reynolds' book, apparently he never really decided, swaying first one way, then the other as his fixation and growing madness took hold. One of his last entries was his description of how he'd meant to kill her if she'd gone with him into Miss Penwithen's house – and his frustration that she hadn't. It was one of the few instances where his own emotions showed. And there the record ended.

As for the phone calls, Sinclair had left a copy of what Jen was supposed to say and in that sense she was his accomplice. She herself had used Newcomb as her cover – borrowing his car, for example, when she went to a public phone box, although she never told him what she wanted it for and never involved him in anything more than that. His non-appearance on the night of the murder had been an unexpected blow. She had asked him specifically to change the date for her meeting (again a precaution in case something went wrong) and had great difficulty in escaping for a few moments from her house, forced into using her own car to make the phone call to Caddick. It was after that failure, on Sinclair's instructions, that she informed Newcomb, quite clearly, that if he didn't carry out her instructions to the letter in future she would tell the authorities all about his past. What she didn't tell Sinclair and what he only found out by accident, was that, in an unguarded moment, she had revealed Sinclair's involvement with her, suggesting to Newcomb that she was 'under Sinclair's orders' – possibly her way of building up a defence in case they were ever caught. That mistake signed Newcomb's death warrant as well as hers.

While Jen used the phone calls to inject her venom, Sinclair relied on his observations about various people to anticipate their reactions. This was especially true in the assessment of Derrymore. Sinclair guessed that Derrymore would ignore the messages and for his pains probably get into trouble later (a good example of the way Sinclair's mind worked and the depth of his understanding).

One last thing about those calls. After all the fuss had died down, a timid lady came forward to confess she'd seen a strange car parked outside her house on that fateful Tuesday night. It had only been there a few minutes and she hadn't made anything of it. But she lived round the corner from the phone box at Lostwithiel – and the car was a great grey Mercedes, so out of place that's why she'd noticed it.

There were other odds and ends to tidy up, of course, other suspects in the case, who, even if they were innocent of the main crimes, still had to deal in their own way with the results. Mrs Barker was guilty perhaps of nothing worse than voyeurism. She was too old to take part in the sexual rites of Mrs Murdock's club, but that didn't stop her going – her method of paying her husband back.

She and Elsie both moved away and their houses were sold. They had never been friends and they didn't stay in touch. Eden went abroad, where his mother may have eventually joined him, after the source of money in his bank account had been explained. Of course he'd been getting cash – and his step-father had been paying it, to keep him silent and not make a fuss. 'Better me than his women,' Eden said defiantly when it was pointed out he was talking blackmail here. But as his mother seemed not to care, and his step-father wasn't there to press charges, the matter was dropped. And he may have had a point. Although not in this case. Whatever Betty Caddick had done to deceive her husband, she'd never taken money for it, although her lover would have lavished it on her if she'd let him.

Dave Caddick continued to work at the sawmill. He sometimes was seen using the wedge that almost caused his conviction for murder, and when he had a drop too much to drink (for that original night out at the Fox and Goose seemed to have broken some inhibition and he became a regular) he used to swear that without Mr Reynolds he'd be a dead duck; a man couldn't have a better friend than a writer fellow with his head screwed on the right way.

The sex club vanished overnight, or went underground, and its members, suitably cautioned, were glad to get off lightly. Grange Manor stayed empty for a long time and was bought by the council. Jen Murdock must have turned in her grave to learn it was to become an old people's home.

The bookshop was closed and eventually reverted to a house as it had been when Miss Penwithen first came to live next door. For a while it and Grange Manor were much in the public eye, but gradually interest died, as it always does. So that left only the three main characters.

First Derrymore. He was again commended for bravery, but he also faced an inquiry, as he had guessed he would. It was harder on Mazie than on him. 'You were only doing what was best,' she said and would have told the commission so, if he hadn't persuaded her to stay at home. In the end common sense prevailed. He was let off with a caution, and again praised for his concern. But whether he would stay on the force and whether he would leave the village still hung in the balance. He'd had a drubbing, as he put it, and needed time to think. Sinclair's knowledge and use of village gossip had disillusioned him; he still couldn't get over it.

'You should stay,' Sally encouraged him. 'They still need

you. And if I'm to live in the village, I'd like to think you were close at hand.'

Sally had already told him that she couldn't marry him now; she couldn't marry anyone. She used the word 'marry', although that had never been even mentioned between them, because she sensed for a man like Derrymore marriage was the only thing that mattered; he wouldn't be content with an affair. And neither would she.

She had waited until after the commission's findings as she didn't want to give too many blows at once, but he had assured her that either way wouldn't have mattered. Somehow he wasn't put out about her refusal as much as she feared. Despite his indecision about his professional future, he had found a new purpose; he would never let go, no matter what she said.

'I'll be here if you need me,' he'd said, and she knew he meant it. It made things more difficult for her, but that was the way it was.

As for her and Reynolds, here the vital decision was not hers to make. And although she thought she knew the depth of his feelings she also knew by now that he couldn't or wouldn't speak of them unless he felt certain that Derrymore had relinquished his claim. Derrymore was his best friend; and he himself was no Lancelot.

One evening they sat together on the terrace in Reynolds' garden, the last chapters of his new book on the bench between them. She'd finished typing the manuscript and they had been discussing it – she thought it would be one of his best, he himself wasn't sure. It had cost him too much effort.

By now it was high summer. The sky was clear, one couldn't even imagine what rain was like, and fog had gone until autumn. The scent of sweat peas mingled with the smell of fresh-cut grass that floated from the fields behind them and swallows were twittering on the roof of the neighbouring barn.

Studying the contours of Sally's face when she wasn't looking, Reynolds wondered, as he did each time he saw her, how much she had been changed by the events of these last months. She seemed to walk as confidently as before, she seemed to smile as readily, but to his way of thinking she had grown taller – or it might have been the gathering twilight that made her look tall and thin. He sensed in her something deep that hadn't been there, something resolute and strong.

'I'm taking your advice,' he said after a long silence. 'I'm thinking of writing a new kind of book. It's about real people with real emotions, how they handle them and each other – and not a crime in sight. I hope I get it right. I may even go away and stay a while in Rab's cottage for inspiration. It's still empty.'

'Then you'll have to learn to be as tidy as he was,' she laughed. 'Of course you'll get it right. Don't fret.' Underneath he guessed she was worrying whether he'd be back, although she didn't say so. She wouldn't put pressure on him, just as Derrymore wouldn't put pressure on her. And she wasn't the sort of person to play one man off the other. It wasn't her style.

She had closed her eyes against the sun. In his imagination he ran his fingers down her face, as if trying to remember its contours. In his imagination he almost heard her say, 'I can wait, I'm not afraid.'

The words conjured up the evening in her little flat when she'd said the same thing. Then he had replied that he on the other hand was full of fears. As he was now. Of hurting her again, of leading her into danger, of being what he was, too old to change.

Sally might want to argue against what he was thinking, but she was too wise to do so. And because she was a young and active woman, she wouldn't just sit and mope. 'I've come to a decision as well,' she told him, 'or rather two. It's taken some courage, and means I've finally asked my father for his money, which probably pleases him. Miss Penwithen's cottage is for sale . . .'

'And you've bought it?' He sat up. 'Good for you,' he said, 'And the second?'

'Oh that,' she said. 'I'm going to take a leaf out of your book. I like detecting work so much I may make it my new career.'

He laughed and again said, 'Good for you.' But he eyed her more speculatively as if wondering, 'Can you really stand the course?' What he did ask was, for she had told him about her dreams, 'You won't mind seeing Miss Penwithen's ghost?'

She smiled again. 'Remember, I already have. And she is a gentle one. I know she'll be glad to have me in her house.'

'And Sinclair?'

It was the first time the name had been mentioned. She looked at him thoughtfully. 'You know,' she said, 'when we were together he wasn't all bad. I think in his way he was almost fond of me. He saw me as his student and himself as a professor. And you know something else. For all his hatred and jealousy of you, he never doubted for a moment that you couldn't find out where we were and come after us. So in spite of all his cleverness, he gave you credit for what you really are.'

He waved the compliment away and put his arm along the wall as if letting it rest on her shoulder. 'Do you remember,' he said, 'you asked how people could communicate if they wouldn't say anything to let you close? Sometimes you don't need to speak at all.'

Like us, he meant. It gave hope.